FORBIDDEN DEVIL

A NASHVILLE DEVILS NOVEL

MELISSA IVERS

Copyright © 2020 by Melissa Ivers

All rights reserved.

No part of this book may be reproduced or used in any form or by any electronic or mechanical means, including information storage and retrieval systems, without written permission from the author, except for the use of brief quotations in a book review. For more information, email address: melissa.ivers.author@gmail.com

This is a work of fiction. The names, characters, businesses, places, events, locales, and incidents are the products of the author's imagination or have been used fictitiously and are not to be construed as real. Any resemblance to actual persons, living or dead, actual events, locales or organizations is entirely coincidental.

Forbidden Devil

Cover Designer: Sarah Hansen

Editor: Whitney's Book Works

Formatting: KM Rives

For the readers who love second chances

1

JAZLYN

THE BALLOTS WERE SENT OUT, votes cast, and results tallied. The consensus, ladies and gentlemen—*drum roll, please*—the general manager is a giant dick. Side note—probably overcompensating for a small one.

Resident asshole in question, Adam Barrett, GM of the Nashville Devils hockey team, sits across the conference room table from my brother and I in an awkward stare down. To say I could slash the tension with a machete would be a gross understatement.

Damn, I'd love to have one of those right now. Self-defense is alive and well in Tennessee.

While Adam is a pretty decent GM, he's a shit human being.

"I don't know what you both expect from me." Adam plants his hands on the long mahogany table and leans toward us. His chair creaks beneath him, and he lets out a frustrated sigh. Every word he speaks drips with contempt. "It's not in my job description to babysit two over-privileged rich kids who can't fathom what it means to own a hockey franchise, let alone run it."

I shift in my chair and my pulse skyrockets, as the heated glare from Adam settles on me. His hardened brown eyes bore into my soul, and I swear I can hear his teeth crack beneath the pressure of his clenched jaw.

It's a good thing looks can't actually kill. If they could, my lifeless corpse would slouch to the floor.

I did not wear my kickass heels to die in them.

Adam will have to glare me to death another day.

He'd been my father's right-hand man for years, and for the life of me, I don't understand why. Not that my father and I had a particularly close relationship. Growing up, I was always my mother's problem. Even after they divorced, he was too busy to spend real quality time with his children. But if the rumors are true, he was just as difficult as Adam, and Adam is a dumpster fire. Being an asshole must be a fairly common trait in the upper echelons of men's professional hockey.

I glance at my brother. Gordon's widened eyes and rigid posture reflect the same shock I feel.

Well, this meeting is off to a fantastic start.

Gordon and I set up this appointment with every intention of aligning ourselves with Adam, wanting to get the upper management team on the same page before our ownership was announced to the country. Somewhere in the last five minutes, the train left the station, derailed, and plowed into a fireworks factory.

I eye him like I would a ticking time bomb. I'm sure he won't physically explode, even though the pulsing vein on the side of his forehead indicates otherwise. "We're not trying to cause you more work."

"It doesn't matter. You're going to," Adam growls.

I hold my hands up in surrender. "Listen, Adam—"

"What would a spoiled princess like you know about hockey, anyway? You probably wouldn't know a puck if it hit you in the face." He gestures toward me, his hand sweeping out before it falls back to the table with a loud thump.

Considering I grew up playing hockey, I can only assume his observation is based purely on the fact I have a vagina and not my actual experience with the sport. I'm also pretty sure he knows that.

He's a fucking prick.

"I did play hockey. In the Olympics."

"On the *women's* team. We all know how different it is from real hockey."

I steal a glance at Gordon. His green eyes sharpen, his nostrils flare, and his lips press together in a firm line. He's always the first one to come to my defense. Not that I can't stand up for myself, but in his mind, no one messes with his little sister. Adam is either completely oblivious, or doesn't give a shit, because he turns to him next.

"And you, Gordie." He spits out the name like my brother doesn't deserve to share a name with the great hockey legend. "You're just some washed up has-been who couldn't make it in pro-hockey. You're sure as shit not going to hack it here."

My spine straightens, and I throw my shoulders back as the blood simmers in my veins. If there's anyone who needs to eat a bag of dicks, it's this guy.

Gordon is a lot of things, but a washed up has-been isn't one of them. The only reason he isn't playing professional hockey is a devastating knee injury. Otherwise, he'd still be out there week after week tearing up the ice.

He stands, towering over Adam with his bulky six-foot-three frame. The muscle in his jaw tics before he leans over and slaps his hands flat on the table. The sound echoes off the walls as he pins Adam with a glare, and I give him a mental high five. It's a total power move to put Adam back in his place.

He needs to learn he's no longer in charge around here.

"Unfortunately for you, *Mr. Barrett*, our father left the hockey team to us. In case you don't understand, that means you now answer to Jazlyn and me. It would be in your best interest to keep future comments about our perceived shortcomings to yourself." Gordon straightens, smoothing a hand down his tie. "Unless, of course, you'd like to search for another NHL team to work for. I don't know anyone who's looking for a new GM right now, and with last season's record, you don't look too good."

Adam's face turns a satisfying shade of red as he jumps to his feet. "What the hell was your father thinking? You two are going to be the end of this team. You're both a laughingstock. Don't think we aren't all waiting for you to fail." With one last glare at Gordon, then me, Adam turns and stalks out of the room, slamming the door behind him.

My fists clench under the table so hard my nails dig into my palms. I want nothing more than to charge into his office and tear him a new asshole. But regardless of how I feel about Adam, we need him. My father's closed mind and selfishness brought the Devils to the bottom. They finished the previous season with the second worst record in the league. Pair those stats with two inexperienced owners, no general manager in their right mind would consider joining the organization right now. We need to win, and win often, to entice even a half-decent GM to replace Adam.

That means my best option is to swallow my pride and let it go. Even if my brain is screaming at me to clean house.

Gordon releases a long breath, unbuttons his black suit jacket, and collapses into his seat. Dark circles rim his eyes, and there's a noticeable slouch in his shoulders. He looks like he's in need of a serious nap, or maybe a stiff drink. Or both.

I need both.

"That went well," I muse, lacing my fingers together in front of me, and quirk my mouth in a wry smile.

"I don't know, sis. I'm not sure we were in the same meeting."

I hate how Adam makes him sound so defeated, and it riles

me up all over again. I shoot to my feet, sending my chair rolling several feet backward. "You know what? Fuck that guy. I don't give a shit what he says. We're going to turn this team around. This is *our* legacy, Gordon. We're going to take the Devils out of the bottom and make them winners. We're going to prove everyone wrong, including that fancy suit wearing asshole." My voice steels with resolve as I point towards the door where Adam made his recent exit.

Gordon slumps even lower and runs a hand down his face. "I hope you're right, Jazz. I really hope you're right."

"I think you should know by now, brother, I'm always right." My lips curl up in a smirk, and I cock my hip against the table.

Am I cocky? Yes. A little self-assured? Right now, absolutely.

But the gauntlet has been thrown, and there's no way in hell I'm not picking it up. Just need to figure out how to run a hockey franchise while simultaneously building a good team and getting wins.

Couldn't be too hard. Probably. Right?

Gordon shakes his head, chuckling. "I wish we could just fire him."

"Trust me, I know the feeling. Unfortunately, unless we can start winning, I don't think we stand a chance at recruiting anyone."

"True enough." Gordon makes his way to the door of the conference room. "I'm going to make some calls to a few friends of mine and see what our options are for replacing him."

I nod. "Good idea. Keep me posted."

Anger and restlessness boil through me. Sitting down in my office chair to stew for the next few hours doesn't seem very productive. A good walk around the stadium will help me get my bearings and settle the storm brewing inside.

Adam's right about one thing. I have no idea what it takes to run a hockey team. For the better part of my twenty-eight years of life, I've been on the ice. The front of the house is foreign to me, and I didn't ask for it. I didn't expect to have a hockey team suddenly thrown in my lap. I didn't expect to have to move my entire life for Dad's dying wish, or for his dying wish to land me as co-owner of his hockey team.

I certainly didn't expect to be in a position where I would be completely disregarded and disrespected because of my gender. Our ownership hasn't even been made public yet. If Adam's reaction is any indication, I'm in for a media shit show.

Great.

I make it downstairs, sure I'll be able to find the workout room and, with it, a punching bag. Maybe giving it hell for a few minutes will improve my mood. Better it than Adam's face. I clench and unclench my fists. I haven't been this pissed in a long time.

Lost in my violent thoughts, I round a corner and run into a solid wall of muscle. The impact sends me staggering in my heels, and I might have fallen on my ass if two hands didn't reach out to steady me.

"I'm so sorry."

My muscles tense, and my heart pounds in my chest. I know that voice. It's deep and gritty, yet smooth and hypnotizing. It's a voice I could get lost in. And have. The meeting with Adam threw me off balance, and I forgot about him being here.

As one of my players.

"I almost ran you over. Are you okay?" A flicker of recognition sparks in his light blue eyes, and his hands drop to his sides.

Lincoln Dallas.

A missed opportunity if there ever was one. One look at him, one innocent touch, has my nipples peaked and my panties soaked. My body remembers him too.

He's one of the sexiest men I've ever laid eyes on. His tall, muscled body, full lips, and chiseled jaw are a gift to women everywhere. The hockey gods have been kind to him. Unlike some of the other hockey players, he doesn't look like he just got knocked around a few times after meeting the wrong end of a hockey stick.

"Jazz?" Lincoln's mouth tilts to a frown. "What are you doing here?"

I cross my arms over my chest, trying—and failing—to get my damn heart rate under control. Shit, it's like I'm in middle school with the way my body's reacting—racing heart, fluttery stomach, damp palms. I take a deep breath, release it slowly and count to ten. Get it together. "Hello to you too, Linc."

His eyes flash to my cleavage before meeting my gaze. "Sorry. I'm just surprised. It's been a long time."

I drop my arms. As satisfying as it is having Lincoln eying my boobs, it's not the best time. Now that I'm his new boss, there would likely never be a good time. "It has. Six years, I think." I don't think. I know damn well how long it's been since the last time I laid eyes on him.

I haven't stopped thinking about him since.

He grabs my hand and gives it a squeeze, effectively jump-starting my body from its sexual hiatus. It's like being hooked up to a car battery. Tingles race across my hand and down my spine, right to that bundle of nerves no man can ever seem to find. My body aches for more of his touch. His fingers brush along the length of mine, teasing my flesh in light caresses. No one but Lincoln has ever made my body light up like a cheap carnival game—and it makes him dangerous to my current position.

"I was sorry to hear about your dad, but it's good to see you." His voice deepens as his eyes travel the length of my body. "If you're going to be here for a few days and need someone to talk to or maybe get your mind off things, I'm here for you. I'd love to catch up."

I can think of a number of ways Lincoln can get my mind off things, starting with—*Abort. Abort.* Rule number one of hockey team ownership: no fraternization with the players. I need to get out of here fast before I lose myself in his husky words and steely gaze.

Adam and Eve's corruption came in the form of an apple. That man—that sexy-as-fuck hockey playing man—could easily become mine.

"It's good to see you too, but, um...I have to run. I'll see you around."

Lincoln's eyebrows draw together, and before he can utter another word, I turn around and bolt back to my office, far away from temptation, as fast as my black Prada heels can take me.

2

LINCOLN

GET YOUR MIND OFF THINGS. I can't believe that's what I said to her. *Hello folks, I'm the biggest dumbass known to man.* I might as well have invited her back to my place for a quick fuck. *Get your mind off things.* Yeah, that's exactly what not to say to a woman whose father just died. *Way to fucking go, dipshit.*

Not just any woman either. Jazlyn fucking Benson.

Fuck me, I didn't think I'd ever see her again. And I've already fucked up my attempt at a second chance.

A woman who'd always had a starring role in my dreams and the top spot in my spank bank, right above the half-dressed Victoria's Secret models.

Now, I've gone and ruined any chance I had at a reunion with those five little words. Get your mind off things. Fuck. Grade-A asshole right here. Maybe I need to order two beers from the bartender and start double fisting. That might make me feel marginally better.

Jazlyn fucking Benson.

"Hey there, big boy." A sultry-looking blonde sidles up along my right side, brushing my arm with hers in a soft caress. Big boy, really? As cheesy as that shit is, it probably works on more men than a line like that should. The fragile ego of men, I suppose.

I shake her off without so much as a glance.

Now I know Jazz is here, there's only one woman whose touch my dick wants, who sets me on fire with nothing but a simple stroke of flesh. Thinking about how her body bumped into mine, her soft breasts pressing into my chest, has my balls aching for release.

The woman next to me elicits nothing. Zilch. I doubt she even has a remote interest in me, beyond my career choice anyway. Most of these women don't.

After I left the group to grab a beer, she must've sensed weakness and circled in like a shark hunting its prey. I shift to reclaim my space and perch my arms up on the gleaming copper bar. Instead of responding, I keep my eyes on the bartender, hoping he'll feel the weight of my stare and head my direction.

She hasn't introduced herself, and I don't need to know her name. In fact, I have no intention of letting this conversation continue any further. Don't get me wrong, she could have a riveting personality. But even someone with half a brain would know what she's after has nothing to do with friendly conversation.

Just in case there's any question about what exactly she's offering tonight, she sticks out what I could only guess are surgically enhanced breasts and proceeds to stroke my bicep with a lazy index finger. No doubt I'm supposed to be thinking about her doing this to my cock.

Hard pass.

"Looking for some company tonight?" She smiles, fluttering her eyelashes like I'm a tool who'd be hypnotized with her eye dancing.

Even if I'm looking for a booty call tonight, it wouldn't be with her. Instead, I'd hunt down the woman I scared off earlier when I offered to *get her mind off things*. I wouldn't touch this chick with someone else's dick. Don't get me wrong, she looks nice enough. Petite, thin, but completely fake right down to her bleached, shoulder-length hair. A perfect contrast to the slightly orange-tinted spray tan layering her skin. Even her perfect smile looks fake. Something I'm sure she plasters on to get what she wants from men.

She also looks familiar enough, I'd bet my right testicle several members of the team have already enjoyed her 'company.'

With a career making me semi-famous, it's not unusual for women to come on to me. And trust me when I say casual is all they're ever looking for. Aside from introductions and trivial small talk, there isn't much conversation after an invitation back to their place. Their eyes are busy focusing on the large bulge in my pocket—my wallet—and any other perks that could possibly come their way.

A few years ago, I probably wouldn't have given two shits. I'd have gone back to her place and fucked her until we were both boneless and sated. Now, I'm bored with one-night stands. Casual flings don't do it for me anymore. I need something real. I'm ready to settle down into a relationship. I can't remember the last time I had one of those, and I'm not sure high school counts, but I'm ready. After our run-in in the hallway and our unfinished past, there's only one lady I want to fill the role of girlfriend.

That is, if I can make up for sticking my foot in my mouth. And I don't even know how long she'll be in town.

"I'm sorry." I flash her a smile that's gotten me out of trouble with the ladies more times than I can count. "Boys night tonight. Looks like I'm busy."

She frowns and a brief flicker of disappointment flashes across her features, but she's quick to slip her mask back in place. "No problem. Maybe next time."

Not a chance.

Giving my arm a slight squeeze, she slinks off to find herself some fresh man meat to sink her teeth into.

After another good minute and a half, the bartender makes his way over to me, beer in hand and a tight smile across his face. Normally, I'd be a little irritated it took that long to pour a damn beer, but I feel a little bad for the guy. It's pretty lively for a Friday afternoon, at least half the real estate around the bar is claimed and most of the tables are occupied. Poor guy is working alone.

"Thanks, man." I nod to him as he hands me my drink before moving on to another customer.

I take a hefty swallow, a local IPA that goes down smooth, and move to sit back down at a high-top table with my teammates at the local pub, Whiskey and Rye. It's a little hole in the wall, but as one of the few bars within walking distance to the arena, it's a favorite hangout spot for most of the team.

A warning about the little puck bunny at the bar dies in my throat as a breaking news report flashes across the big screen of the nearest TV, stealing my attention. Some jackoff news anchor starts blabbing about the fate of the Nashville Devils, the south's most *beloved* NHL hockey team.

I was traded here two years ago in an attempt to revitalize the team, and while it didn't work, I have some good teammates and have tried to make the best of it. We're not the greatest, but we're certainly not the worst.

We didn't finish dead last in the league, but we were definitely in the bottom five. With retirement and contract expirations, we've lost our team captain and a couple other solid teammates. Left with a mediocre coach, rookies, and only a few good players, the upcoming season doesn't look hopeful. We need a damn miracle to even land the wild card slot in the playoffs.

But instead of focusing on rebuilding and recruiting some key players, our whole franchise has been turned upside down.

Under new management.

Effective immediately.

Oliver Benson, sole owner of the Nashville Devils, retired hockey player and all-around asshole, died almost a week ago at the young age of 54. Cirrhosis of the liver apparently, because while hockey is a sport, drinking is not.

It's no secret Benson and I weren't the best of friends, so I'm not going to pretend to be broken up about his death. He wasn't involved much with the players and always acted like he was better than us. Didn't help he and I had some history together. He often lost his cool where I was concerned. We got into a few heated arguments about some stupid bullshit because he refused to move past my indiscretion with his daughter. It must have been a blow to his pride when the GM struck a deal resulting in my trade to his team. In exchange for a center and his long-standing goalie, he was able to cement me here with a contract preventing any movement for two years.

Two years that just ran out.

"Can y'all believe this shit?" Tag Harris, Devils teammate and native Kentucky boy, brings his beer to his lips and about drains half the glass. "Who leaves a hockey team to his kids? They're barely older'n us." He lets out a loud sigh while running a hand through his shoulder-length, blonde hair.

"Wait. What did you say?" I whip around to stare at him. That would mean—

Tag points to the TV. "Just announced that SOB Benson left the team to his two fuckin' kids."

My heart soars in my chest. Jazz isn't here for only a few days. She's here for good.

But she's also being dissected by the media, and they're not painting her in a positive light.

Not saying women don't have a place in hockey or managing a sports team. But I know for a fact, aside from us, there are no other teams with a woman in the owner's box or in the management suite.

It's going to be a challenge for her.

Tag scratches his fingers over his stubbled chin. "Although, I like Gordie. He's been doin' a good job."

Gordon Benson has been helping with team logistics over the summer after a knee blowout ruined his professional career last season. We'd played against him while he was in Chicago. He's built like a beast and is one tough motherfucker. Unfortunately, I don't think being a hockey player won't prepare him for any responsibilities as a team owner.

"I don't know, guys. Might not be bad to have her skating around the rink every day." Owen McIver elbows Ian McIver, his Irish twin, younger by eleven months, and motions towards the bank of televisions behind the bar. The pair are known as the Bruiser Brothers, two of the toughest defensemen in the league, on and off the ice. While they have slightly different facial features, they both have the same short, light brown hair, dark blue eyes, and are built like brick shithouses.

Ian laughs and gives his brother a fist bump. "Rather have her rolling around my bed than skating around the rink, though."

Fisting my hands under the table, I clench my jaw as possessiveness floods my body. I know these guys are playing around, but I'll be damned if anyone else has Jazz in their bed. Shit. Where the fuck did that come from? She isn't mine. Far from it, in fact.

Turning my head, I try my hardest not to gape at the woman who's staring at me from the TV. The woman I'd poorly propositioned mere hours ago. I need to get it together and play it cool. No need to draw any unwanted attention to myself or bring to light I may have a prior history with our new lady boss.

Jazlyn fucking Benson. Colliding with me twice in one day.

I'd like to say seeing her on TV doesn't have much effect on me, but that would make me full of shit. Just looking at her face with her bright green eyes and very kissable lips are like a hit to the gut. It's the same reaction I had earlier when I mowed her down in the hallway. She's older but looks better, if that's even possible. Her hair is longer too. Thick, wavy chestnut hair that felt like silk between my fingers.

Well, fuck.

I shift around in the chair and give myself a quick adjustment.

Seeing her around the rink is going to be interesting. Not to mention having her as my boss. Just looking at her face on a TV screen has me half hard. Not a good precursor to a proper employer-employee relationship.

It doesn't help I never got what I desired when it came to Jazz. What I craved. Never got her naked and underneath me, to feel her soft skin around me. Never got to hear her moan my name while I did wicked things to her body. Didn't even get to fall asleep with her in my arms only to wake up and bury my cock in her sweet pussy over and over again.

I'd gotten permission from the NHL to play in the Olympics six years ago, and while in Sochi, we dated for close to a month. Stupid ass me thought she was the *one*. No girl made me feel the way she did, before or since. We took things slow, neither one of us wanting to be buried under the intensity of our connection. So, we talked. A lot. We spent most of our free time together, getting to know each other, before we shared some not so innocent touches and several undeniably hot kisses. Kisses that were practically into my soul. All culminating into a few short minutes of bliss where her body shifted under mine, and I was mere moments away from claiming her before her jackass of a father walked in on us.

He pulled me aside and had a few choice words to say before

he sent me packing. Mainly how much damage I would inevitably do to her professional career by being a distraction. The asshole even threatened to get me cut from my own team and blackballed from the NHL. I'm still not sure if he would've done it, since he was drunk off his ass when he delivered the threat, but he had the clout to do so. And I couldn't take that chance.

When the Olympics ended, we parted ways and lost touch. Both of us buried in our careers, and, with her father's threat hanging over my head, I was able to convince myself being with her wasn't as special as I thought.

None of it mattered now, she and Gordon have the power to trade me at will. At the end of the day, I have my own livelihood to think about. I can't let a pretty face—or hell, even some good teammates—keep me on a bottom league team. Any attempt at pursuing a relationship with Jazz would inevitably result in hurt feelings and a swift exit on my account. I'll have to tell my agent to keep his ears open for trade opportunities before the deadline in February.

With my two-year-no-movement clause up, there's a good chance I could land a team on the road to the Stanley Cup. I've had my eye on that bad boy since I was drafted into the NHL eleven years ago, at the ripe age of eighteen. Back then, I was nothing but a wide-eyed kid with a bright future and a hell of a slap shot. I've put in the hard work and grown as a player. It's my time. And if I want to make my dream come true, I need to get on a winning team.

And the Devils aren't it.

"Awfully quiet over there, Dallas." Tag pulls my attention away from my thoughts. "What do you think about all this?"

I think I'll have to invest in a sturdier cup if Jazz planned on hanging out during practice. I'd hate to embarrass myself while skating drills.

"At this point, who knows. We didn't do so good last season, so any kind of change might be good for the team. Or we could all be screwed. It's not like ownership ever really mattered before. Oliver was a dick."

Ian slaps my back. "Thanks for those words of wisdom, Linc. You're like our very own Socrates."

"No problem, I'll be here all week." I chuckle.

"There's never been a woman owner," Tag points out.

"Or a lady GM, or coach," Owen adds.

I tap my fingers along the edge of the table. "Doesn't mean it couldn't work. Jazlyn grew up with hockey. She can't screw things up too bad. All I know is our job hasn't changed. We still need to work hard, stay focused, and when the time comes, try to win some damn games. Maybe with some divine intervention, we can manage to do better than we did last year."

Yep. Just have to stay focused. Keep my head down, nose to the grindstone. Win some games.

Get traded to a team within reach of the cup.

Nothing to it.

After running into Jazz today, I have a feeling the season is going to be anything but easy. In fact, there's a good chance she's going to become one hell of a distraction.

3

JAZLYN

IT'S ALWAYS five o'clock somewhere, the magical hour declaring it's now socially acceptable to kick back with a drink. Lucky for me, the clock strikes five in Nashville. After the week I've had, I need a drink—or seven. Seven was more my dad's style, though.

I'm perched against the kitchen island, clad in leggings and a loose sweater, so relieved to be rid of my power suit and heels. Gordon moves around the kitchen with grace and efficiency, something you wouldn't expect from a monster of a former hockey player. I'd ask if he needs help gathering our supplies but have no idea where anything is in this monstrous kitchen. Gordon, on the other hand, seems to know where everything is.

"I'm glad you know where all this shit is. I spent ten minutes this morning looking for a spoon." I speak to Gordon's back as he reaches up and easily plucks two tumblers from the top shelf of the cabinet. He's a giant. Damn him. I hoisted my five-foot-seven ass up on the counter yesterday just to grab one of those glasses. I fell on dismount and thought I was going to break my neck.

Gordon snorts, pulling out his favorite Kentucky bourbon, Angel's Envy. "Yeah, well, when Dad forces you to move in for months, you learn where things are real fast."

"Maybe you can make me one of those maps like in Harry Potter." I'm kidding. Mostly.

The house is way more than one man would ever need, even if his ego was the size of a small country. Years ago, I dubbed this place the Benson Estate for two reasons: it's sheer enormity and how my dad's face contorted in anger when I called it that. He thought naming something an 'estate' made it sound 'country' whatever the hell that meant. Dear old dad built this place because he was a go big or go home kind of guy. According to him, there was no better way to show off status and success than by besting everyone around him. Which meant the biggest house in the neighborhood, the fastest cars, and the youngest girlfriends. Anything less was completely unacceptable to a larger-than-life man like Oliver Benson. To most people, it might have suggested he was compensating for something. I don't want to know either way—gross.

"I can't figure out how to make the map appear ordinary when a non-Benson tries to read it. Can't have something like that falling into the wrong hands." Gordon shrugs.

I bark out a laugh. "My brother, the dork."

Gordon's smile widens. "You're the one who made me watch the movies. So, what does that make you?"

"Awesome," I answer with a laugh.

A wry smile breaks across his face as he hands me two fingers of bourbon with a large ice ball. This is the first time in quite a while Gordon appears lighthearted. Ever since his accident on the ice, he's acted like he has a hockey stick lodged permanently up his ass.

He still has a lingering limp. Most of the time it's not noticeable, but when he's relaxed at home, it's more pronounced. I suspect he's trying to maintain his tough guy image for the public. An image our dad hammered us to maintain outside of closed doors.

"How's your knee treating you? Are you still doing rehab?"

Gordon eyes me cautiously, as if debating how much to share. He's never been much to talk about his health issues, he doesn't like it when I worry about him. After a few ticks, he sighs. "The doctor says I have a few months left. My muscles are getting stronger, and I almost have full range of motion. It won't be long before the limp is gone, and I can be back to normal."

"Normal is overrated."

Gordon grunts, his way of ending the conversation.

He's one of the lucky few who landed an NHL contract after a lifetime of hard work, talent, and training from our father who was an NHL superstar in his own right. A career which ended the second after he was boarded on the ice and took a stick to the knee by an opposing player with an ax to grind. The other player was given a game misconduct while Gordon was carried off the ice by an athletic trainer and immediately greeted by the team doctor.

Once Gordon was out of surgery to reconstruct the ligaments in his knee and well enough to travel, he was strong-armed by our father to move down to Nashville and finish his recovery. Giving up his penthouse in downtown Chicago for a backyard guest house was a hard decision. Not to mention, he was trading his bachelor ways for a stubborn ass father who would rather drink himself to death than spend time with either of us. Gordon put up with the bullshit better than me. I could barely spend a week with our father without considering patricide.

Biting the bullet, I toss back the amber liquid, trying to ignore the burning in my throat. Gordon takes a long slow sip. Even though our dad was an overachiever with his drinking, Gordon and I both still enjoy the occasional drink to relax and unwind. We're both careful not to drink in excess and certainly not daily.

"I'm certainly glad to be out of the office." Gordon's long fingers play along the edge of his tumbler. "If I had to do one more press conference or deal with Adam's shit again, I would've snapped."

I chuckle trying to imagine my brother losing control and decking a sports correspondent. "I would've bailed you out of jail. Woulda been worth it to see you punch one of those journalists in the face."

I was tempted to punch a reporter myself. The media outlets had a field day at our expense this week. TV, radio, you name it, raked us over the coals. After our chat with Adam, I realized we didn't even have support from within our own organization. Not only are we the youngest and most inexperienced owners of a professional sports team, but I'm a woman. As much as I like to think my vagina is negligible, the rest of the world doesn't agree. If I'm being honest with myself, it's been the biggest pushback.

"I think I would've rather punched Adam in the face." Gordon's jade eyes darken, and his fingers flex into a fist.

"That would've been satisfying. Especially after he told us we'd be the end of the franchise. We both know it wouldn't have been a smart move, though. Without him, there wouldn't be a management team. Plus, you'd end up in jail as someone's bitch, and I'd be stuck running the team myself."

Gordon grumbles, "Might be worth it."

"It might." I laugh. "But I do think we need to start looking for a new general manager as soon as we can. I know we talked about releasing Adam from his contract after two years, but something tells me he won't ride out his time quietly."

"More like a hurricane raging through South Florida."

Adam had stormed into Gordon's office shortly after reaming us out in the conference room, demanding an early release from his contract. He had four years left. Gordon and I entertained the idea of releasing him right there, but neither one of us were prepared to deal with player negotiations, sponsorship deals, and the ins and outs of running a franchise. We settled on cutting his contract in half, leaving all of us unhappy.

When it came to my father's legacy, I never considered being a team co-owner with Gordon. I always thought Gordon would be the most obvious choice to take over ownership of the Devils. Even though we both grew up with hockey, Dad pushed Gordon the hardest. He was Dad's number one. I was just an afterthought. Did it matter I played hockey too? Of course not. Even though I was a damn good player. Not only did I get a full-ride scholarship for hockey at Dartmouth, but I made team USA and medaled at the Olympics. Twice. Dad paid more attention then, attending games and helping with sponsorship deals. I'd like to think there was a part of him there to support me, but I know he used his presence in the games to boost his public image and ticket sales. I liked having his attention for once, so I turned a blind eye to his motives.

He never wanted to spend time with me at the arena either. I absolutely wasn't allowed where there was a chance I'd have a run-in with any of his prized hockey players. A rule in full effect once I turned sixteen. He'd told me I was a distraction to the men, and any advances they might make would be my fault. According to my father, professional athletes couldn't control their wandering dicks. He would know.

I pour myself another splash of bourbon, hoping it'll help me relax. "Problem number one, we need a head coach."

Gordon groans, sitting down at the island, running a hand through his short chestnut hair.

"I know it's not good to have your coach quit right before pre-season games, but I'm glad that asshole Burton is gone."

"I hear Price and Eustes aren't too happy right now." Gordon trails his fingers along his jaw before tapping his index finger on his bottom lip. "I'd offer to help out, but I don't know jack shit about coaching a team. The media would love that. Inexperienced owner appoints himself as a coach, team loses every game."

I eye him tentatively, an idea popping into my head. "What about Weller?"

His eyes widen, and he chokes on his drink. "Mick Weller? Wasn't he booted to the minor leagues?"

"He was. The GM out of Phoenix didn't appreciate him sleeping with his very recent ex-wife. I've crossed paths with him a few times. He's a fighter and won't be down long. A guy like that," I lean toward Gordon, "pushed out of his position because of a slight indiscretion. He's gonna be hungry. He'll be looking for redemption. Plus, he's a great coach. Really knows how to push the players."

"And you think he'll fight for us?" Gordon arches an eyebrow.

"Why wouldn't he? I bet you anything he's working overtime right now trying to get on with an NHL team before the season officially starts."

Silence settles over us as Gordon drums his fingers on the counter. "Let's touch base with him tomorrow and get Adam in the loop. How do you feel about Foster Craig? With Daniels gone, we need another center. He's a free agent right now."

"Out of Vancouver?" I sit down next to Gordon as he nods. "Leader in assists, good face-off percentage, solid player. You've played against him, right?"

"Yeah. The guy is fierce on the ice. He works hard, good skills, and is a total team player. I think he'll play well with Dallas and Harris."

I avoid eye contact with Gordon and toss back the rest of my bourbon as my heart starts to race.

I'm sure I should admit Lincoln Dallas and I have history together. Maybe something along the lines of: *I dated your right winger, and after running into him yesterday, I want to jump his bones, which may prove problematic for us in the future.* I know I should say something, it's the right thing to do. But I can't make my mouth form the words.

I haven't seen Lincoln since the last night of the Olympics. Not any fault of my own either. He kinda disappeared. Until yesterday when I rammed into him because my dumb ass couldn't watch where I was going. Must've made a great impression. *It's been so long since I've seen you, let me trample you to death in the underbelly of the arena.* Could I be more of a spazz? Doubtful.

Since the official announcement of our ownership, everything is different. Not only am I his boss, but I have to be nothing but professional if I want to be taken seriously. I will absolutely be held to higher standards than the men around me. There's no way I could date anyone, let alone one of my players. Which is kinda bullshit. It doesn't matter my stomach flutters like a teenage girl at the thought of seeing him again. My hormones will have to take a backseat to my career. If the press ever got wind there was hanky-panky going on at the top of the Devil's franchise, they would officially nominate my vagina for VP of player relations.

And then she'd be fired.

He probably doesn't harbor any feelings for me, anyway. Players like him could get any girl they want. And usually do.

"I think they would complement each other well on the ice." I set my glass down and take a deep breath. "What about Devin Lane? Dad left the team weak on the left side. Harris is good, but he can't be on the ice the whole game."

Gordon nods in agreement. "I'll have Adam reach out. Anyone on the team you'd like to trade out?"

I chew on my thumb nail, needing a minute to think. "I'm not sure if we should make any player changes right away. It might be smart to let the new coach weed these guys out."

"Probably smart. They lost several players at the end of last season, so it's like we have a brand-new team."

"Agreed. They didn't play well last year. My expectations aren't very high."

Hell, they need to be, though.

While my brother and I inherited the hockey franchise, it's far from a done deal. Oliver Benson made sure it came with stipulations. Neither of us are allowed to sell our portion of the Devils for two seasons and have to attend all home games. The icing on the cake: we have to make it to the playoffs by the second year of ownership or we'll be forced to sell to an undisclosed associate. At least the old bastard was generous enough to give us two seasons.

If the way the team played last year is any indication, we're in for a bumpy ride. Hell, we'd need a damn miracle to even get near the playoffs.

As it is, we have no coach, a disgruntled GM, and a disjointed team. And it seems my libido wants the one thing it can't have. A silver-eyed hockey player with a body made for sin.

Down girl, he's not for you.

But fuck me, there's a part of me that wants him to be.

4

JAZLYN

"Alright, are you ready to meet your team?" Gordon turns to Mick Weller, our new head coach, and I with a smile as the elevator door closes. He runs a hand down the length of his silk tie, black to match the rest of his all-black suit, and looks at us expectantly.

"Oh, absolutely." Mick rubs his palms together.

He's excited, like a kid on Christmas morning standing in front of a whole mess of presents. Mick was itching to get back in the NHL, as predicted. After our phone conversation Saturday, it took all of two point five seconds for him to accept the position and insist on starting with the team on Monday's scheduled practice.

Mick's eyes are bright. "I can't tell you how excited I am to be back in the big leagues."

Smoothing my hands over the slight flare of my hips, I eye myself in the polished mirrors lining the elevator.

I look good.

Professional with a side of sexy. Just because I want to be taken seriously doesn't mean I can't make a statement. I can do the job of a man, and look good doing it.

My black fitted skirt stops just above the knee and has a small slit up the back, perfect for showing off what I've been told is my best asset. Key word here being ass. My dark green blouse brightens the green of my eyes while enhancing the curve of my breasts. Black four-inch "don't fuck with me" pumps complete the look.

Nevermind the lion's den, I'm marching straight into a room full of Devils.

"More than ready." I look up at Gordon while a slow smile spreads across my face, and I give him a wink.

Gordon lets out a low laugh. He knows exactly what that look means.

Game on.

My look today is calculated. Everyone is doubting my ability to lead simply because I'm a woman. Well, a woman is exactly what they're going to get. I have no intention of blending into this man's world by wearing a pantsuit or whatever else would make me look more masculine. So, I'll showcase my curves when I can and put my femininity on display. I'm not going to change who I am for anyone.

The locker room comes into view, and my pulse quickens. My palms dampen with sweat, and my throat tightens. The weight of this is monumental—we're making history here. Not just within the team, but the whole damn league.

Whether they like it or not.

And trust me, there's still plenty of opposition. Opinions are flying around in full force instead of dying down. My brother and I were front and center when I flipped to the sports channel this morning. Many question my father's sanity in leaving the team to us, insinuating he wasn't mentally competent due to the alcoholism. Or he was hammered when he made the will. Others claim he no longer had any respect for the hockey league and our ownership is nothing but a big middle finger to the entire organization.

I have one response. *Screw them.* The naysayers, the chauvinists, and everyone else against us can kiss my perfectly rounded ass. It's all bullshit. I have two jobs. One—turn this group of burly individuals into a team. Two—transform said team into champions.

"Let's do this," I whisper more to myself than the men flanking me.

The players rustle in their seats, their loud-as-fuck voices silenced as we make our way into the room and up to the front.

I'm prepared for the looks of curiosity I receive from most of the athletes and even the few looks of disdain. What throws me off balance and leaves me digging deep for some semblance of control is the scorching light blue gaze belonging to the one and only Lincoln Dallas. He leans against the wall, arms crossed and expression unreadable. He's too sexy for his own good, and I feel my panties dampening already.

Of course, I knew he'd be here. But fuck, our relationship was six years ago. I've moved on.

Mostly.

He probably hasn't thought of me since then. Internet searches from the few times I've Googled him confirm he's dated other women. I've certainly dated other men.

I'll have nothing except professional interactions with him.

Only, the look he's giving me incinerates my panties and has my stomach twisting in knots.

This doesn't feel very professional.

I can feel his eyes devouring my body, and I take the opportunity to engage in an appraisal of my own. Women everywhere will be outraged if I don't take a second to admire how his dark blue Henley hugs all those delicious muscles in his arms and across his chest. And those thighs…his dark jeans do nothing to hide the fact his perfectly muscled legs look like they were carved from stone. Maybe by Michelangelo himself.

I bet he'll have no problem holding me up against a wall, driving into me over and over while I chant his name and hold onto his wavy dark brown hair by the fistful.

Lincoln's eyes snap back to mine as an involuntary shiver crawls up my spine, and he quirks up a corner of his mouth in a sly half-smile. I shift my legs to dull the growing ache between them and break eye contact.

Gordon, never one to waste time, dives right in. "Thank you all for coming in early. My father's passing came as a shock to all of us, and I want to personally thank everyone for their condolences. As you've heard by now, Oliver Benson left the team to my sister and me. I'm aware we're the youngest owners in the league. I'm also aware the media's crucifying us because Jazz is a woman." Gordon pauses, looking around the room, meeting each player's eyes. It's a look I've been on the receiving end of as a teenager—he's challenging them to say something. "For the life of me, I can't figure out why either of those things matter. My dad moved from a player, to a coach, and finally to an owner where he ran this team for years. Tell me, how many times did he make it into the playoffs? How many cups did he bring home? The answer to both questions is zero." Gordon holds up his hand in the form of an 'O'. "Can someone please tell me where the team finished last season?"

"Second to last in the league," Owen McIver, a powerful defenseman, calls out from the center of the room.

"That's right. My dad was a good player but didn't always make the best decisions as an owner. He was disconnected from the team. I'd say it's well past time for a change." Gordon steps back.

I step up to take his place. "We want to move on from mediocrity and make this a winning team. As Gordon accurately pointed out, I lack a certain piece of anatomy swinging between my legs. But it doesn't mean I don't have what it takes to get us in line for the playoffs."

I hear a muffled snicker from the back of the room and look up to see Kevin Craft and Joe Vale eyeing the floor, each with a hand blocking their grins. Their jokes don't bother me, even if it is at my expense. I don't expect to get immediate support from all the men on the team. Results will win them over, not words.

"Like you, I've been playing hockey most of my life. I played for Dartmouth and brought home a silver and a gold medal for this country at two different Olympic games. And up until about two weeks ago, was one of the trainers for team USA. I assure you, both my brother and I want what's best for this team. Right now, we're focusing on talent for both the team and the coaching staff. I'm sure most of you have heard Coach Burton is no longer with us. He served the Devils well for the past several years but decided to take his career in a different direction. I'm pleased, however, to introduce Mick Weller, former assistant coach for the Phoenix Lightning as your new head coach."

Mick takes a step forward. "I'm grateful to the Bensons for the opportunity to lead this team. I'm excited to be working with all of you and look forward to turning things around. Now, I can talk about myself all day, you can ask any of my ex-girlfriends," he flashes the group a quick smile, "but I think we can get to know more about each other out on the ice. I'm ready to start practice, I'll see you on the ice in ten."

After a quick shake of my hand, followed by Gordon's, Mick is out the door. Multiple conversations start up as the team stands and makes their way to the locker rooms. Gordon is off to the side in deep conversation with one of the assistant coaches.

I see Lincoln out of the corner of my eye. He waits until most of the players are gone before he pushes himself from the wall and heads in my direction. I thank a couple of the guys who hung back to offer their congratulations before Lincoln pauses beside me.

"Good to see you again, Jazz." He leans down, whispering in my ear, close enough that his breath brushes my neck. His lips so close covers my flesh in goosebumps, and he sweeps his fingers across my inner elbow.

Electricity shoots up my arm and straight to my downstairs. Torturously, he trails his fingers down my arm and across my hand leaving fire in their wake.

His voice is husky in my ear. "Congratulations, boss."

Seconds later, Lincoln disappears, leaving me standing here with my mouth gaped open like an idiot. A million thoughts run through my head.

All of them dirty.

So much for keeping everything strictly professional. One small touch turns me into a panting, horny mess. I need a good orgasm from my battery-operated friend and a nice long conversation to convince my vajayjay Lincoln Dallas is completely forbidden.

Because he is.

In every fucking way.

5

LINCOLN

What the fuck was that?

Of course, I had to put my hands on her. Damn dick took control of my body.

Touching Jazlyn had been a mistake. A mistake I'd give anything to repeat until we're both gloriously naked.

But a mistake, nonetheless.

Fifteen minutes have passed, and I swear I can still feel her soft skin beneath my fingertips.

I know her position with the Devils is precarious. Hell, the media is still dragging her name through the mud at every opportunity just because she sits down to pee. Most of the men on the team have the same opinion, and I'm already fucking sick of it. Her gender has nothing to do with what she can do as an owner. She'll have to work twice as hard to prove herself. Unfortunately, it means there's no way in hell Jazz will ever consider anything with a player. Her fragile reputation wouldn't be able to withstand it.

She would forever be marked with her own scarlet letter, one standing for unprofessional. Everyone would know her as the hockey owner who couldn't keep her legs together.

Of course, I'm the asshole who wants to play with fire. I know damn well trying to start anything with her will end with both of us getting burned. Her with the media and me with a shitty trade. Still, I can't help myself. Being so close, it almost physically pains me not to touch her. Now, the loss of her skin underneath mine feels like I'm missing a part of myself.

But after how I tucked tail and ran after the Olympics, she may not want anything to do with me.

Fuck.

I grab my stick—ahem—hockey stick and follow my teammates out on the ice, gathering around our new coach for what I'm sure will be some kind of come to Jesus talk.

"Can you believe that bitch canned Coach Burton?" Kevin whispers to Joe. Both of these guys are standing in front of me, not giving a shit who hears them. I know what they said about Jazz at the meeting, and there's no doubt she's the bitch in this scenario.

My fingers curl and uncurl into tight fists at my side. I'm seconds away from knocking some sense into these two idiots. Starting a fight immediately after meeting the new coach will certainly give him a lasting impression, just not the one I want to make if I have any desire to play. I rein in my temper and nearly have to bite my tongue to keep quiet.

"I heard he told her there was no way he was going to be controlled by—"

Whatever Joe is going to respond with is cut off by the sound of Coach Weller clearing his throat.

"Alright, guys, listen up. I know some of you aren't happy with all of these changes being made. I don't expect you all to like me right off the bat, but I do expect your respect. Same goes with the new owners. After we run through some drills, I'll be calling each of you individually to come and talk to me. This is your time to express any concerns you have or ask me any questions. There will be no ramifications for anything brought up. I'll also be letting you know my expectations of you. As for me, you can expect I will try my damnedest to make this a winning team. Even if it means recommending players be cut from the roster or traded out. I'm available day or night if any one of you gets into trouble. Please do not hesitate to call me. If you have a problem with any one of us on the coaching staff or a teammate, come to my office and we will find a solution. Any questions?"

He's met with the shuffling of skates. These guys can talk all the bullshit they want to each other, but when it comes down to it, they aren't man enough to speak up in front of the team. These one-on-one meetings are sure going to be interesting.

"Well, then I guess we better get started." Coach Weller divides us into teams and starts practice with puck handling and passing.

Practice is intense with drills, and by the time I walk into Coach Weller's office, I'm dripping with sweat. Tension thickens the atmosphere, and I edge toward his desk, the hairs on the back of my neck sticking up.

"Dallas, please take a seat," Weller says tersely, running a hand through his hair and rubbing the back of his neck. "Alright, lay it on me."

"Excuse me?" Cautiously, I lower myself into the uncomfortable armchair on the other side of his desk. "Am I missing something here, Coach?"

Weller sighs and sags a bit in his chair. "Sorry, Lincoln, the past few meetings haven't exactly gone as planned. Are there any issues or concerns you have with the team or how it's being run?"

"At the risk of sounding like an ass kisser, Phoenix struggled every season until they recruited you. Now they're sitting pretty in the top of their division, and I can't wait to see what you can do with this team. The owners have just stepped into their role, so we won't know how effective their leadership is for at least a few months. The only thing we can do is sit back and wait."

"Well, Dallas." Weller sits up a bit straighter in his chair and laces his fingers together in front of him. "I think you may be the most level-headed man on this team."

"Thank you, Coach. Either shit works out or it doesn't. People are full of surprises."

"That they are." A slow smile stretches across his face, and his eyes look unfocused, like his thoughts have drifted elsewhere. He gives himself a shake and proceeds, "So, I've been watching footage from last year's games and I noticed Coach Burton underutilized you. You're a quick thinker, fast skater, and you don't miss a beat when you take a hit. Lincoln, you're a strong player and dominate the puck when you have the ice time. Unfortunately for you, it looked like Burton played favorites and held you back on the second string. I'm starting you as the first line right wing. Don't let me down, Dallas."

"You got it, Coach." I stand and quickly accept his handshake, feeling a pleasant tightness in my chest. It feels good to be recognized after years of hard work. I have long suspected Coach Burton of favoritism, no doubt under Oliver Benson's influence. That fucker didn't want me on his team from day one.

"You can send Harris in next. Oh, and Dallas, keep in mind, I'll be looking for a team captain."

Team Captain.

That would put me in a great position for a trade. Maybe even make me look good enough to be traded to Chicago. They're in line for the cup and close to my family.

My mom and my younger brother, Liam, still live in Clarendon Hills, a suburb of the windy city. I keep in touch as much as I can through video calls and text messages, and because we don't see each other as often, we make sure to get together when I travel that way for games.

Moving there, I'd be able to help Liam train for the draft and be there to keep my mom company once he leaves.

With a curt nod, I leave the office feeling much better about the team and where I fit in it.

I'm feeling a lot better about a trade.

6

JAZLYN

If I have to listen to one more dumbass man tell me to wear a pantsuit and let my brother do all the talking, I'm going to lose my fucking shit. It's not that I have a personal grudge against pants. I just refuse to pander to the media, and they want me to blend in with the men and keep my mouth shut like a good girl. News flash, I'm not that kind of girl. A pair of pants won't fix this media storm. I need professional help.

Find a PR person, they say. It'll be fun, they say. Well, they're a bunch of fucking liars. This is pure misery. I'm not sure what the fourth circle of Hell consists of, but it has to be better than this. I've already interviewed five of these pricks, and I'm positive this stuffed shirt sitting on the other side of my desk won't be any different.

I initially balked over finding someone to take over the public relations nightmare I'd found myself in, but considering what Coach Weller told me after his player meetings a few days ago, I promptly changed my mind. Knowing so many of the players felt so strongly about my being here pisses me off. And I'll do whatever it takes to fix it, including finding someone to take over public relations and help improve both my image and the image of the team. I can't stand by and let the media keep twisting reality, especially when it affects the morale of so many players.

"So." I take a deep breath, trying like hell to calm my tits before continuing. "What steps would you recommend the Devils' organization take to improve our media presence?"

"Well, Miss Benson." Dave…wait…Dan…? Anyway, this guy, who's name likely started with 'D', rubs his palms down his thighs. He seems nervous. And he should be. I have a good feeling he's about to say something stupid. "It seems the media has a problem with your gender, as I'm sure you're aware. I think it would be best addressed if you let your brother lead the press conferences for a while, and you took a backseat role for interviews and corporate events."

Donald…Doug…Oh what the hell, Dick is way more suitable at this point. Dick looks at me for confirmation. I give him none. If he wants to walk through the land mines, he could be my guest. He's not getting my help.

I'm pretty sure at this point, I've successfully ground my teeth into dust. And is my eye twitching? I am almost at my breaking point. The chances of me finding a PR person at this point are slim to none.

Despite the fact my eyes are shooting lasers into his body, he continues. "Don't get me wrong, Miss Benson, you're an attractive woman. But I think, in this case, you should consider toning things down." *Don't say pantsuit. For the love of all things holy, don't say it.* "It might be good, for the time being, if you wore a pantsuit to fit in with your male counterparts."

There it is, folks. This is the moment where I lose my shit and end up serving a life sentence for murder. No more heels, home-cooked food, comfy beds, sex with men…

Mustering all the patience I have left, I stand up and point at the closed door. It's been a while since the last time I had some good dick, and I'm sure as hell not going to jail without getting more. Murder is off the table.

I'm disappointed. Dick would have made a lovely corpse.

"I suggest you remove yourself from my office immediately. I will not hide who or what I am. I have half a mind to plant my foot so far up your ass that every time you brush your teeth, you'll be shining my shoe."

"Sorry to waste your time." His voice trembles as his hands fumble with his briefcase before he flees from the room.

Releasing a long breath, I flop back down in my chair like a deflated balloon. I lean forward and thunk my forehead on my desk, letting out a loud groan. My office door opens and closes with a quick click of the doorknob, and I hear shuffling. Probably Gordie coming in to laugh at my misery.

"What do you want, Gordie? Before you make fun of me, let me wallow in self-pity for a few more seconds."

"Who am I to interrupt a good wallow in self-pity?" I'm so deep in the dismal PR nightmare it takes me a second to register an amused feminine voice with a slight southern accent. She is, indeed, not my brother.

Pushing myself up from my desk, confusion draws my brows together as I take in Business Barbie standing on the other side of my desk, practically dripping from head to toe in pale pink. Petite and gorgeous, she has breasts that seem a little too large for her frame and perfectly tanned skin. Her honey blonde hair falls straight past her shoulders to the middle of her back. Crystal blue eyes sparkle with what looks to be amusement.

I have absolutely no idea who she is or why she's in my office.

Lucky for the both of us, she doesn't miss a beat as she takes a step forward and extends her hand for a handshake.

"Sorry to barge in on you like this. I assumed the cryin' man running from your office meant your interview with him was over. I'm Lucille Hurst, PR specialist from Coomer Associates, but you can call me Lucy. Your assistant penciled me in at the last minute. I'm also gonna assume she didn't let you know I was comin'."

Nice firm handshake. Not a limp wrist handshake like the men gave me. Her smooth skin hints at an expensive moisturizer. I'll have to ask her about that later. "Nice to meet you, Lucy. Your assumptions on both accounts are correct. Please have a seat. Unless you're going to suggest I start wearing pants to fit in with all the men around here."

"Heavens, no. Pants definitely have their place, but I prefer skirts and dresses." Lucy laughs, plopping herself down in front of me and runs a hand down her own skirt for emphasis. "Just 'cause no one likes the fact you're a woman doesn't mean you need to hide it."

Thank you, Jesus. Finally, someone who doesn't need to ask the Wizard of Oz for a brain.

Someone who understands.

Lucy's a breath of fresh air.

She shifts in her chair, crossing her ankles and leans forward. "And I would never tell you what to wear unless it was truly horrendous. What you need is someone to help you put a positive spin on everything that goes out to the media. Give 'em something else to focus on. Someone to be present not only at interviews with you and your brother, but with the players. Right now, they're all liabilities. You don't know what any one of 'em would say to a reporter. You also need some nice charity events. Things that will get you and your brother involved in the community. Events you can wear all manner of dresses to."

She hits the nail on the head. There's no telling what the players say about me behind closed doors. The last thing I need is private locker room talk making its way to a press conference and ending up on the evening news. I've also been thinking about getting involved in some charities but didn't know where to start.

"I assume you have a few ideas there?"

"You assume correctly, and as soon as you hire me to represent the Devils, I'll gladly share."

I tilt my head back and laugh, "I like you, Lucy. I think you'll fit in just fine around here."

A sly grin stretches across Lucy's face. "Do you mean I'm hired?"

"Welcome to the team, Ms. Hurst. It'll be refreshing to have another woman around here to keep these men in line. Speaking of, I've got a practice to drop in on. Would you care to join me while I have my assistant get all the paperwork together?"

A look I can only describe as pure bliss flashes across Lucy's face. "I won't turn that down. I love hockey just as much as I love sweet tea. And I'll give you a hint, us Georgia gals drink a lot of sweet tea."

Twenty minutes into practice, I realize Lucy is not only easy to talk to, she makes for a great distraction. Not once do I have to force myself to look away from Lincoln to focus on the rest of the team. Okay, fine, it happens twice. But it's a great improvement from the last practice I attended.

The Devils are improving but don't fully function as a team, yet. Quite a few players could benefit from some skills sessions. Not that I want to name names right now. This week I'll be going over contracts, reviewing players' stats, and getting more familiar with how they play and work together. I watched some of their games last year so at least I have something to start with.

"There's something about grown men slammin' each other into the boards I just love!" Lucy claps her hands with excitement as the McIver brothers collide with Kevin Craft, smashing his body into the glass.

I can't help the laugh that bubbles out of me as Kevin falls backwards. "I can certainly see the appeal."

Kevin pulls himself up on his skates, but instead of joining the other players, he stands still and glares over at us. Message received. Kevin Craft is a douche.

"Oh my, he is a treat." Lucy turns in her chair to face me. "I'm going to step out on a limb here and say he's not your number one fan."

"You'd be correct. He's been the most vocal against my part in ownership."

"Bless his heart. So, let's get back to these fundraisers. I was thinkin' we could start with a casino type event with prize giveaways that can include game tickets, signed merchandise, lessons with an individual player, and facility tours. I've got a company I work with who can set us up with all the games and dealers. The proceeds can be donated to several different charities, but I would strongly suggest lookin' into Growing Families. They've been struggling to expand their program in Nashville and a large donation here would make the biggest impact. Not to mention, there are several underserved areas of the city where an expansion would help connect those kids in need with good mentors."

I nod my head in agreement. "Sounds great. I was thinking of doing something to help kids, and this sounds perfect. Although, we should probably run everything by Gordon and make sure he's on board. What's our timeline?"

"I was thinking close to Halloween. That gives us around two months to get the word out and get it all set up. Plus," Lucy lowers her voice and leans in toward me, "we're close enough to the holidays and that tends to make people looser with their wallets."

Oh yes, Lucy and I are going to get along just fine. Not only is she clever, she radiates confidence.

I chuckle. "Ruthless, I love it."

Lucy opens her mouth to reply when a thunderous boom on the glass interrupts us. Both our heads swing just in time to see Lincoln release his teammate from the boards.

He raises his head, meeting my eyes. A flash of heat swims through me, and I clench my legs together trying to stifle the reaction he has on my body.

Damn him.

Damn my libido.

His eyes never leave mine as he starts to skate backwards toward the center of the ice.

"No. No. No. No. No." Lucy's scolding reminds me of my mom after I asked for something no less than six times in a row.

I meet her wide-eyed stare. "Don't look at me like that. There is nothing going on there."

Her gaze sharpens on me and the corner of her mouth lifts in a half smile. "That didn't look like nothing. Do you know how it would look if you started dating one of your players?"

I sigh. "A PR nightmare, I know. We knew each other years ago. It was nothing. We've barely said two words to each other since I took over ownership."

"The way you keep sayin' it's nothing makes it sound like something." Lucy's laugh is light and teasing.

"Whatever it was doesn't matter. It would be career suicide to get involved with any of my players. Therefore, absolutely nothing will happen between us."

Lucy turns back to watch the action on the ice with a smile on her face. "There's that word again."

7

LINCOLN

Tension is high as I try like hell to dominate the game. My fingers fly across the controller, pressing buttons in rapid sequence, while insults fling like confetti through my headset. There are two punks ahead of me, leading in kills, but I'm catching up.

"Don't make me come over there and tell your mother what kind of language you're using," I bite into my microphone after a boy, who sounds no older than twelve, unleashed a profanity ridden tirade directed at me. It was, of course, after I delivered a well-executed head shot. I fight the urge to tell him where to stick his controller. The last thing I need is this kid's mom showing up at my door, demanding I apologize for telling her precious baby to shove something up his ass.

The front door to my apartment opens and closes moments before I hear a male voice call out. "Honey, I'm home."

After muting my headset, I answer, "Just let yourself in, Tag. No need to knock or anything." I lower my voice to a mumble. "Not like this is my private space."

I'm kidding. Mostly.

When I was traded to Nashville, I opted to move into The

Mill, a set of luxury apartments close to the arena, owned by the Devils' organization and rented exclusively to players. Most of the single guys on the team live here. It came fully furnished and seemed like a no brainer to me. A career in hockey is erratic at best. Trades are swift and players are often given a few days to uproot their lives and relocate to their new city.

Being so close to most of my teammates is both a blessing and a curse. Some of these guys have become like a second family to me, especially Tag. We spend a lot of time together and support each other in our personal lives. It also means they drop by unannounced at any given time, which doesn't always leave a whole lot of privacy. I think I see more naked ass here than in the locker room at the arena. Walking in on a guy passed out on his floor, naked as the day he was born, is an image that stays with you no matter how hard you try to bleach your eyeballs. Lobotomy is the next logical step, but it seems a little extreme.

"What're ya up to?" Tag plants his hip against the couch, crosses his arms over his chest, and eyes me with a smirk.

"Playing Call of Duty against other talented adult males. Definitely not losing to foul-mouthed kids if that's what you're thinking."

Tag throws his head back and laughs. "Well, turn that crap off. I'm here to take your lucky ass to lunch before we head to practice. In case you haven't heard, I'm quite the catch."

The thought of another practice makes my muscles ache. It's Friday, and I'm itching for a break over the weekend. Pre-season games start next week, and the new coach has been working us nonstop since our Monday meet and greet. Today will be no different. Training in the weight room followed by drills and a scrimmage. Either Coach has a sick sense of humor or he wants to make sure all of us are too tired to cause any trouble at his welcome party tonight. A party all coaches and management will be attending.

Including the owners.

My balls ache for release at the thought of seeing Jazz tonight. Preferably while pounding into that hot body of hers.

Except she's off limits.

Forbidden.

Not only does she own my contract but can trade me to another shit team. While I have my agent at the ready to scout other organizations, I want a trade to be my choice. Right now, I have my sights set on a team with the skills to make the playoffs.

Doesn't mean a guy can't have some dirty fantasies.

I still have both my hands.

Turning off the game, I stand and stretch my arms over my head. "Are you getting hard up for a date, Tag?"

"You do have a pretty face." Tag eyes me speculatively. "But don't get your hopes up, Dallas, you're not my type. Too much below the belt and not enough above it."

"What a shame." I grab my practice bag and slip on my shoes. "Wait. Are you saying I'm dumb?"

Tag snickers. "I wasn't, but I might be thinkin' it now."

Shooting Tag a look out of the corner of my eye, I toss him an extra stick, which he catches easily.

"We've got the new trade starting with us today." I close the door behind us and head down the wide hallway to the elevator.

"And you say I'm the girl in this relationship," Tag scoffs. "You always have all the gossip."

A smile plays on my lips. "If you paid attention, you'd know about new players. And yeah, you are the girl. You look much better in a dress."

"Damn right I do. Your legs are shit."

8

LINCOLN

Not sure what I expected walking into Coach Weller's welcome party, but it sure isn't him tossing back tequila shots with Adam and Gordon. For one, I've been under the impression Adam isn't enamored with either of the new owners. Owen might have overheard the end of a certain meeting where Adam referred to Jazz and Gordon as inevitable failures. Two, well, our latest head coach doesn't strike me a tequila guy. More of a scotch drinker.

Nodding my way through the crowd, I make my way toward the guys. Tag, Owen, and Ian flank our most recent trade, Foster Craig. Foster is our new center, fresh off the plane from Vancouver. He stands tall, like most of us, but his physique is more lean than overly muscular. Hell of a skater too, the fastest on the team, which earned him a few sneers from some of the veterans. Not to mention he looks like a rugged blonde model *and* has a British accent. Basically, every girl's kryptonite. He's going to have to beat all the women off with a stick.

Judging by the look on his face, I think I know which stick he'd prefer to use.

"Hello, ladies." I clap Ian and Owen on the shoulders before leaning over them to signal the bartender for a beer.

Ian elbows me in the ribs, which only makes me lean into him more, and he narrows his eyes. "What took you so long? Couldn't figure out what to wear? Had to fix your makeup?"

"Of course. Couldn't let you bitches completely outshine me. Tag has such beautiful soft hair, you and your brother have the pretty blue eyes, and don't get me started on the newbie. A British accent?" I lean my head back and groan for effect. "You're killing me here. All I have is my pretty face."

Foster hands me a beer, clinking his bottle against mine before taking a sip. "Cheers. And what a pretty face it is, mate. Just give me a minute to revel in its glory."

"I don't know why I hang out with all ya'll." Tag snickers, shaking his head. "Wasn't the last James Bond played by some Craig guy?"

Foster's eyes narrow. "Daniel Craig, yes?"

Owen breaks into a fit of giggles that would put a schoolgirl to shame. He's so amused by his own joke he's struggling to get his words out through the laughter. "I think that makes you the team's official James Bond. I thought Christmas only comes once a year. Shocking. Positively shocking."

Foster groans. Loudly.

"Don't mind my brother, he cracks himself up," Ian snorts. "Sometimes I think our poor mom should have quit after one."

Ian, Owen, and Tag hunker down to fill Foster in on all the dirty team details. Terrible attitudes, bad players, who makes the plays, what they think of the coach and the team. A conversation any other time I would have been all about. This particular moment, however, the door of the bar opens like the gates of heaven, and I swear I hear angels singing.

Fucking hell.

Jazz.

I want to haul her off somewhere private and kiss her senseless. I want a taste of her, and my body doesn't care if we're surrounded by the team. And more than that, I want to talk to her. See how things are going and how she's dealing with all the change.

As much as I try to resist, I can't keep my eyes off of her.

Wanting something with every fiber of your body and knowing you'll never get it is pure fucking torture. I must be a masochist because as hard as I try, I can't make myself turn a blind eye to everything that is Jazz.

She looks great tonight. One of those tight skirts that drive me crazy. This time it's gray paired with a black sleeveless blouse, cut to show off a slight amount of cleavage. Enough that I'm left with water pooling in my open mouth and an itch to find out if her skin tastes as good as I remember. Her chestnut hair, down in loose waves around her shoulders, has me longing to run my hands through those silky strands. Her black heels give her a few inches, but I would still need to lift her up to align my naughty anatomy with hers.

I shouldn't let my head wander like that.

Either one of them.

But as long as I don't act on anything, this is my own little harmless fantasy. Just a beautiful woman and all the filthy, dirty things I'd like to do to her.

Jazlyn spots her brother and joins him and some of the coaching staff by the side of the bar. One of the assistants slithers over to her and places his hand on the small of her back. His bulbous head lowers to her ear in intimate conversation.

Something unbidden and dark crawls up my spine and holds me in place.

I have no right to feel this way, no right to want to chop off his hand, and certainly no right to feel like he's touching what's mine.

Needing to turn away before my feelings etch on my face, I direct myself back to the teammates in front of me.

"How are you likin' things here in Nashville?" Tag asks Foster.

"I suspect it will be a much warmer winter than what I'm used to." His accent is light and smooth as he takes a quick sip of his Manhattan. "And the sights here are bloody gorgeous."

Foster smiles at two blondes sitting at a table nearby. Both busty and wearing dresses that look painted on. They whisper to each other and smile back, sending a message I can only interpret to mean they're both interested in whatever he offers. Simultaneously.

"Alright, Bond." Tag grabs his shoulders and redirects his gaze in our direction. "Plenty of time to hook-up with the ladies later. Right now, it's time to get to know your new teammates over a pool tournament."

"Which basically means you losers give me your money while I kick your ass." Ian laughs and follows Owen and Tag over to the pool tables while Foster and I linger behind.

He throws a couple more looks I can only describe as smoldering at the blondes.

Ian calls over his shoulder. "Let's go, Lincoln. Bond? My wallet is feeling thin."

I steal one last glance at Jazz. The douche who put his hands on her is now long gone, presumably with both his hands intact. Jazz looks bored and steps back from her brother, who's in an animated conversation with Coach Weller. She raises her white wine to her glossy pink lips for a slow sip, letting her eyes flit across the room until they meet mine.

She lowers her glass and gives me a shy smile. The knowledge it's just for me sucker punches me in the gut. I don't know what about her makes me feel this way. No woman has ever been able to hold my attention as long as Jazz. She's under my skin and on a constant loop running through my brain since she skated her way back in my life.

Fuck, maybe the past six years.

I should've never listened to her prick of a father. Letting her go was, quite possibly, one of the stupidest things I've done.

"Lincoln, you coming?" Ignoring Foster gets me pelted in the face with a wadded-up napkin. "You might as well forget about that one. She's way out of your league, mate."

I tear my eyes from Jazz and narrow them at Foster. "What the fuck are you talking about?"

He throws his head back and laughs. "Just what I said, Linc. She owns your arse. Quite literally. I don't think I need to tell you how twisted it could end up. Don't worry. Your secret is safe with me."

"Shut up, Bond."

"Tell me, are you going to pass her a note in class? Maybe ask her to the school disco?" Foster throws his arm over my shoulders and leads me over to the pool tables. "Would you like me to ask her friends if she's mentioned wanting to see your dangly-bits?"

"You're an asshole. I hope you know that." I give Foster a playful shove.

He laughs again. "Yeah, but right now, I'm your arsehole, and I believe that refrigerator-sized man challenged us to a pool tournament."

9

JAZLYN

My eyes land on Lincoln's broad shoulders as he leans over the green-felted pool table and travel down the sculpted muscles of his back before landing on a delectable, perfectly muscled, ass. Even my grandmother would've sat back and appreciated the sight. I have to hold myself in place, my fingers begging to latch on to his flawless butt.

Professionally speaking, of course.

"See anything interestin' over there?" Lucy's teasing voice sounds over my shoulder, and I jump.

Busted.

Of course, she'd show up right as I'm admiring Lincoln's form as he bends over to take his shot. I could lie and say it's for research. However, researching how Lincoln's ass looks when he's slightly bent, how the pool cue slowly slides through his fingers, or how the muscles in his shoulders bunch as he takes his shot, is probably not a valid excuse.

I turn around with a bright smile plastered on my now heated face. I can tell her it's nothing, but it would only garner more scrutiny.

"Hey there, Lucy. I was just checking out the game over

there." I gesture toward the players. "You know, at the pool table. Those Bruiser Brothers are pool sharks." I cock my head to the side. "Although, I'm not sure which one is the better player. How are you doing?" Yes, I'm rambling, but if it keeps Lucy distracted, I'll count that as a win. "You look great, by the way, but do you ever wear colors other than pink?"

I motion toward her dress, which is a dark pink, sleeveless sheath paired with matching pink pumps. The woman is Elle Woods incarnate.

Lucy throws her head back and laughs, capturing the attention of several men. "Don't think I don't know a distraction when I see one, Miss Benson. But yes, most of what I own is pink."

"Well then, how about I offer you a drink, or perhaps several, and we never speak of this again?" I hold out my arm, which Lucy accepts, and we stroll toward the bar together.

"Several would be splendid."

Maneuvering Lucy around a group of rookies, who blatantly check us out, I toss an icy look over my shoulder. Not on the menu, boys. There are plenty of puck bunnies around the arena who would love a warm bed and a young hot stud, but not me. I only have eyes for one, and even he's too much to handle.

"Hey, Lucy," Gordon calls out, waving us over to where he stands with Adam. "I didn't see you come in. Glad you could join us."

Lucy greets them with a quick handshake. "Glad to be invited."

I throw Gordon a questioning look. I'll never understand how he can stomach being around Adam for an extended period of time, even in a professional way. The sooner we get to the playoffs and can find a replacement, the better. As if he heard my unspoken hatred, my dearest brother looks at me with wide Bambi eyes and shrugs his shoulders slightly, feigning his innocence. He isn't fooling me. I grew up with him making the same exact face. He's never as innocent as he tries to portray.

"You ladies look lovely." Adam must be three sheets to the wind to offer up any sort or compliment where I'm involved.

Gordon leans toward Lucy, a charming smile stretches across his face. "Tell me more about this Vegas style fundraiser idea you have."

Lucy's eyes sparkle before she launches into a full discussion about the charity night, starting with how important the Big Brothers Big Sisters organization is to the community. Adam and I may as well not exist.

I frown at Adam and cross my arms. I don't know what his motivation is for hanging out with Gordon tonight, but I don't like it. The assistant coach and trainers he's known for years are here. So, why hang out with someone you've been so vocal against? He's up to no good, I have little doubt.

"When someone compliments you, it's only appropriate to say, *thank you*," Adam murmurs, reaching out to brush a wave of hair over my shoulder.

I force myself not to flinch from his touch, not wanting him to think he has the upper hand. "Thank you, Adam. You also look nice tonight." I end the fake compliment with a delightful smile I plaster on my face for special assholes like him. If he wants to play nice, I'm game. Since we work in the same office, I should probably practice being civil.

"Thank you, Jazlyn." Adam smooths a hand down his dark blue pinstripe suit jacket. "Have you gotten to meet our new addition?"

"Foster?" I shake my head. "Not yet. He's going to be a good one."

"I agree, he'll be a great asset to the team."

I toy with the zipper on my purse and avoid looking Adam in

the eyes. "I appreciate your hard work getting his contract. I know it wasn't easy."

"It wasn't. I see you added some girl power to the crew," Adam scoffs.

My eyes snap up to his and see him watching Lucy with a predatory gaze. Leave it up to him to ruin a nice moment.

I move my body, placing it between his prying eyes and her body. "She's perfectly qualified to handle the Devils' public relations," I hiss. "It's *not* in my agenda to hire or fire people based on their gender. I don't know what you have against women, but believe it or not, Adam, we are perfectly capable of doing things outside the kitchen."

Adam rests his hand on my shoulder, making my skin crawl as he leans in close. He lowers his vile mouth to my ear. "Of course, you can do things outside the kitchen. There's also the bedroom." He chuckles, and all I want is out of his hold and far away from him. "I bet I could fuck that smug look right off your face. Then, we'll see who calls the shots."

What.

The.

Fuck.

Shock runs through me, and I fall into stunned silence for the first time in my life. Did he just say what I think he did?

Son of a bitch.

Keeping my eyes on Adam, I pull away as he trails his hand across my back before dropping it at his side. Every single moment his hand was on me twisted my stomach almost to the point of hurling. I fix him with a scathing stare, my fingers flexing at my sides. I want to punch the bastard in the mouth right there in front of everybody.

No amount of alcohol makes a comment like that appropriate, and since I'm so determined to be a fucking lady, there's no way I'll make a scene in front of the entire organization. Even if I want to choke the life out of him with the dark blue Gucci tie already looped enticingly around his throat. What little credibility I have would go up in smoke.

This fucker has me backed into a corner, and he knows it.

I force my hands to relax at my sides and tighten my lips together in a flat line. I itch to fire Adam. To throw him right out on his pinstriped ass. Once we make it to the playoffs, that fantasy will become reality. I have to grit my teeth and deal with it until we can replace him.

Adam raises his eyebrows, his lips curling in a sly smile. Before I can retort, he brushes past me. "Come on, Gordon, let's see if you can beat me at darts."

He wins this verbal sparring round. I'll be prepared next time. He's going down. And not in any way he insinuated. That's just vile.

If I had to choose between setting myself on fire and sexy time with Adam, I'd be begging someone for a lighter and gasoline.

"Did I miss somethin'?" Lucy looks between my scowl and Adam's retreating back.

"Just an asshole being an asshole," I grind out through gritted teeth. Although, asshole doesn't seem like a strong enough word to describe the maggot-riddled trash pit that is Adam Barrett.

Lucy looks around once more and leans in. "Anything I need to worry about or will come out down the road?"

I shake my head. "No, he's just trying to get the upper hand on me."

Lucy purses her lips together and studies me for a moment. "I don't think I care very much for him."

"Join the club, Lucy. I'd fire him if I could replace him right now."

She nods her head. "I'm gonna run to the lady's room before

we start drinkin'. I reckon I had too much water today. I'll be back in a jiff."

With a groan, I rub my hands over my face and through my hair. This night went downhill fast. I lean against the bar and take out my phone, intent on distracting myself with email or social media. Before I can turn the damn thing on, I feel body heat licking along my back.

I spin on my heel, a scathing retort on the tip of my tongue and freeze, mouth open slightly in surprise.

Lincoln.

"You look like you could use a drink." The rough timbre of his voice quickly drains the icy anger from my body and replaces it with scorching lust. It's a pure shot of liquid pheromones straight to my downstairs. He stands directly in front of me, hands shoved in his dark blue jean pockets, his smile tight as he scans my face before sweeping down my body, his gaze resting on my phone. "Are you not having a good time, Jazlyn?"

I hate the way my stomach flutters every time he forms my name with those soft, kissable lips of his. Hate the way his black buttoned-up shirt stretches across his chest, clinging to his hard-earned muscles. And definitely hate how his ice-blue eyes rake over my body, tightening my nipples and commanding my heart to race. Damn my traitorous body.

"I could use some more wine." I take a deep breath. "You look like a pretty decent pool player."

He glances over to the players still hustling the table. "You saw that, huh?" His smile widens, eyes never leaving mine as he signals to the bartender. "I wasn't aware you were watching me."

Busted. Again. Heat crawls up my neck and spreads across my cheeks. "Well, I mean, I wasn't watching. I just…it looked like an interesting game."

"I bet it did." He winks at me, his smile widening even more.

Seriously, just shoot me on the spot. Maybe if I'm lucky, the earth will open and swallow me whole.

Lincoln looks down before meeting my eyes. "I'm sorry about your dad. These past two weeks have been kinda crazy, and I haven't been able to tell you that. So, how are you doing with everything? This must be a major adjustment."

I nod, accepting a glass of white wine from the bartender before he hands a bottle of beer to Lincoln.

Without missing a beat, Lincoln places his hand on my lower back and leads me away from the bar. Any protest I have dies on my lips. It feels as if his hand belongs there, like it's an extension of my flesh, and it removes the slimy feeling left by Adam's hand. In all honesty, he could've led me back to his place for a naked rendezvous, and I wouldn't have thought twice. Which makes Lincoln Dallas dangerous.

Where Adam makes me lose my temper, Lincoln makes me lose my sense.

I close my eyes for a second and let myself enjoy the warm tingling sensation left by his hand as he leads me to a small alcove at the back of the bar. It's pretty private. Too private, and if my legs worked, I'd think about rejoining the crowd.

He looks down at me expectantly. I blink, my brain coming back online. Oh, right, he asked me about my dad and is waiting for a response. *Good job, Jazz.*

Add lack of brain function to the growing list of why I need to steer clear of Lincoln.

Damn him and his magical touch. Surely, the draw to him is because we can't be together. If he weren't completely and totally forbidden, then maybe the sight of him wouldn't have heat flooding my body. Though, it's doubtful. No one has ever made me feel the way Lincoln Dallas does.

"Thanks." I'm not sure how much to divulge. Talking about this with one of my players is probably a huge no-no. I hesitate, but then my stupid mouth opens, and everything tumbles out. Dangerous indeed. "His passing was sudden, but we were never really close. Of course, I'm sad he's gone, but I think I'm sadder knowing I'll never get to have the kind of relationship with him I always wanted." I take a breath to stop myself from rambling. "Getting the team was a surprise, for sure, but Gordon and I are figuring it out as we go. Some times are harder than others."

He brings his beer bottle to his lips. The way his throat moves, working up and down as he swallows several mouthfuls, has me momentarily entranced. I briefly wonder how it would feel to trail my tongue up the side of his neck.

Or anywhere else.

Everywhere else.

"Getting rid of Coach Burton right before the season started was pretty ballsy. Weller is good, though. He was a good choice."

Lincoln's approval isn't necessary. I know it was a good choice. So does Gordon. But there's a part of me, a miniscule part, that cartwheels anyway.

"When we inherited the team, we saw a chance to finally make some changes. It's no secret the Devils have been struggling for a while." Leaning in toward him, I lower my voice to make sure this conversation stays private. "Coach Burton couldn't get out of his own way long enough to see he was leading the team in the wrong direction. We're already in an uphill battle trying to rebuild while also figuring out how to win. Burton wasn't going to change with us. We already have enough challenges coming from within the organization, so it only made sense for him to go."

Lincoln studies me for a moment. "I might have heard Adam isn't your number one fan."

"That's the understatement of the century," I scoff. "But unfortunately, we need a GM so I can't fire him even though he's a massive asshole and nothing would make me happier."

Lincoln nods in agreement.

"There's just so much riding on this for me. I have to prove to myself and everyone else out there that I can do this."

At some point during our conversation, Lincoln had edged closer. Or had I moved closer? It doesn't matter. The warmth from his body radiates around me, cocooning me, caressing my body, making my head dizzy and my knees weak. Robbing me of all sense.

Again.

Only a foot separates us, but it feels like my body is pressed tightly against him. He takes up more space than he should, and it makes me feel small, vulnerable.

He takes our drinks, puts them on a nearby table, and reaches out to rub his large hands up and down my upper arms, sending tremors down my body and turning me to putty.

"If there's anything I can do to help, I'm here for you, Jazz." His voice is low. Consoling. Intimate.

It's so...unexpected. And sweet. And inappropriate, considering I'm very much his boss. His boss who already decided not to date anyone. Especially a Devil.

"Lincoln, I—" Whatever I'm going to say flees my mind as some partygoer pushes into me from behind. I fall forward and catch myself, palms flat against Lincoln's well-defined chest. "I'm so sorry."

Trying to push myself from his muscled body, my heel wobbles, and I sink further into him, running my hands down his washboard stomach.

"Oh shit. I'm sorry. I'm so sorry." Heat floods my cheeks. After embarrassing myself in front of him twice in the span of a few minutes, it's probably time to call it a night and go home.

"It's okay, Jazz." His whispered breath brushes along the shell of my ear, his hands circle my waist and roam up my back. "Next time you want to feel me up, all you have to do is ask. Maybe buy me dinner first."

"Ha. Ha. Ha." Instead of coming out sarcastic, it comes out light and airy.

I swallow past the puck-sized lump in my throat. His eyes darken, his gaze smolders as he takes me in with a hunger that makes my whole body tremble. He leans closer to me, only a small space now separating his lips from mine. Breathing ceases to be a possibility under the heat of his gaze, yet my heart thumps wildly in my chest. The air around us buzzes with a palpable energy, and my hands tighten in his shirt.

To push him away?

To pull him closer?

I don't know if the gap between us is my worst enemy or my best friend.

In this moment, it doesn't matter he's one of my players. Doesn't matter if we're surrounded by the whole damn team. Doesn't matter I can lose everything. I know I need him closer. Need to feel his lips on mine. Need him to light up my body and set it on fire in ways I haven't felt in a very long time.

I look up, see the fire behind his blue eyes, and plead with him to walk away. To end whatever's happening. He'd have to be the one to snap out of the moment. I'm not strong enough to resist this pull of his.

Every cell in my body is chanting his name, building up a storm only he could conquer.

He sighs, the puff of air leaving his lips, and tickling the stray hair around my face.

"I know, Jazz. I know." Soft lips brush against my cheek for a fleeting moment. Lincoln runs his hands down my back before he turns and disappears into the crowd.

10

JAZLYN

The guys are playing like fucking amateurs. I played better in high school with vertigo and a double ear infection. It's like watching a minor league team who can't get their legs underneath them or hit a goal to save their damn lives. Calling the Devils a professional hockey team is an insult to the rest of the league.

"Oh, come on!" I push out of my chair and storm to the front of the owner's box. I'm not sure what I hope to gain by getting closer to the ice, but I need to do something to stem my anxiety. I should hide in the bathroom until this mess of a game is finished. "It's like they're working to *not* touch the puck."

Gordon snorts behind me, a response that's completely unwanted and unhelpful.

I grip the metal partition, my knuckles white and my fingertips numb as I look out at the half empty stadium. All I can focus on is the ice below and the twelve players working against each other for control of the puck. We're getting our asses handed to us on a silver platter by the Boston Blazers. They're good, but damn.

I look over my shoulder for a moment of reprieve from the travesty on the ice. "How can you just sit there?" When I glance back, Boston, yet again, makes it past our goalie and into the net. We practically have a sign above the crossbar, 'Open for Business-All Pucks Welcome'.

It's a wonder we manage to fill up half the fucking arena. I guess people like hockey regardless of how terrible the team plays. Although, looking down there are more Blazer fans than Devils.

Impressive show of local support for our first home game.

It's only the first preseason game, so it usually isn't a big deal. Preseason games are just warmups for the regular season, but to us it *is* a big deal. This is our first game as owners, and I want to make a good impression, to show we can hang with the other teams, to prove Gordon and I belong among the other owners. I'm not delusional enough to think we would win the game, but I'd been optimistic we'd at least give the Blazers a run for their money. Instead, we're complete hosers.

Not only are the plays sloppy, but their failure to work together directly results in their inability to get a little rubber disk in the damn net. We're certainly making an impression, not the impression I want, but at least it's clear as day now for the other teams.

The Nashville Devils suck pucks.

We don't need to make it to the playoffs this year, but next year's a whole different animal. We *had* to make it next year. If we don't, we lose the team. Something neither I, nor Gordon, will ever let happen without a fight.

"All you're doing is getting yourself worked up. There's nothing we can do from up here." His voice sounds strained, as if he's talking through clenched teeth.

I peer over my shoulder to see his gaze fixed on the ice, his hand absently rubbing his injured knee. "Is it hard for you to watch knowing you can't play anymore?"

He looks down at his affected limb, as if surprised by his own contact, and slowly raises his eyes to meet mine. "Yes." He pauses and shifts uncomfortably in his seat. "I was taught my whole life to live and breathe hockey. Who am I if I can't play?"

"You're Gordon fucking Benson. I know life dealt you a shitty hand and you had to give up what you loved. I hate that for you, I truly do. But now, you're more than a great player. You can make a difference to this team, to hockey as a whole. You need to figure out a new way to live hockey, figure out where you fit."

Gordon eyes me. One eyebrow arches in question. "Do you know where you fit?"

Good question. My brows furrow in consideration before turning back to the ice. "I don't know yet, Gordie."

"I guess that's something we can figure out together." Gordon joins me at the rail and squeezes my shoulder before chuckling. "This game really is terrible, isn't it? Dallas, Foster, and Harris look like the only ones with pulses out there."

"I know. They really do." Despite my best effort, I can't keep my eyes off Lincoln. Even when I lose sight of him, my eyes trailing the puck, they always find their way back to number eight.

With thirty seconds left on the clock, the Boston center snatches the puck from the boards and scores one last goal to end the game 5-0.

"Maybe we should meet with Weller tomorrow. He looks like he's about to have a stroke on the bench."

It might be a slight exaggeration, but it isn't far off. He's red faced and his arms are waving around like one of those wavy armed inflatable tube men. If I wasn't afraid he'd rip my head off, I'd suggest he stand in front of the arena to help us advertise.

I nod with a chuckle. "Agreed. I have some drills I want to run by him anyway. They really helped when we were getting ready for the Olympics."

"Sounds good." Gordon squeezes my shoulder once more

before nearly knocking the air out of my lungs with a slap to the back. "I'm going to stop by Whiskey and Rye. After this clusterfuck, I need a drink. Wanna join?"

His offer tempted me. I could use the friendly atmosphere more than the drink. But after that terrible loss, I'm not sure I'll be good company. "Nah. I've got a few things I want to do here. I'll see you at home."

"Sounds good. Try not to work too much."

There really isn't any work to do. I just want some time alone to think. After waving Gordon off, I find myself in my office in front of my hockey gear. Before I can think better of it, I grab the gear bag from the floor behind my desk and head for the practice rink on the backside of the arena.

I need to let loose. I need to get on the ice.

The cold air swirls around the rink, rejuvenating me as I grab my hockey stick and step out onto the freshly smoothed ice. I had changed into a loose sweater and leggings, not wanting to skate around in a skirt and blouse. While I may look nice, it isn't the least bit functional.

As soon as my skates hit the frozen surface, my shoulders relax, and I can feel the tension leave my body. Hair whips around my face, the air biting my cheeks the faster I skate. I barrel around the rink, the scraping sound from my skates as they cut against the ice is music to my ears. Sweat pricks the back of my neck, my lungs heave with exertion and burn from the cool air, but I feel grounded. Skirting around some of the pucks left on the ice, I line up to take some shots. Puck after puck flies down the ice and toward the empty net.

My ego's been shattered by the loss, and it's nice to let it go for a moment and just be. Sports writers are going to revel in our spectacular defeat. They'd already predicted the loss against Boston along with the rest of the damn season. It seems unlikely we'll lose every game, but it stings, nonetheless. Gordon and I are officially branded as losers. Only getting wins, and lots of them, will prove everyone wrong.

Then, there's the delicious, six-foot-four, muscled, hockey player that's been shoved into the back corner of my brain and consumed any space I had left. I have no idea what to do about Lincoln. I'd almost begged the man to kiss me at the bar last Friday. Hell, I'd almost mounted him in front of the whole team.

I spent the whole weekend tangled up in my sheets, trying to purge the image of Lincoln's hard body thrusting into mine. Slow and savoring and then fast and hard. The dirty things he would whisper against my lips after the sun had set and darkness enveloped us. Just the thought sends shivers down my spine.

The pleasure he would wring from me would most likely be brutal, intense, and all-consuming. Things he can't give me in the world I live in.

"It's not a fair fight when there's no goalie."

My body jolts and I circle around as the devil himself taunts me from behind the boards. His grip on the edge, the way he leans in slightly, bunching up the muscles in his upper body, has my stomach in knots. I can't tear my eyes away from that stupid perfect smile either. There isn't a damn thing wrong with that man, and it pisses me off.

"You wanna talk about it?"

"Shouldn't you be icing down after the game?" Accomplishing a near impossible feat, I pry my eyes from him and eye the pucks at my feet. I absolutely don't want to talk to him about the reasons we should stay away from each other, why he disappeared all those years ago, or how I shouldn't react to him the way I do. Tonight's game is a much safer topic. Nothing about that will send my libido into overdrive.

"Shouldn't you be at home?" He smiles again and cocks a brow, taunting me silently.

I laugh, hitting another puck at the net. "Fair question, I suppose."

"Maybe a little one-on-one instead?" His cocky voice dares me to deny him.

Fogging breath catches in my throat as I meet Lincoln's gaze. He really is one of the sexiest men I've ever met. Standing outside the rink, fresh from the showers, his dark hair still wet and pushed back from his forehead, he radiates masculinity. His black sweats hang low on his hips. A long sleeve, white tee fits snug around his biceps and clings to his chest in a way that makes me want to rip it to shreds just to see more skin. It rises when he stretches his arms to show off his chiseled abs and a thin trail of dark hair leads my eyes straight to the promised land.

I lick my lips, as if he's my favorite dinner and I haven't eaten in a week. "I wouldn't want to embarrass you."

Lincoln cocks his head to the side, keeps his arms raised above his head for much longer than what's appropriate, and quirks his mouth up in a smile. "I think I can handle myself."

"Men." I roll my eyes and try not to stare while he bends down to lace up the skates he pulled from his bag.

He glides up to me, stops less than an inch away, making me hyper aware of his every move. He reaches up and tucks a stray wave of hair behind my ear, trailing his fingertips along the lobe and down the side of my neck. My pulse hammers, and my breath catches in my throat.

Once again, panties ruined.

"I promise to be a perfect gentleman." His breath ghosts across my cheek.

It isn't him I'm worried about.

"Like Friday night?" My hand flies to my mouth as if it could shove the words back in. My brain-to-mouth filter short-circuited. Friday night needs to stay locked away. Acknowledging we almost kissed would be like opening Pandora's box. As it is, the box had been cracked open, and the demon broke loose to wreak havoc on my hormones. That box, like my box, needs to stay closed. "Forget I said that."

His light blue eyes turn stormy. I don't trust myself not to do anything stupid, like kiss him or ask if he thought about me since the Olympics. So, I do the next best thing, I turn around and skate away as fast as my legs can go.

"Nice try." He laughs, the sound drifting closer as he catches up to me. "If I remember correctly, I've always been faster than you."

"Didn't do you much good tonight."

Lincoln cuts me off on the ice and turns to face me so he's skating backwards.

Show off.

He smirks. "It didn't. We played like shit. Boston handed us our asses. Thanks for bringing that up."

"Too soon?" I toss my head back and laugh. "I think your ego is big enough to handle a little razzing."

A smile sweeps across his face as his eyes brighten mischievously. A look I've seen before. "That's not the only thing on me that's big."

Suddenly unable to put one foot in front of the other, I stumble over my skates and lurch forward. Lincoln's hands shoot out, steadying me before I can fall flat on my face. Heat spreads across my cheeks. "I can't believe you just said that."

"What did I say?" He smirks, raising both eyebrows. "I was talking about my skates. You know, big skates, big feet."

Lincoln the perfect gentleman has vanished. If he'd even been there at all.

"Oh, my God." I lift my hands to cover my inflamed cheeks. I can imagine, in great detail, exactly what part of him is big. How I can make it even bigger. How it would feel in my hands.

It has nothing to do with his feet.

"That's what all the ladies say." He wiggles his brows, another cocky grin on the horizon.

I groan and roll my eyes. "I'm sure they do, Lincoln. Why don't you go flirt with one of them?"

He snorts.

Typical man.

Lincoln slides closer to me, my heart flutters in my chest. I need to skate away, tell him this can never happen, and head home alone. Home is safe. I'm unlikely to rip off his clothes if I'm at home.

Alone.

Raising a hand to the side of my face, he brushes the pad of his thumb across my lower lip. His fingertips trace my jaw line then push into my hair. My entire body clenches, suddenly needy and treacherous. A low moan slices through the silence of the arena, and it takes me a second to realize it came from me.

My stupid skates stick to the ice. I open my mouth but quickly close it. Rarely am I at a loss for words.

"God damn, Jazz." His fingers trail down my neck and dance along my bare flesh. His whispered words husky in my ears. "You make me want to break all the rules."

A shiver twists through my body, and I press my thighs together to try to ease the ache between my legs. Electricity buzzes around us. I'm on the verge of combusting, surprised when the ice beneath our feet doesn't melt.

Dazed, I lean into his heated touch. "There are some rules I can't break, Linc."

His forehead drops to mine, and his breath strokes my lips. Another inch and his mouth would be on mine. His eyes darken, looking more gray than blue as he searches my face. I hold in a whimper, wanting to lose myself in him, but knowing I can't.

Lincoln lets out a long sigh and backs away. I want to pull him back to me, already missing the heat from his body.

"Come on, let me walk you to your car." He turns his back to me and skates to the boards.

Hanging my head, I scrub a hand over my face. *What am I doing?*

I lift my head and skate after Lincoln.

The devil is full of temptation. And temptation has an ass I want to grab with both hands and never let go.

11

LINCOLN

A HEAVY WEIGHT slumps on my shoulder and blonde hair tickles my chin as a head nuzzles against me.

What am I, a body pillow?

I place a hand on the side of Tag's face and gently push. With a light snort, Tag rolls off me and curls up to rest his head against the airplane window. Only an hour into the flight to Colorado and over half these guys are already asleep. We got our asses kicked today in training, so I can't say I blame them.

In light of our loss against Boston, Coach worked us to the bone to prepare for our game against the Denver Knights. I could be passed out too, if I didn't have such trouble sleeping on planes. Unabashedly gawking at the sexy team owner in the tight skirt sitting at the front of the team plane doesn't help either.

She caught me staring soon after takeoff and now carefully avoids my gaze. Doesn't mean I can't stare at her, though.

I may have pushed her too hard last night. I should've kept my hands to myself. Biting back a moan, my hands curl into fists. But fuck. She felt so good. I lose control when I'm around her, and my dick thinks it has the right to call the shots. I guess he and I are overdue for a conversation about what constitutes workplace appropriate behavior around the woman who can derail your career.

My phone vibrates in my pocket, and I quickly fish it out to answer. There's only one person I expect a call from tonight. It's the reason I hooked up to the plane's WiFi as soon as we got in the air.

"Hey, man."

"Hey, Linc. How's my favorite brother doing?" Liam answers back.

I straighten in my chair and move the phone to my right side, away from Tag, the slumbering princess. "Good. Heading to Denver for our second preseason. Our first game was a total shit show. How did yours go tonight?"

"We won, of course. We do have the best high school center in the state. I meant me, if it wasn't clear." The excitement is palpable in his voice.

Liam is a hell of a hockey player. I had no doubts they'd win their game.

"I hear he's modest too."

"And handsome," he adds.

I chuckle. "Must get that from his brother."

He groans loudly in disagreement. "He wishes. I'm much better looking. Hold on." Liam's muffled voice drifts to the background as he speaks to someone else. "Oh, hey, I've got to run. Mom's calling me."

"Tell her I said hi. Miss you."

A shadow falls over me, and I glance up. Gorgeous green eyes lock with mine. Isn't this nice. Seems I'm finally worthy of some eye contact.

Her black button-up blouse is snug across her breasts, complimenting a tight red knee-length skirt and a pair of glossy black heels. Jazz is sexy as hell.

What I wouldn't give to have her handle my hockey stick.

"Miss you too," Liam quips.

"Bye." I slip the phone back in my pocket, my gaze never leaving hers.

Jazlyn pauses beside me. "Talking to your girlfriend?"

The terse tone of her voice offends me. Hell, her accusation offends me even more. Does she really think I'd almost kiss her if I had a girlfriend?

Before I have a chance to refute her accusation, she whips that wavy hair over her shoulder and stalks to the back of the plane. Twisting in my chair, I watch her walk away, her ass swaying side to side with each step.

Sure, I like having her around, but not quite as much as I like watching her leave. My cock stiffens at the thought of bending her over one of these uncomfortable chairs and fucking her like I imagine she needs to be fucked. Hard and fast. I'd grab myself a handful of silky chestnut hair and have her arching against me like a cat in heat.

I hope my little pussy cat doesn't think I'll let her have the last word. I have plenty to say. Unbuckling my seatbelt, I push out of my seat and follow her to the back of the plane.

After walking in the back cabin, I close the curtain, blocking us from the snoring players and any prying eyes. She has her back to me, pouring herself a shot of bourbon in one of those classy, clear plastic cups. I sneak up behind her and place my hands on the counter on either side of her, caging her in.

Let her try to walk away from me this time.

It's a total alpha move, and right now, I'm king. I'm minutes away from thumping my chest and dragging her back to my cave.

Jazz stiffens her spine, her drink abandoned on the counter as she spins around to face me. Her eyes light up, mouth opens slightly, and all I can imagine is pumping my dick in between those pouty lips.

I've got you now, kitten.

I smile down at her and raise my brows. "If you wanted to know if I was single, you could've just asked."

Her gaze narrows and darkens. The shallowness of her breathing and the way her skin jumps when I touch her prove she's just as affected as I am.

She runs her bottom lip through her teeth. It comes out glistening and slightly plump from being bit. Jesus, that turns me on like a flip of a switch. Moves like that are going to get her kissed. That lip will be raked between my teeth after I suck its rounded flesh into my mouth. My cock jumps, no doubt trying to punch through the zipper and bury itself in that sweet junction between her thighs.

"I didn't ask, because I didn't want to know." She looks up at me, her tone indignant. "Nor do I care."

I stroke the back of my hand down her arm. Her emerald eyes flare, flickering with surprise before smoldering with heat. She can act annoyed all she wants, but her body responds to me. "I don't believe that for a second, kitten."

"You can believe whatever you want." She jerks her arm away from me. "What if I have a boyfriend?"

"Do you?" Thinking of her with another man forces the question out as a growl. I don't like those thoughts one bit. No other man has a right to touch her. Not when she's mine. She doesn't know it yet, and I don't quite understand it, but I need to have her. And I don't share.

"Yes," she whispers.

"Are you sure?" My hands, needing to do something, needing to claim her, start to wander. I'm no longer in control—those damn dick beaters have a mind of their own. They slide up her back, over her shoulders, and wind themselves in her soft hair.

"I mean, I could." Her words come out breathless, and she releases a low moan.

She trembles under my touch, and I pull her closer. One of my hands skims her jaw and the other fists her hair. These stupid ass hands are going to get us both in trouble.

"Lincoln, we—"

My fist tightens its grip in her hair, pulling her head back. A shudder quakes through her body, and she lets out a strangled half moan, half sob. Her mouth parts, and I need to know if she tastes as delicious now as she did six years ago.

I lean in and skim my mouth over the curve of her bottom lip. I expect her to push me away, to shut it down, but she doesn't. That's all the permission I need, so I take more. The kiss consists of gentle bites and teasing licks before I suck her pouty bottom lip in my mouth. She gasps and I take full advantage, pushing in and sweeping my tongue into her warmth and exploring every damn inch.

I'm well and truly fucked.

She doesn't taste like she did six years ago. She tastes better. Like a sweet tropical fruit. It tops my dirtiest fantasies, whispers wicked desires into my ear, and promises me the best, heart-pounding, world-shattering sex of my life.

I'll never get enough of her.

It isn't the risk of being caught or knowing we are breaking the rules, it's Jazz. I'm drowning in her. It may make me a selfish bastard, but I need more.

Her little moans have me hard as a fucking rock. I grind against her, pushing her back against the counter, letting her feel what she does to me. Her hands clutch at my shoulders, pulling my chest tight against her breasts. She kisses me like her life depends on it. And maybe it does. She meets me lick for lick, stroke for fucking stroke, holding nothing back as I thrust in her mouth.

This is, hands down, the hottest kiss of my life.

One taste of her and I can feel my control slipping away. I'm close to coming in my pants over a kiss.

Hell, it's almost better than sex.

Lust curls inside me, twisting up my spine, taking over my brain. It takes all the restraint I have not to drop to my knees, push up her skirt and bury my face in what I'm sure would be the sweetest pussy known to man.

She tears away, eyes wide, lips swollen. Her open palms land on my chest and shove. I don't budge. With a frustrated huff, her hands jerk away from my pecs and start to rearrange her perfectly placed skirt.

"That can't happen again. What were you thinking?"

My jaw twitches, pissed she'd pull away from me, from my touch. "If you're looking for an apology, you're asking the wrong man. I'm not sorry about a damn thing."

Her eyes narrow on me, and she slaps at my hands as I reach out to grasp her. "That's not the point, Lincoln. It. Can. Never. Happen. Again."

Shit. Of course, it can't.

Fuck, I want to pull her back to me, feel her along the length of my body, but it would only make her angry. Right now, she's off balance, and I hope that means she'll be thinking about me when she walks off this plane. If I could stay in her head, then maybe, just maybe, I'll be able to convince her to give us another chance.

I force myself to back up. "I understand. Can't let the media get hold of something like this. Don't want the players to think you're playing favorites."

Jazz nods, her expression closed off.

As much as I'd love to sink into her body—and trust me, I would—I realize I want to reclaim what we once had. I want the closeness. The conversations. The trust. I want everything from her.

So, I swallow my pride. Now isn't the time to push her. I've made the first move, and now it's up to her.

"See you around, Jazz." I give her hand a squeeze before stalking back to my seat.

I understand where she's coming from. I know what a relationship could cost the both of us. Potentially our careers.

And whether or not she can admit it, she wants this, me, just as much as I want her. The passion and desperation when she kissed me back showed me that. I plan to show her I can be exactly what she needs.

And no one has to know.

Not the team, not the media, not even her own damn brother.

I can be her dirty little secret.

12

JAZLYN

I sit at my desk, grinding my teeth together, willing my computer screen to spontaneously burst into flame. Clicking the mouse with way more force than necessary, I send what feels like the thousandth email of the day. My eyes burn, and the back of my head throbs. It's past time to go home, but I still have several more pressing emails to respond to.

Confining myself in my office, I allowed myself to be pissy pretty much all day. It isn't the computer's fault, even if I do want to take out all my frustrations by smashing it to smithereens with my hockey stick.

There are several of these frustrations weighing on me at the moment.

It's no shock, we lost the game in Denver yesterday. The final score was an embarrassing 6-0. There's a part of me that thinks they weren't playing their best just to stick it to the man. Or in this case, the woman. I may have been born on a Wednesday, but it sure as hell wasn't last Wednesday. I know damn good and well the team still hasn't bought into the concept of having a lady owner. What I didn't know is how much that was affecting their play.

According to the media, my presence in the building is directly to blame, as I'm labeled both a nuisance and a distraction. My favorite part of the news last night was when the reporter stated that hockey was meant to have periods, not the owners. Way to stay classy, channel five.

Coach Weller is trying his hardest with the guys but has been very clear the team is lacking. He's adamant they're missing a critical element, something they need if they want to win any games. Internal leadership. Since the start of the preseason, no one from within the team has stepped forward to grab the reins, becoming the team captain. And until one of the players takes charge and unifies the team, they're doomed to lose.

He could yell at them until he's blue in the face—and he often did—it won't make a shit of a difference. They need one of their own to take the leap and move them forward.

There's one player I want to take charge. However, it has nothing to do with the team and everything to do with my lady boner.

I raise my hand to my bottom lip, sweeping my fingers across it. The same bottom lip Lincoln so expertly sucked into his mouth and held between his teeth. I squeeze my thighs together at the sudden burst of heat at my core.

His kiss is everything I remembered it to be, hot and hungry. His tongue demanded entrance into my mouth where he devoured me like he was starved. It teased and caressed, making me desperate for more. Desperate for his hands on my body, to strip him out of his clothes, to feel his skin on mine. I lost myself in that damn kiss. A kiss that shouldn't have happened, but I was powerless to resist. I should have stopped it. Pushed him away. Anything. I'm his boss for Christ's sake. Letting him get close to me is not okay.

I knew what was happening the whole time, and I just stood there brainless, letting my fucking vagina call the shots. She's a

Forbidden Devil | 87

desperate bitch and can't be in charge. My image is too important. Being seen as a respectable and responsible franchise owner is everything to me, and I only have one chance to not screw it up.

He also walked away from me six years ago and never looked back. I can't risk everything for someone who can leave so easily.

So naturally, there's only one thing to do. I've avoided him like the plague since we got off the plane. Prompting me to flee into a nearby elevator when he walked into the hotel lobby and making sure to be the last one to board our return flight home. I'll continue to do so until I figure out what the hell I'm going to do.

Then, there's Adam.

Still an asshole. Still open in his dislike for me. As a matter of fact, the shit bag just sent me an email, dripping with condescension, requesting a meeting tomorrow to discuss my position with upper management and to find my fit with the organization. I have no doubt he wants to put me in my place, maybe even offer a reminder of what he suggested to do to get the smug look off my face. If he isn't careful, his balls are going to find themselves at the wrong end of my size seven Jimmy Choos.

The corner of my eye twitches, my hands clenched at my sides. Normal reactions whenever I think of Adam. He always manages to piss me off with minimal effort.

I push myself away from my computer and stand.

There's one problem on my list I could eliminate right now. I'm not going to wait for tomorrow to meet with Adam. This is my organization, and he needs to learn he isn't in charge of me. Which means meeting on my time.

Not his.

Walking the short distance to his workspace, I notice every office but ours is dark. Seems everyone aside from Adam and I have gone home. Lincoln is long gone. He left shortly after practice. I may have caught a glimpse of his shaggy brown hair and broad shoulders striding through the player's parking lot from my window. No doubt he'll have plans tonight. Maybe even a Thursday night dinner date. The clawing at the pit of my stomach is just hunger, not at all an insane jealousy at the thought of him with another woman.

Even Gordon left an hour ago. Must be nice to have a life.

Adam's door is closed, not unusual as he doesn't like to be disturbed while working, even at the late hour. I don't hesitate to bring up a fist and give the door a few short thwaps. No response, but also not unusual.

My hand falters on the doorknob for a brief moment, and I debate retreating back to my office. *Don't be stupid*, I chide myself, *he asked for a damn meeting*. With a deep breath, I turn the knob, push on the door, and freeze in my tracks.

Oh.

My.

Fucking.

God.

Adam stands behind the desk, suit jacket discarded, tie loose around his neck, hair disheveled, and mouth opened slightly. His hands grip the hips of a blonde woman as he pummels her from behind. Doggy style at its worst.

Slap. Slap. Slap.

With her hands planted on the desk in front of her, she pushes back against him with wild abandon. Her breasts, clad in a red lacy bra, sway with every bruising thrust.

I slap my hand over my mouth, eyes wide open. There's no way I will ever unsee this.

She takes this moment to raise her head, looking directly at me, her hazel eyes never wavering, like she's unsurprised by my interruption. Recognition jolts through me.

"Candace," I breathe out.

Candace is one of the staff physical therapists. Up until now, I thought she was one of the most proficient therapists on staff. She's always available for injuries, never out of line with any of the players, and the coaches have nothing but good things to say about her. She's between a rock and a hard place now. Quite literally. There's no way she can argue she's in his office to help him with an ache in his lower back.

More like an ache in his balls.

Taking a step back, my eyes snap up to meet Adam's. His face is impassive. He raises his eyebrows and then winks. The asshole actually winks at me while he's playing hide the salami with an employee.

I'm going to lose my lunch all over my five-hundred-dollar shoes.

There are two good options here. I can run back to the safety of my office. A place I know for sure has no exposed genitals. Or I can demand he cease doing the nasty with his subordinate and report them both to human resources.

Adam would eat that shit up, making it clear I couldn't handle myself in this world of men. That I have to run to HR and get them to fight my battles for me. He would love it if I gave him another reason to discount me as a woman.

Closing the door with a bang, I pull up my big girl panties, grab ahold of my dignity and flee to my office. My heart is racing like I just ran the Boston marathon. I can't believe I walked in on Adam going to Pound Town. What in the actual fuck? The only thing that could possibly make this situation worse would've been direct eye contact with his trouser snake.

Gag.

Needing a distraction, I open up my eighties Spotify playlist and let Billie Joel banish the disturbing images from my brain. Maybe this Uptown Girl can manage to focus on the rest of these emails. As a reward, I plan to offer myself a glass of wine from my dad's private stash. Whatever it takes to make me forget the atrocity that happened over Adam's desk tonight.

Gordon and I agreed to keep Adam in place for the next two years, but I'm not sure I can keep dealing with all his bullshit. He has a job in Pittsburg lined up with his old team if we release him from his contract at the end of this season. Consequences be damned, I'm ready to release him tonight. I need to have Gordon reach back out to his assistant general manager buddy. He and I will be having a conversation about this, and soon.

Forty minutes later, my emails have all been returned, and my work for the day is done. Opening the door so very slowly, I peer down the hallway. The lights are out in Adam's office.

I look up to the ceiling. *Thank you, Jesus.*

Breathing out a sigh of relief, I make my way out of the building and into the cool night air. The back door is heavy and closes behind me with a thud. The parking lot is empty, except for my Porsche Cayenne and the nighttime security guard, Dan. He's an older man, who started working stadium security when he retired from the police force. Claimed he needed some action in his life.

"Good evening, Miss Benson." Dan's two fingered wave greets me from the steering wheel of his golf cart before he stops it beside me. "Burning the midnight oil, I see."

I smile down at him. "Good evening, Dan. You know work never ends. And I've asked you at least ten times to call me Jazz."

"And yet I continue to decline, Miss Benson," he teases, his smile wrinkling the tanned skin around his dark brown eyes.

I can't help but laugh. "Goodnight, Dan."

"Goodnight, Miss Benson," he calls over his shoulder, already driving away.

Getting closer to my SUV, I see a white piece of paper stuck under the windshield wiper, the ends blowing around in the gentle breeze. Weird, I didn't think businesses still advertised like that.

Grabbing the note, I notice there's no company logo or list of services, instead there's a handwritten note.

You are nothing but a spoiled little rich bitch. You are the worst thing to ever happen to this team. No one, and I mean no one, wants you here. If you know what's good for you, you'll pack your shit and leave Tennessee.

13

JAZLYN

"I thought I'd find you in here." Lucy pops her head into my office with a sweet as pie smile.

I grin back and make a sweeping gesture with my hands. "Well, Lucy, this is my office. I'm not sure where else I would be."

"Maybe watchin' practice." Lucy walks up to my desk tapping her rose-colored lips, which predictably match her entire outfit, right down to her heels. "I wonder why you're not down there today. Could it be we're avoidin' someone?"

I narrow my eyes at her, wondering what she could possibly know. As it is, I'm currently avoiding three someones.

Lincoln is trouble. Sex on a stick, I want to put my mouth all over him, kinda trouble. HR would have a field day writing incident reports on all the indecent things I want to do with that man.

Adam is another walking violation. He tried to talk to me this morning, and I made a lame excuse so I could run off to my office like the adult I am. And then there's the receiver of his snake charming expedition. I know Candace will be downstairs with the team, and I'm not quite ready to face her after watching her romp with the trouser snake. I could report the entire situation to HR, seeing as how their rendezvous is wildly inappropriate, but it would make me a gigantic hypocrite.

It's not like I threw Lincoln down in my office chair and rode him until my thighs quivered and his balls were empty. But damn if I don't want to. Besides, we did something on the plane, a plane filled with our co-workers, that crossed all sorts of workplace boundaries. I can't even call what happened kissing because it felt like so much more. It left me feeling raw and exposed, yet utterly complete and fulfilled. It's like he fucked my mind and my mouth thirty-two thousand feet in the air.

"I'm not talking about who or what I'm avoiding. Especially in my office."

Lucy grabs my purse and holds it out to me. "Then, it's a good thing we aren't stayin' in your office. It's high time we had a girls' day."

I laugh, snagging my purse and throwing it over my shoulder. "What kind of girls' day?"

"As it turns out, I've made an appointment for us today to taste different whiskeys and whiskey cocktails for our upcoming casino night fundraiser."

"Where are we having this tasting?"

"The Sinful Gentleman Distillery." Lucy beams. "I don't know if you know this about me, Jazz, but I have a weakness for gentlemen built for sin."

I throw my head back and laugh. I can't imagine pink-loving Lucy doing anything sinful, yet the gentleman part isn't surprising. A custom-tailored suit wearing businessman is right up her alley. "Somehow I don't see you walking on the wild side. Doesn't matter how sinfully delicious he might be."

"We all have our secrets." Lucy holds my gaze with one brow quirked up.

"The Sinful Gentleman it is." I grab Lucy's arm and steer her out the door. "I've heard good things."

Distraction. What I need is a good distraction. From my life. From the things I want and can't have. And most of all from Lucy, who is strangely quiet on the ride to the distillery. No doubt waiting until I have some alcohol in me before attacking me with questions.

"Hello, ladies, and welcome to the Sinful Gentleman."

Two tall, blond, and exquisitely handsome gentlemen greet us at the door with wide smiles. Their lean physiques are apparent, even in jeans and distillery t-shirts. If I have to guess, I'd say they're close to our age.

Don't know if all their guests get this welcome or if Lucy is getting special favors already. With how good looking they are, I'm not sure I mind either way.

"I'm Reed, and this is my younger brother, Hudson, the founders of the Sinful Gentleman."

Reed, the taller of the two, has a warm smile and gorgeous hazel eyes. Hudson's hair is longer and held back in a ponytail, his eyes, more brown than green, assess us both before resting on Lucy.

"I like this special treatment." Lucy nudges me with her elbow. "If I knew you provided such personalized services, I'd have stopped by ages ago."

I chuckle, shaking my head. I thought Lucy picked this place based on their reputation for great signature cocktails, now it seems like maybe she had something else in mind when she made this appointment.

"Of course, Miss Hurst. I'd love to make you feel special." Hudson takes a step forward, grabs Lucy's hand, and brings it to his lips for a slow kiss.

I roll my eyes and extend my hand to Reed. "I'm not sure what's happening here, but I'm Jazlyn Benson."

Reed takes my hand and holds it in his a tad longer than what's acceptable for a normal handshake. "The pleasure is mine, Jazlyn. We've been expecting the two of you. It's not often we get someone as important as you through our doors. We want to make sure we give you an experience to remember."

Smooth. He is definitely smooth.

"If your whiskey is half as good as those dimples, I'm sold." Lucy points at the dimples framing Hudson's smile.

Hudson places Lucy's hand on his arm and walks her into the next room. "It's better than the dimples, but not as heavenly as you."

I laugh as Reed and I follow them into a small bar area where, despite it being the middle of a workday, there are a few people scattered throughout this masterpiece of a room.

"Wow." I look at Reed after taking in the brick walls, barrel accents, and liquor displays. "This is gorgeous."

Reed's cheeks turn pink. "Thank you. We've both worked really hard to get here."

"I believe it."

"Lots of late nights, sipping whiskey, finding the perfect blend."

I chuckle, laying a light hand on his arm. "That sounds absolutely dreadful."

"Now, if you ladies will take a seat," Hudson winks, his dimples appearing at the edges of his smile, "we'll bring out the good stuff."

"What do you think?" Lucy turns to me once the brothers are out of hearing range. "They're cute."

I scoff. I know what she's doing, and I'm not playing this game.

"Reed is nice."

"Hudson seems smitten with you. You should go for it." I'm not going to touch anything else with a ten-foot pole. I already have enough problems where men are concerned. No need to make things more complicated.

Lucy bats her eyes at me. "You're very good at avoidance. It's a good thing I'm persistent."

"Fine, Reed is hot." I huff out a breath. "Does that make you happy?"

"A little." Lucy smiles and flicks her eyes on something behind me.

I groan and lean forward, covering my face. "He's behind me, right?"

"Yes, ma'am." Reed smiles and puts down a barrel plank serving tray holding various shots. He hands me the first shot with a wink. "A gorgeous blush, more striking than my finest whiskey. And if you haven't noticed yet, I'm very attached to my whiskey."

I slide down in my chair, heat blooming on my cheeks. I'm going to murder Lucy later.

As we take our first sip, Reed explains the different flavors. His passion for whiskey is apparent as he goes over the different blends and what combinations we should taste. Lucy and I sip when instructed, enjoying the smooth liquor.

"I think this one's my favorite." I take another sip of the last whiskey. "I love the honey flavor."

Reed leans towards me, his arm resting on the back of my chair. "It's my favorite too. The flavor really blooms on your tongue."

The way he accentuates tongue isn't lost on me, and I feel my cheeks heating again. Maybe dating someone like him would be safe. The media wouldn't give two shits if Reed and I were caught having a night out on the town.

It would be nice and boring.

No scandal.

Too bad safe doesn't make my lady parts light up like the Fourth of July.

"I don't know, I like the Signature Gentleman. It's all smokey and that's kinda sexy." Lucy smirks.

"Did you call for me, princess?" Hudson saunters to the table with several drinks in hand. "This here's our version of a whiskey smash. We do citrus, blackberry, raspberry lime, strawberry, and peach."

I grab the blackberry and take a drink, the smooth heat burning its way to my stomach. "Oh, this is so good. I could drink this all day."

Hudson holds the citrus out to Lucy. "Y'all are more than welcome to stay here all day."

"Give me more of these and you might have a deal." I laugh.

Reed exchanges my drink for a light amber drink with jalapenos floating in it. "You only like that one because you haven't tried my spicy vanilla lemonade."

It's heavenly, but strong. I can already feel it sloshing around in my brain after one sip. "That one's dangerous. It's the kinda drink that sneaks up on you and knocks you on your ass."

Lucy snags it out of my hands. "Yeah, this is good. A couple of these would loosen you right up."

"I can make this for us if you agree to have dinner with me." Reed smiles at me.

As good looking as he is, I feel nothing. "You men are certainly charmers."

Although, at this point, I can't tell if they're always like this or just putting on a show to make sure we give them our business. Too bad for them, my vagina doesn't call all the shots. She's not swayed by a pretty smile and flirty words. Unless Lincoln's the one whispering those things in my ear. She tingles with delight, like the betraying bitch she is. Damn you, vagina.

With a few more flirtatious looks, Reed and Hudson clear the table and excuse themselves to get a few more drinks to sample.

"I will say, Hudson and Reed are mighty hospitable." Lucy takes another sip of her whiskey smash.

"That's because Hudson really wants to get in your pants. He can't keep his eyes off you." I point over to the bar where Hudson is, in fact, sneaking a glance in her direction.

"We could always go on a double date."

"Now, Luce, you know I shouldn't be dating anyone right now."

Lucy clucks her tongue, disapproval eminent in the way she slowly shakes her head at me. "I don't think there would be anything wrong with dating someone completely unrelated to hockey."

I let out a deep breath and drop my forehead to the table.

"Have you had enough liquor to talk yet? I know somethin' is bothering you, Jazz. We don't know each other well yet, but I'd like to think we're friends." Lucy looks genuinely concerned, and in the short time we've known each other, she's always been nice.

Still, I'm hesitant to say a damn word.

"Well," I'm not sure where to begin or how much to disclose, "let's say hypothetically, there was a team owner who had a player they were interested in. You know, for more than his hockey skills and stats on ESPN."

"Like his bedroom skills. Go on."

"Would there be any way for them to actually be together without it blowing up in anyone's face?"

Lucy pops her chin on her hand and studies me. "Well, in a situation such as that, there will always be some sort of backlash. If it were a player on a different team, the media attention would be less and there wouldn't be as much speculation about favoritism and abuse of power. If we're talking about two people in the same organization, then I wouldn't advise makin' anything public unless I was sure it was going to last."

I take a long sip of water, letting the coolness quench my frazzled nerves. "And what if it does?"

"Then, you ignore the media because it's none of their damn business anyway. You deserve to be happy."

"You and I both know it's not easy to ignore the media."

"True." Lucy laughs. "You just have to make sure he's worth it. You'd be risking not only a media scandal, but an upset of team dynamics and disrespect from your peers."

"Hypothetically, of course." I give her a pointed look.

Lucy arches an eyebrow, one that says 'hypothetical, my ass.'

"Of course. But as your friend and public relations consultant, I expect you to tell me if the situation arises."

I don't know if spending time with Lincoln is worth all the potential complications. Being with him makes me feel sexy and desired. With our history, I feel I can be myself with him and not just the person I need to be for the organization. I could be more. More than some new owner trying to keep her head above water and earn everyone's respect. More than a small disturbance in my dad's big shadow. That is, if he stuck around this time.

I have plans for the Devils and have no intentions of selling in two years. We *will* make the damn playoffs, and Gordon and I will keep the team. I can't let anyone's feelings interfere with these plans.

Even if those feelings are my own.

14

LINCOLN

If I thought last season was bad, it's nothing compared to the five-alarm dumpster fire I've found myself in. It's the last preseason game, and it looks like we are going to lose. Again. We're one period away from holding the record for most preseason losses.

It's fucking embarrassing.

Tag places a hand on my shoulder as we trudge into the locker room for our last intermission, and I shrug it off. I don't need any of his 'it'll be okay' bullshit right now because everything is not okay.

Kevin Craft and his merry band of idiots are still spouting all this sexist bullshit about Jazz. Not everyone is buying into his claims that she's a Devil temptress with the sole purpose of destroying the team, but there are enough people on the fence that it's causing a major disruption. His ramblings are keeping everyone disjointed, which is why we're playing like pure garbage.

In addition to all the shit with the team, my personal life is also in the crapper. Including my nonexistent relationship with Jazz. It has been a week since I kissed her on the plane. Anyone care to guess how many times I've seen her since? A big, fat, whopping zero. Every time I catch a flash of her rich brown hair or her piercing green eyes, she's gone just as fast. I'm not a stupid man; I know she's avoiding me. And it pisses me off. It has all my caveman instincts fighting their way to the forefront of my brain, wanting nothing more than to stomp up to her office, sling her over my shoulder and carry her home. I could say I just want to talk to her, but even I know that's bullshit. I want to mount her, fuck her, claim her, make sure she knows she belongs to me.

Coach Weller clears his throat. "We haven't lost this game yet. We still have the third period, we can come back and win this thing. I know this has been a rocky start to the season—"

"Yeah, it has. None of us want to work for some bitch and her brother sidekick." Kevin leans over and gives Joe Vale a fist bump.

Several players nod in agreement. I feel my blood boiling with the need to defend Jazz. Everything he's saying is wrong on multiple levels. Kevin is asking for a fight, and I may not be strong enough to deny him this time.

Tag stands and stares pointedly at Kevin. "You just don't like the fact she's a woman and her balls are bigger than yours."

"You're right." Kevin stands and stares back at Tag. "I don't like that she's a woman, and I'm not the only one. There's a reason women haven't been a part of this league. We play at a different level, it's tougher and faster. A woman can't understand how we play, what we go through, and it's destroying our team."

"You're what's tearing this team apart, Kevin." I level him with a hard gaze. "You're nothing but a sexist prick, and you're toxic to this team."

Kevin turns and puffs out his chest, his face turning red. "Go fuck yourself, Lincoln."

"You need to shut up and listen, Kevin. All of you do. I know Jazlyn and Gordon taking over has caused a huge upset. The media is out there making a big deal about her being a woman and then you have this jackoff in your ear parroting everything they say." I gesture to Kevin, take a deep breath and look over at the coach for support.

Coach Weller stands with his arms crossed and his mouth in a tight line. He meets my gaze, but his emotions are walled off. I don't know if I'm in the proverbial penalty box or if he's in agreement with what I said. No doubt, I'll get a talking to after this game.

I step out to the center of the room and look around, making eye contact with the other players before continuing. "It doesn't seem like most of you have a problem with Gordon, just Jazlyn. Let me remind you, she's played hockey. Not only has she played, but she has two fucking Olympic medals. It's ridiculous she's being discounted because of what's between her legs."

Most of the guys are looking directly at me, but some have their heads downcast, staring at their skates. I hope they feel a little ashamed.

"You don't trust her, and I get it. This is something new, and we don't know if it's going to work. But has she done anything so far to hurt this team?" I pause to give them the opportunity to speak their mind, but of course, not a single one of the sexist bastards speaks up. Even Kevin keeps his mouth shut and sits his ass down as he glares at me. "As far as I can tell, she helped recruit a new coach, a better coach. And Craig, one of the fastest skaters in the league. None of us have a say in ownership, and it's past time we start moving on. Sitting around whining and bitching about something we can't control isn't helping. It's a waste of time." I glare directly at Kevin. "We need to pull our hockey sticks out of our asses, put our heads together, and unify as a team. Anything less and we don't even stand a chance of getting to the playoffs."

"He's right." Foster points his stick around the room. "You

tossers have forgotten what it means to be part of a team. Everyone thinks we're a bunch of hosers. I think it's about time we go prove them wrong."

With nothing more to say, I turn and stride back to the ice. We have one more period to go, and I'll be damned if I'm going to lose another game.

I crash into Kunznetsov, throwing him into the boards. Our sticks bang together as we slash at the puck, fighting for possession. He has it but not for long. He's pushing against me, shouldering me out of the way, but I'm pushing right back.

He wants the win, but I want it more.

I drive him back into the boards, sweep my stick, and take off with the biscuit. The defense rushes toward me, leaving Tag open. I flick a pass across the ice and watch as Tag takes control of the puck and circles the goalie.

His stick rears back—and the puck goes sailing through the air. My heart pounds as I propel myself forward, skating around Bradford and Schultz, to line myself up for a rebound.

Clink.

The puck hits the bottom of the crossbar at the top of the net. Jankowski stands helpless as the puck drops in.

The horn bellows, crowd erupts, and I barrel into Tag, throwing my arms around him and pounding him on the back. I can make out his wide smile underneath his helmet. It's a damn good shot and gives us a large enough lead that with only a minute left, there's no way North Carolina can catch up.

Every muscle in my body screams at me as I trudge into the locker room. My legs burn from exertion, and I'm drenched in sweat, desperately needing a cool shower. I move toward my stall slowly, still in awe, having witnessed a minor miracle. I feel lighter than I have in days. We won the game. Coach forced Kevin to ride the bench for the last period. With his negativity gone, the plays seemed effortless. The Bruiser Brothers kept the other team nailed to the boards, Foster scored a beautiful goal with a long slapshot, and Tag and I turned their goaltender into a sieve.

"God, it feels good to win." Ian strides up beside me, his helmet dangling from his hand.

Owen flanks my other side, playing a game of catch with his gloves. "I almost forgot how that felt. You know, maybe we should do it more often."

I laugh, lowering and shaking my head. "I think that's what we get paid to do."

"What do you think, Ian?" Owen looks past me to the other side. "You reckon he's right?"

"I don't know, Owen. It seems pretty legit to me."

"You're both idiots." I push them away and throw my gloves and helmet in my locker. "Don't you have—"

"Dallas." Coach's voice booms through the locker room. I freeze, hands at the bottom of my jersey and my eyes move from Owen's to his. He stands at the doorway to his office, arms crossed over his chest, lips drawn in a tight line, and eyes narrowed. "I want you in my office before you leave."

Dread hits me like a bucket of cold water. I give a quick nod. "Yes, Coach."

With one last scan of the room, he turns on his heel, disappearing back into his office, slamming the door with a loud bang.

Owen tosses one of his gloves, hitting my back. "Someone's in trouble."

I tug my jersey over my head. He's likely right, but there isn't much I can do about it. I stood up for someone who isn't here to defend herself and have no regrets. I just hope it won't cost me play time. "I imagine I'm going to get my ass handed to me for my tirade earlier."

"If it makes you feel any better, it needed to be said." Owen sits down in front of his locker and unties his skates. He shoots a look to Kevin, who sits on the far side of the locker room, refusing to look our way. "That asshole would rather talk out of his ass than shut up and play hockey. I think it's getting on everyone's nerves."

My breezers hit the floor and I look over at Owen. "Yeah, but I stepped on Coach's toes to do it. I should've let him handle it."

Owen shrugs and pulls off his skates.

Anxiety settles into the pit of my stomach as I finish getting undressed and head for the showers. I'm undoubtedly in trouble, the question is how much. Best case scenario, Coach gives me a slap on the wrist and lectures me for speaking out of turn. Worst case scenario, Coach would bench me until he decides I've learned my lesson. He didn't bench me for the last bit of this game, but it doesn't mean he can't change his mind.

I cringe, stepping under the cool stream of water in the shower stall. The next game is the first of the season. No way I want to sit there like a duster, watching all the action I can't have. I can only cross my fingers and hope for the best. Maybe the win tonight will soften Coach up a bit.

After showering and getting dressed, it's time to face the music. I stalled as much as I could. Shoulders squared and head held high, I make my way into the coach's office, closing the door lightly behind me.

Coach Weller has his head down, buried in paperwork.

"Coach, you asked to speak with me?"

His eyes shoot up to meet mine. I shift under his gaze, and my shoulders slump as I wait for the bad news.

"I'm sorry, Coach, I was completely out of line. I know that I—"

"Lincoln, stop." He raises his hand, interrupting me.

My heart rate increases, and my palms begin to sweat. He's about to hand me my ass. Or maybe something else? He grabs something out of his desk drawer and extends his arm to hand it to me.

"Coach?"

He opens his hand to reveal the captain's letter. "You've earned it, Lincoln."

The pounding of my pulse hammers in my ears and my hands feel clammy as I reach out and grab the C, the soft material brushing across my fingertips. All I can do is stand here and stare at it. I'm at a loss for words.

"This team has been missing a leader, and we weren't sure anyone was going to step up. You've got a good head on your shoulders, and the other men respect you. I expect you to set a good example for them. I'll let you know when I need you to attend a coach's meeting and Miss Hurst, the new PR lady, will inform you when your attendance will be needed for post-game interviews. Don't worry, I also have to attend, and Miss Hurst will be there to make sure we don't say anything stupid. Not her words exactly, but the meaning was there."

Say anything stupid? I'm not sure I can say anything at all. I came in here expecting to get a good ass chewing for both hijacking our intermission pow wow and telling off a teammate. Even if Kevin is overpaid and underproductive. Not to mention a huge asshole.

Becoming the team captain comes with responsibility. I couldn't be a media liability and would have to set a good example for all the guys on the team. I'm not a drama queen like some of these other guys, so that won't be a problem. If I have any hope of being traded to a better team with an actual chance at the Stanley Cup, I'll jump at anything that increases my worth as a player.

Shit.

It's also another reason against being with Jazz.

I extend my hand for a shake. "Thank you, Coach. This really means a lot."

He keeps my hand in a firm grip. "Like I said, you earned it. Now, get outta here. I've got more work that's not going to do itself."

"Have a good night, Coach."

"You too."

That certainly turned out different than I expected. I find myself in a much better mood than I'd been all week. The locker room is empty as I grab my bag and make my way outside. There's a chill in the night air and a few cars in the parking lot, but only one aside from my own I instantly recognize.

However, the car doesn't excite me nearly as much as the high heeled vixen standing beside it with her head buried in her phone. My cock stirs to life at the sight of that tight black skirt and those creamy legs. I suppress a groan in my throat. I want nothing more than to hike that skirt up her thighs and bury my face in her sweet pussy right there on the hood of her SUV.

The uneasy expression I see on her face as I near her pulls my mind out of the gutter and leashes my semi.

Her bottom lip is caught between her teeth, her brows drawn together, and she shifts back and forth uncomfortably. She's worried and alone. Alone in a darkened parking lot. We'd be having words, not only is my ego still sore about her fleeing from me every chance she has, but I don't like the idea of her being out in a dark parking lot alone. Dangerous things happen to lone women at night, and I'd be damned if I let her put herself at risk.

I jog to close the gap between us. By the time she notices me, I'm already at her elbow, the survival skills in this woman are sub-par. I shake my head. She isn't even paying attention to her surroundings. I swallow down the urge to pin her on her stomach across the hood of her SUV, flip up that skirt, and turn her ass red.

"Hey, Jazz. I thought you'd have been long gone once you saw me come out the door. You know, seeing as how you've been avoiding me," I tease, flashing her a smile, trying to appear more relaxed than I am.

She shifts on her feet. "Sorry, I thought it was for the best. It wouldn't be good for us to be seen together."

"And why is that, Jazz?" I lean against the driver's side door, cross my arms over my chest and give her a sly smile. "Is it that maybe next time you'll be begging to kiss me? Or are you afraid next time a kiss won't be enough?"

Her eyes widen, and I fight the urge to laugh.

"You…I…We can't…"

"Relax, kitten, I'm messing with you." My smile quickly fades, and I narrow my eyes. "What exactly are you doing out here alone? In the parking lot. At night."

"It's nothing. Don't worry about it. You should go home." Jazz takes her bottom lip into her mouth and nibbles on it, looking at me with those bright green eyes.

If she thinks acting like some innocent little girl is going to make me turn around and walk away, she's sadly mistaken. I no longer give two flying fucks about what she wants. I'm not going anywhere.

15

JAZLYN

OH SHIT. Playful Lincoln is gone. The heat from his glare settles on me as I shift in my heels, my feet aren't necessarily uncomfortable, but I am.

"I'm waiting on a tow truck and a car."

I don't think it's possible for his eyes to narrow anymore, but he proves me wrong. "What's wrong with your car?"

"Um."

Boy is he pissed. His jaw tics and the muscles in his arms flex like he's restraining himself from reaching out and grabbing me.

"Jazz," he growls my name through clenched teeth.

I sigh, and my shoulders slump. "My tires are flat."

"Tires? As in plural?" Lincoln pushes away from my Porsche and stalks around the SUV in disbelief while I stand by the hood, watching and waiting for him to tell me what I already know.

Like I'd be mistaken that *all* of my tires are flat. I'm a woman, not a moron. "All four of them. Yes."

"What the fuck happened, Jazz?" His voice is now a little more than a growl, and it would be frightening had it been anyone other than Lincoln.

"I have no idea. They were like this when I came out."

Lincoln kneels down to inspect the tire next to me, lighting it with his phone. His voice is laced with bewilderment. "Jazz, these look like they've been slashed. What the fuck? Who would do this?"

"I've been asking myself the same question for the past ten minutes." I hold my finger up and count the people in my life that hate me because I have a vagina and not a flaccid dick between my legs. "There's obviously Adam, but he likes to torture me in person. This doesn't seem like his style. There's a long list of people, players and fans, who would love nothing more than to fuck with me. I don't know if there's a correlation to the note, but—"

Lincoln springs to his feet. His fists curl at his sides, his nostrils flare, and his chest heaves with each breath. "What. Fucking. Note?"

I wince, and his feral look makes me want to spill the beans. Damn my big mouth. I hadn't meant to tell anyone about it. I don't want anyone to worry about something that's more than likely an idle threat.

"It's nothing. Forget I mentioned it."

"Jazz." I can barely make out my name as he snarls it at me.

"It's no biggie, Lincoln." I reach out, smoothing my hand down his arm, trying and failing to calm his beast. "I had a threatening note on my car the other day. It basically told me to leave town or else. It's not the first note I've gotten. Probably some crackpot with too much time on his hands."

His eyes close, and his chest rises and falls with each forced breath.

"Are you okay?" I eye him tentatively. If he doesn't calm down, he's going to give himself a stroke.

"No, I'm not okay." His eyes pop open, the light blue irises harden to steel. His voice is gruff, like every word must be pushed out. "Did you give any of these notes over to security? Does anyone know?"

I shake my head.

"Christ." He runs his hands down his face. "Cancel your car."

"What?"

"Cancel the fucking car service, Jazz. I'm sure the tow truck is almost here and as soon as we get your car hooked up, I'm taking you home. Hand me your keys." He puts a hand out, palm up, and stares at me.

"You're not taking me home." I cross my arms over my chest and stare back, daring him to make a move. Getting in a car with Lincoln alone and then going to my house where I know damn well Gordon is gone for the night is not a smart idea.

Lincoln advances on me, and before I can protest, he lifts me off my feet and throws me over his shoulder. I'm hanging upside down with an up close and personal view of Lincoln's perfect denim clad ass.

And I couldn't be less pleased.

"What the hell are you doing?" I let out a high-pitched squeal. This isn't happening. I must be having one of those out of body experiences because in real life Lincoln has no right to pick me up and take me wherever he wants. I'd been avoiding him all week, for fuck's sake. He obviously couldn't take a hint and leave well enough alone.

"What's it look like I'm doing?" His arm bands across the back of my legs and a heavy hand lands on my ass. "I'm getting you in my car because like it or not, I am taking you home. I'm not letting you go anywhere alone after you've been threatened and had your tires slashed."

"You can't manhandle me to get your way, Lincoln. The tow truck guy is going to be here any minute and think you're abducting me or something. Put me down."

This caveman routine is out of line. It's not covered as

acceptable behavior in the workplace handbook. The last thing I need is for someone from the organization to pull up and catch a glimpse of Lincoln carrying me off to his lair like some hockey playing Tarzan. They'd either think I'm some sex slave or being kidnapped. Neither one is great for public opinion.

"Lincoln, I don't think you're listening to me. You cannot pick me up and move me where you want me." I push myself up from his back to try and brace myself. I don't think being hauled over someone's shoulder like some business-attired damsel in distress would be so bumpy, but it is. I can feel every step Lincoln takes as he makes his way to his vehicle.

His hand leaves my ass as he fishes his car key out of his pocket and unlocks it with the click of a button. He shifts me into the passenger seat of his gray Range Rover and holds out his hand. "When your safety is involved, I can and I will. Now give me your keys."

I shoot Lincoln what I hope is a ball-withering look before slamming my keys into his hand, hard. He winces slightly, but it doesn't give me the satisfaction I want. He smiles, flashing his teeth, before he gives me his sexy backside and saunters over to my Porsche to meet the tow truck driver who is, of course, just pulling into the parking lot. He couldn't have been here two minutes ago to prevent caveman Linc.

My pulse hammers as I watch Lincoln talk to the tow truck driver. How dare he throw me over his shoulder like I'm a sack of potatoes. Like I would fall for something like that. It's domineering and aggressive, a total alpha move, and completely sexy.

No, inappropriate.

Fuck, who am I kidding?

I can still feel the heat from his large hand resting on the curve of my ass. It would have been better if we were both naked and he was carrying me to his bed. Heat pools between my thighs, and I shift in the seat to dull the ache at my core. I'll have to slake my lust with my vibrating bedmate later tonight.

Lincoln slides into the Rover. "Address?" His voice is curt.

He's still pissed.

Apparently, bossy Lincoln is still in charge, and as much as I try to deny it, this domineering attitude dampens my panties. But still, I'm not ready to have him all up in my personal space. Gordon won't be home until tomorrow, and if Lincoln comes in, well, he's right. A kiss won't be enough. Which is why he won't be coming inside. He can drop me off in the driveway, see me off safely, and leave.

I sigh in resignation, rattle off my address, and use my phone to cancel my car.

We drive over in silence, only the soft hum of a local country station to lighten the tension. He spends the trip with his eyes forward, jaw clenched, and a death grip on the steering wheel. He only relaxes when he pulls into my driveway and parks.

"Wow. This place is huge." Lincoln lets out a low whistle.

"It's my dad's place." I shrug. "Gordon and I will probably sell it soon. It's way too big for the two of us."

"Is Gordon here?" He cocks a brow and looks at me for an answer I don't know if I want to give.

"No, he's on the other side of the country. Went to meet up with some of the scouts. He won't be back until tomorrow afternoon."

Lincoln turns off the engine, and to my horror, opens his car door.

"What do you think you're doing?" I whip around to face him, but he's already out of the SUV.

No. No. No. This can't happen. In no way shape or form can this happen. He shouldn't be leaving his vehicle. I wonder if I'm strong enough to shove his ass back inside.

"What does it look like?" His mouth quirks up in a panty-melting smile.

Whose panties?

Mine.

"It looks like you're inviting yourself into my house." My feet hit the pavement, and I hurry to catch up to him as he stalks toward the door. I could refuse to open it. Shit, he still has my keys. What are the chances I can body check him, grab the keys, and rush inside?

Lincoln smiles, pulling my damn keys from his pocket. "Since you're such a piss poor host, I had to invite myself." His smile transforms into a frown, and his voice deepens. "You've had notes threatening you, and your tires were slashed tonight. I'm not leaving you here alone. If something happened to you, I'd never be able to forgive myself."

I stand there, in the middle of my walkway, staring at him like he sprouted two heads. His reasoning is sweet, I'll give him that. But the word 'danger' lights up in neon and flashes in my head.

I'd feel safer with someone here. Walking out after work to find my tires slashed was a bit jarring. But being alone with Lincoln is far worse. I'm not stupid. I know—I fucking know—if he even sets a foot in this house, we're going to do more than kiss.

Fuck it. Knowing I won't be spending the night in this big house by myself is a relief. I'll just have to make sure we keep our hands to ourselves.

God help us.

I snatch my keys out of his hand and push past him to the door, mumbling, "Don't think you're sleeping in my room."

He leans in close, his breath a whisper across the skin on the back of my neck. "Wouldn't dream of it, kitten."

Oh, sweet baby Jesus, this man. He's going to get me in trouble in more ways than one. A cold shower sounds like a great idea. Especially since I need to put a little distance between Lincoln and me. After being thrown over his shoulder, all I can feel is the heat of his hands roaming over my body. I want him to touch me in other places.

Naughty places.

I need to cool the fuck off.

I feel a little self-conscious walking back into my living room in a Devils tank top and loose cotton shorts. I have an image to uphold for my players and debated putting on one of my business outfits, but it would feel a little ridiculous sitting down to watch TV in a skirt and blouse. Besides, I don't even think a parka would keep that man's eyes off me.

Lincoln looks like he made himself at home with his arms resting along the back of the couch and his feet propped on the overpriced ebony coffee table as he watches TV. His shoes are off, and his biceps flex under the short sleeves of his dark blue t-shirt. He looks sexy as fuck, and the heat is back, only this time in full force. What is it about the domestic scene that gets me so hot and bothered? If he laid out on the couch completely naked, I'd have a downright wet dream on my hands.

"You played a great game tonight. It really was an awesome win." I sit down on the other end of the couch, careful to keep some distance between us. "I forgot to mention that earlier."

My cheeks heat as Lincoln's eyes wander my body, paying particular attention to my breasts. "I understand, Jazz. You've had a pretty stressful night."

"It wasn't all bad." I clear my throat and damn myself for saying something so stupid and abjectly forward.

Lincoln's lips quirk up in a smirk. "I hope that means you decided you liked me showing up in the parking lot."

I bring my index finger to my bottom lip and tap it like I'm deep in thought. "Hmm, maybe."

"I had a nice surprise tonight."

I turn so I'm facing him. "Ha ha. Yes. You've weaseled your way in my house. Trust me, I wasn't expecting that tonight either."

Lincoln flashes a smile, his eyes lighting up. "As nice as you make that sound. That's not it. You're looking at the new team captain."

"Congratulations, Linc!" Before I can think of all the reasons I shouldn't, I launch myself at Lincoln, wrapping my arms around his neck.

Lincoln's momentarily immobile before his strong arms wrap around my waist and tug me to him. His hands trail up by back and hold me firmly in place. It feels natural to melt into him as he wraps me up.

I don't want to go anywhere.

I graze my nose along the curve of his neck and inhale. He smells so damn good, like something earthy and quintessentially male. It makes me want to rip open his shirt and lick the column of his neck, but I figure that will cross the line. More so than what I'm already doing.

"I'm worried about you." Lincoln's voice is gruff, and his fingers dance along my spine, tangling in my hair. He tugs, lifting my face from his neck, and captures my gaze. His eyes darken, turning a rich gray as he lowers his lips towards mine.

I know I started it, throwing my arms around him and running my nose along his neck like some loose-moralled trollop, but I can't let this go any further.

I pull my head back while I'm still able to function. I can't get in any deeper with him. The line I swore would remain intact had already been crossed when he kissed me on the plane. "Lincoln—"

"No one has to know anything you don't want them to. What happens between us can stay here." His hand tightens in my hair sending shivers to my throbbing core and wetting my panties. Damn him, and damn the rules. I have expectations set on me from the league, the franchise and myself. It isn't fair. Why does he have to be one of my players?

"I don't think this is a good idea."

"Jazz." Lincoln stares down at me, the intensity of his gaze slicing right through every barrier I have. "I don't like being on the sidelines. I don't like thinking there's someone after you. It turns me inside out and triggers every protective instinct I have. I know it's not reasonable. But I need this. I need you."

"I think—"

"That's the problem, Jazz. No more thinking. Turn that brain of yours off. Let me take care of you tonight." He brushes his lips against mine in a quick, teasing kiss.

"So, what... we keep it a secret?" My sex clenches in anticipation.

There's a chance we could keep this whole thing a secret, but there's also a chance we would end up on the front-page news.

You miss one hundred percent of the shots you never take, thanks a lot Wayne Gretzky. Not the time for your motivational messages. He also said, *not doing it is certainly the best way to not getting it.*

And damn if I don't want it right now.

Consequences be damned.

He feathers kisses along my jaw. "If it means I get to touch you, kiss you, taste you, then absolutely."

Lincoln captures my mouth with his, running his tongue along my bottom lip until I open to him. His kiss is dominating. Consuming. He kisses like I hope he fucks. Slow, hard, deep, and demanding.

He shifts us on the couch until I'm underneath him, his lips never leaving mine. His knee wedges between my legs, and I open to him.

Having Lincoln Dallas between my legs with his tongue on mine is pure heaven.

I moan into his mouth as he works his hips against me, rubbing my sensitive clit with his denim covered cock. My tongue slides against his, and I clutch at his shoulders, digging into his shirt, longing to touch his skin.

His hand slides under my tank top and up to my breast. I arch my back, pushing against it. My body is tense, waiting for his touch. He teases my nipple with light circles before pinching the nub with enough pressure to make it hurt so good. I cry out and grind against him.

"Fuck, Jazz. I can't wait to touch all of you." Lincoln trails open-mouth kisses down my neck, nipping slightly. He slides down the couch and hooks his fingers into the waistband of my shorts and panties. He hesitates, his eyes flicking to mine for a brief second before he pulls the material down my legs and tosses it behind him.

There's no way I'm stopping him. The house could be on fire, and I wouldn't give a shit.

Lincoln runs his hands along my inner thighs as he stares down at me. "You're the sexiest fucking thing I've even seen. Your pussy is perfect." He licks his lips in a slow tease before drawing his lower lip in his mouth and drawing it between his teeth. "It looks like a greedy little cunt. Glistening, quivering, begging for my finger, my tongue, and my cock. I bet it's so fucking wet for me." He looks up my body, meeting my eyes, his voice gruff. "Are you wet for me, kitten?"

My jaw drops in shock. Lincoln Dallas is a legit dirty talker. I've never had a man talk to me like that before, but damn if I don't love it. Those husky, filthy words of his are only making me wetter.

I smirk at him, opening my legs wider. I'm already going to Hell. I might as well enjoy the ride. "Why don't you find out?"

His chuckle turns into a groan, as he parts the seam of my sex with his fingers. "Fuck. You're soaked for me." He removes his finger, brings it up to his mouth, and sucks on it. "Delicious. I want to taste you. I want you on my tongue and between my lips. Consider this an apology for how hard I'm going to fuck you next time I get you underneath me."

"Oh, God." My voice comes out desperate and needy, I barely recognize it. "Lincoln."

"I've got you. Hold onto something, kitten. I'm about to fuck you with my tongue."

Oh. Fuck.

Lincoln pushes my legs open wider and lowers his mouth. I cry out and reach above me, grabbing onto the cushion as Lincoln fastens his lips to my clit and sucks it into his mouth. He alternates between short bursts and hard tugs of suction. My back arches, and my hips buck against him as he spears me with his tongue. Moving in and out slowly, driving me absolutely wild with his controlled pace.

He rakes his teeth over my clit before releasing it and rubbing it back and forth with his tongue. Lust tunnels through my veins, setting my body on fire and burning hotter as he moves his mouth against me. The pleasure builds, and I know I won't last much longer.

I moan and whimper as Lincoln circles my entrance with his finger before plunging it inside. My body tightens around him as he moves that thick digit in and out of me.

"You're so tight," he groans. "Your pussy is gonna feel so good milking my dick. I'll start off slow, dragging my cock in and out of you like I did with my tongue. Your cunt's so fucking good you'll have me losing control in no time. Then hard, fast, punishing, just like a naughty little girl like you needs. But right now—now I need you to come for me, Jazz."

He quickens his pace, fucking me hard and fast with his finger while his tongue applies pressure to my swollen clit, kneading it relentlessly. I try to squeeze my thighs together, but he pushes them farther apart instead. My hips jerk uncontrollably and pleasure vibrates through my body, sucking all the air out of my lungs. I scream Lincoln's name as an orgasm tears through me.

I see stars.

Lincoln's hold on my thighs relaxes, but he keeps his mouth fastened to me, lapping at my core. Forcing me to feel every deliciously agonizing lick as I thrash underneath him and ride out the waves of my orgasm.

"I could lick you for hours." Lincoln lifts up and nips at my thigh. "You're addicting."

I peer down at him, his head between my legs, as I struggle to catch my breath. "Maybe if you're trying to kill me?"

"But wouldn't it be a hell of a way to go?" His lips quirk up in a half smirk.

"It would." I sit up and reach for him. "I believe it's your turn for torture."

Lincoln grabs my hands and pulls me in for a kiss. "Sorry to disappoint. I said I was taking care of you tonight, remember?"

I pull back, looking at him in disbelief as I gesture to his obvious erection. "Wait, you don't want me to—"

"Oh, trust me, I do," he interrupts, pulling me back to him and wrapping his arms around me in a tight embrace. "I would love to feel your hands and mouth wrapped around my cock. But we've both had a long day. Let's go to bed. Will you let me hold you tonight?"

Lincoln presses a kiss to my temple before looking into my eyes, searching for an answer. He's so sweet and genuine. It's bound to be my downfall. But when he looks at me, like his entire world could be upended by my answer, I'm powerless to say no. I'm powerless to do a lot of things I should when it comes to that man.

"I thought I said you couldn't sleep in my room?" I tease, brushing my lips over his. They are so soft, I can't get enough.

"I'm okay if we sleep on the couch."

I laugh and grab his hand. "Come on, Casanova. Let's go."

"Hold on." Lincoln bends down and retrieves my shorts and panties. "If I'm going to keep my promise to myself and behave, I'm going to need you to put these back on."

"What fun is that?" I give him a wink before sauntering down the hallway.

"Please Lord give me strength."

I laugh to myself. He's done nothing but torture me since I took over the Devils, I figure turnabout's fair play.

16

LINCOLN

"Make it stop," I groan, pulling Jazz tighter against me and wrapping my arms around her. Waking up with her ass pressed against my dick and her back molded to my chest has to be one of the best things ever.

The incessant ringing of her phone, not so much.

Jazz stretches her body, running her feet along my legs and rubbing herself along the length of my cock, stirring it to life. Who am I kidding? That thing was hard as a rock as soon as I woke up and realized Jazz and I were still in the same bed. This stiffy puts morning wood to shame.

She slaps at my arms banded across her. "You've got to let me up to answer."

"Fine." I sigh, rolling on my back, and giving her a playful swat on the ass before she crawls out of bed.

She narrows her eyes at me and scowls, trying to look intimidating, but I think it's cute.

Jazz's eyes go wide as she grabs the phone off the nightstand. "Shit, it's Gordon. You're not here."

Before I can respond and charmingly tell her I am, in fact, here, she races into the bathroom and shuts the door behind her.

I contemplate if the phone call from Gordon is a cockblock or a favor. I was a very good boy last night. My control is astounding. I'd only wanted to strip Jazz naked about ten times and sink my cock into what was most likely the sweetest pussy I'll ever know, but I resisted. My reward is the biggest pair of blue balls I've ever had. There's a good chance I'll need medical attention later, but it's worth it. Giving in and having sex with Jazz, as much as I'm dying for it, is not smart our first night together. I'm playing the long game and need her to know one night with her isn't enough. However, waking up this morning with her body tight against mine and the light scent of coconut coming from her hair was almost enough to break my resolve.

Jazz comes barreling out of the bathroom like it's on fire. She grabs my shirt off the floor and throws the damn thing at me. If I didn't have cat-like reflexes, she would've hit me in the face.

"What's the emergency?" I sit up, letting the sheets fall to my waist and flex my abs like I'm one of those tropical birds on the Discovery Channel trying to entice a female mate.

Jazz's gaze lingers on my chest and dips to the abs before meeting my eyes. It might work. "Gordon caught an earlier flight. He's on his way here from the airport, and in case you missed the conversation last night, he can't know you were here."

"I'm very aware of our conversation last night." I get out of bed and go in search of my pants. "We agreed to keep this thing between us a secret. And there *is* a thing between us, Jazz." I level her with a glare just in case she's going to try and deny it.

"Yes, Linc, there is something between us." She huffs, jumping into a pair of pants. Damn those tits of hers, much too distracting for the current conversation. "I can't seriously talk to you when you're in your underwear. I can't think straight."

I chuckle at how similar our thoughts are and give her my back, bending over to show off my goods as I pull on my jeans.

Ever so slowly, I turn around and smirk, as I catch her staring at my ass. "Good to know. Next time I want to have a conversation with you, I'll make sure to strip first."

"Very funny." She crosses her arms across her chest making her breasts squeeze together for maximum cleavage.

"I like to think so."

"Put your shirt on."

I chuckle, closing the distance between us, and pulling her into a hug. Her eyes widen before her body melts into mine and her hands explore my chest. My cock instantly responds, hardening between our bodies.

"Linc." Her beautiful green eyes meet mine, and her lips part slightly, letting out a small sigh.

I can't wait another second. My lips crash into hers, and she opens underneath me. I sweep my tongue into her mouth, tasting, teasing, and exploring her warmth. Her little moans drive me wild as I kiss her with a greedy hunger I've never felt before. She meets me with a passion rivaling my own.

She arches her back as I grab her ass and grind her against my erection. It's heavy and throbs with the need for release.

Jazz tears her lips from mine, breathing heavily, her voice a whisper. "Oh, God."

I rest my forehead against hers and struggle to catch my breath. "Just a little something so you don't forget me, kitten." I steal one more quick kiss. "We'll continue this next time. And there will be a next time. I'm not nearly done with you."

I back up, instantly missing the heat from her body, and throw on the rest of my clothes. I take one last look at Jazz. Her hair is mussed from bed, her eyes shining as bright as her smile, and her lips swollen from my kisses.

She's never been so beautiful.

"To be continued." I give Jazz a brief peck on her forehead.

I adjust myself, so walking would be possible, and walk out to the Rover before I change my mind about leaving.

My eyes wander, taking in the neighborhood as I leave. It's a great place to settle down. Since when did I start thinking about settling down? Christ. I'm already letting Jazz interrupt my plan to leave Nashville before the trade deadline.

I know I want to be with her, and I'd like to think this doesn't have an expiration date. A trade might make it easier to be together. I wouldn't be one of her 5, and no one could accuse her of favoring a player that's no longer there.

A large red truck barrels around the bend in the road pulling me away from my white picket fence thoughts. Gordon. Shit.

Nothing would put a roadblock between Jazz and I faster than Gordon telling her he saw me leaving the neighborhood. She'd throw in the towel before we got started. I promised her I'd keep this secret, and that's exactly what I'll do.

I feel along my center console until I find my Oliver Peoples sunglasses. They're a bit of a necessity against the brutal morning sun and will hopefully deter Gordon from looking at me too closely. I slide them over my eyes and lower myself in the seat, cramping my legs under the steering wheel. My stomach flips as the truck rolls past me. Eyes straight ahead. Don't make eye contact. If you don't see him, he can't see you.

Once I'm clear and his truck is nothing but a mirage in my rear-view mirror, I straighten up, throw my sunglasses in the passenger seat, and hightail it home.

I think I'm in the clear as I round the corner of the hallway to my apartment. Until Foster pushes himself off the wall by my door and saunters my way with a smirk on his face. One that says he knows exactly what I was doing last night.

Shit.

Might as well call me Fort Knox. There's no way he's getting any information from me, not that I have a whole lot to give. Yet. I hope I'll have a lot to talk about in the next few weeks. Not that I'd be able to talk about it then either. Doesn't really bother me, though. As long as I get to go to bed with Jazz multiple nights a week, I'll be one happy-as-fuck hockey player.

"There you are, mate." Foster's smile widens until he could have doubled as the joker's twin brother.

I smile and stop several feet from him. "Are you stalking me, Foster? You're really not my type."

"Sorry to bust your bubble, but I'm here to see if you want to hit the gym this morning. And I know your type, Lincoln. You like the unavailable, I-pay-your-wage type of lady." He throws his head back and laughs.

Hilarious.

Nice, he thinks he's cute. Too bad for him, his bullshit only works on the ladies. And I'm no damn lady. My lips flatten into a tight line. I cock a brow and cross my arms over my chest as I wait for him to get himself under control. Any minute now.

Foster throws his hands out toward me. "Sorry. Sorry. Couldn't help myself. I was about to call you when you turned up from, what I'm guessing was, a better night than mine. What's this called? The walk of shame?"

I huff out a laugh and look down at the clothes I was wearing yesterday. I'm pretty sure I'm the walking definition of the walk of shame. Although, I feel none. "This isn't a walk of shame."

"No? Looks like it to me. Didn't I see you in that t-shirt yesterday? Do you want to tell your new mate, Foster, where you were last night? Did you get your leg over?"

"My leg over?" I don't know what the hell that means, some weird ass British slang, but there's no way I am telling him I buried my face in our boss's pussy last night. I could tell him I refused sex and fell asleep holding the world's most beautiful woman, but I'm fairly sure he either wouldn't believe me or demand my man card on the spot.

"Yeah, you know—shagging—sex." Just in case I don't get it, he starts to air hump.

I laugh, uncrossing my arms, and continue moving toward my apartment. "Moving on."

Foster turns around, trailing next to me. "I'll take that as a yes. So, gym?"

"Yeah, let me change. Come on in." After unlocking the door, I open it wide and take a step back. "Ladies first."

"Oh, this is nice. The layout looks a bit familiar, though." Foster chuckles, walking into my apartment.

Very astute observation of him considering all the apartments are the same layout, including his. I lead him to the living room and gesture to the couch. "Make yourself at home. I'll be right back."

I don't wait for his witty reply, knowing damn well he always has one at the ready. He really is a funny bastard.

I cross the apartment and close the door to my bedroom behind me. We have ice time later, so I don't really want to go workout, but I need to keep my brain occupied. If I stay at home all morning, I'll keep reliving last night over and over. And how fucking good it was. How right it felt. How—

My phone cuts through my thoughts.

Dan.

My mostly helpful agent.

"Hey, Dan."

"Hey, Lincoln buddy." Dan is always chipper. It's hard to tell if he's genuine or blowing smoke up my ass. "How's my favorite client doing today?"

I cradle the phone with my shoulder as I change into gym

shorts and a clean shirt. Looks like it's a blowing smoke kinda day. "Got some good news for me, Dan?"

"I do actually. I have three teams so far that are very interested to see how the next couple months go for you. LA and Toronto have expressed interest. They're both on track for the playoffs right now."

Despite Dan's tendency to be a schmoozer, he's very good at his job. He handles a fair amount of high maintenance athletes which probably accounts for his overly sunny disposition. He and I have been working together the past couple years, and he hasn't steered me wrong yet. LA and Toronto are both strong teams. They'll probably at least make the second round of the playoffs. "That's good. Who's the third team?"

"Chicago." He sounds pleased with himself, as he should.

Chicago is a big deal. They lost in the Stanley Cup finals and are favored to win this year. Not to mention, a trade there would put me close to my mom and brother. "Chicago? Are you serious?"

"Would I lie to you?"

"Dan, you're a sports agent. You lie to everyone." My voice is devoid of humor, and I switch the phone to my other ear.

He scoffs. "Lincoln, you wound me."

"Back to Chicago. Are we talking serious interest?" Chicago is my dream team, a good chance at the cup, and I'll be back home. It also isn't in another fucking country. Canada is great and all, but...

"Yeah, they want to secure some trades before the deadline, and you're at the top of their list, thanks to yours truly. All contingent on how the next couple months go, of course. I've got to run, Lincoln. Keep up the good work. I'll talk to you later."

I disconnect the call and stare at my phone. The news is great, could be the opportunity of a lifetime. It's everything I've been working for. I'll have a chance to lay my hand on the cup, and I could be closer to home.

But that's also further away from Jazz. As much as I'd like her and my trade to both work out, I'm not sure they can.

I might have to choose.

17

The Missing Linc: Thanks. I got caught doing the walk of shame yesterday.
Jaz-ersize: Lincoln?
The Missing Linc: Who else did you send on the walk of shame? Did you sleep with anyone else recently?????
Jaz-ersize: ……..Maybe……..
Jaz-ersize: Hahaha.
The Missing Linc: I'm not laughing, and I'm coming to show you I'm not laughing.
Jaz-ersize: Calm down, caveman. I didn't realize you had my number.
The Missing Linc: I called myself from your phone when you fell asleep.
The Missing Linc: Sorry not sorry.
The Missing Linc: When do I get to see you again?
Jaz-ersize: What makes you think I want to see you?
The Missing Linc: I'm coming up.
Jaz-ersize: I was KIDDING. Jeez. So touchy.
The Missing Linc: I'll show you touchy.

The Missing Linc: But seriously. When?
Jaz-ersize: Gordon doesn't have any more trips coming up.
The Missing Linc: <unamused face emoji>
Jaz-ersize: I do have my own room on a separate floor when we have away games.
The Missing Linc: Better.
Jaz-ersize: You know no one can see you.
The Missing Linc: I can be sneaky. Think of me as a ninja.
The Missing Linc: Your sex ninja.
Jaz-ersize: I'm still not sure this is a good idea.
The Missing Linc: It's a great idea. No one will find out. Promise.
The Missing Linc: Plus, my game will suffer if I don't get in that tight pussy of yours.
Jaz-ersize: <laughing face emoji> Are you saying if I don't put out, you'll purposefully suck?
The Missing Linc: <wink face emoji> That's exactly what I'm saying.
The Missing Linc: As the team owner, you should want to do everything in your power to keep your players happy.
Jaz-ersize: All the players?
The Missing Linc: Fuck no.
The Missing Linc: I'm coming up.
Jaz-ersize: You keep saying that, but I still haven't seen a himbo around here anywhere. Weird. <shrug emoji>
The Missing Linc: I don't know what a himbo is, but I'm here.
The Missing Linc: Open the door.
The Missing Linc: Jazz I'm here, open the fucking door.
The Missing Linc: Jazz??
Jaz-ersize: Sorry, the person you are seeking is not taking visitors at this time.

The Missing Linc: I'm going to spank that ass next time I see you.
Jaz-ersize: Maybe I like that. <shrug emoji>
The Missing Linc: You're going to be the end of me.
Jaz-ersize: <Face Throwing Kiss Emoji>

18

JAZLYN

That has to hurt.

I cringe watching Tag Harris take a hit that would make most grown men cry. It's a good thing the guys are tough mother—oh, another hit. Harris retaliates with a body check, sending their center sprawling on the ice.

Helmets thrown aside and gloves are off. I'm staring at a full-on hockey brawl. Red and yellow blur together as fists swing, and blood is spit on the ice.

"Get 'em, boys!" I grip the rail and shout down at the Bruiser Brothers who are right in the middle of the action, and by the look of things, winning. I'm suddenly glad to be in the Phoenix luxury box by myself and not in the private box with the other team's owners.

The game is a brutal one. Going into the game, I expected things to be a little tense, but nothing like this. Gordon's texted me twice to make sure I'm okay.

Penalties are being handed out like business cards. The other team is playing dirty, and the refs aren't going easy on them. It seems the owner of the Phoenix Lightning holds grudges, and he has one hell of a vendetta against Coach Weller. I can't say I understand. It isn't like he's *still* sleeping with the guy's ex-wife, plus they're already divorced. Have been for months. It's a fair play.

My heart rate jacks up as Lincoln skates into the mass of squirming bodies, pulls someone off Tag, and tosses him aside. My breath catches in my throat, and my grip tightens on the rail. He narrowly avoids a punch to the back of the head. Where are the fucking refs? Someone should be breaking this up before one of them has to be carried off the ice.

Jesus. Weller looks like his head is about to explode. I can't hear a thing he's saying, or rather, yelling, and his arms are waving wildly.

The refs finally make their way over, whistles blowing, calling out players like Oprah. You get a penalty. You get a penalty. Everyone gets a penalty. Balcom, the player who threw the first punch, skates to the sin bin to sit out his two-minute penalty, spewing obscenities the whole way. Way to stay classy, Phoenix.

The fans are going crazy, yelling at the refs, and hell, yelling at each other. Several of them have already been escorted out after fighting. The energy in the arena is intense. They may be pissed about the call, but I'm liking these odds. We're three on two with an odd man advantage.

At least for the next five minutes.

The players split apart and skate to their spots for the faceoff. Lincoln looks up in the stands and holds my gaze. I can't make out his face this far away, but something tells me his look means we'll be taking care of our unfinished business. And soon.

Shivers wrack my body, and I clench my thighs together in anticipation.

It's been two weeks since Lincoln buried his face between my legs and gave me the most intense orgasm of my life. But it seems we're back to square one with flirtatious looks and racy text messages. It isn't that I'm avoiding him this time. Season started and, between away games and meetings I unfortunately have to attend, we haven't had any time to get together.

Since Lincoln stepped into his role as captain, we're actually winning some games, making my inner Devil very happy.

Yes!

Foster Craig wins the faceoff and takes the puck right to the attack zone. It gets passed between Lincoln and Tag as they circle the goalie, then back to Foster who lines up for one of his slap shots. His stick shoots back and—crack—the puck sails through the air. The goalie reaches out, the puck tips off the top of his glove and makes it in the net.

The roar from the stands is deafening. The fans are on their feet, some cheering and some yelling. The Devils flank Foster, giving him back slaps and helmet taps as congratulations for a fucking fantastic shot. It didn't win us the game yet, but it gives us a two-point lead. The Devils are skating back to center ice—whoa, punches are launched. Fans are screaming and pointing toward the ice. And another fight breaks out as one of the Lightning players rips off his gloves and charges toward Foster.

It seems blood and violence are the themes of the game as the fighting and rough plays continue for the remainder. The score stays close, Phoenix manages to score at the top of the third period, leaving us with only a one-point lead. Thank God that point is enough, giving us a hard-earned win.

Once post-game interviews are wrapped up, we head to the buses that'll take us back to the hotel.

"Stick close to me." Weller comes up beside me and tugs me close. "Security said Lightning fans are lined up by the buses. They're trying to hold them back, but these idiots don't seem to be able to follow directions."

I glance up at Weller, his nostrils flare and brows crinkle

together. If he's worried, then I need to be careful. "I'll stick close. I'm sure it'll be fine."

Weller gives me a tight nod. "I hope so. I don't think they were very happy with tonight's win."

"I wouldn't be surprised if the owner offered extra incentive to their players for starting fights. It was the roughest game I've seen in a while."

"I know." He sighs, running a hand through his hair. "Before tonight, I would've never thought Paul would have sunk so low, but now—damn, the man has never played a dirty game in his life. If he wanted me to know he was still angry, let's just say message received."

"He could have just sent you a bag of dicks in the mail or some animal shit," I grumble.

Weller turns toward me, eyes wide and a smile playing on his lips. "Are these actual things? Please tell me these are actual things."

"They are completely real things." I laugh and turn the corner, making my way down the hallway before the back exit. "There's a website where you can send your enemies bags of gummy penises. Right there on the bag it tells them to eat a bag of dicks. It's genius. The poo is a different site. I've not been to it but heard you can select various animal shit to be packaged and sent to someone's door."

"This is, hands down, the best thing I've heard all night. I think I'll be making good use of the hotel WiFi tonight."

I'm pretty sure I know someone who's going to be getting a surprise in the mail. I just wish I could be there to see the look on the asshole's face when he opens it. "You're welcome. I'm glad I could help."

We pause at the exit door, and I eye him nervously. We have a few players waiting to walk out behind us, looking good in their game day suits and ties. I don't know what's waiting for us on the other side of the door, but I'm not going to stand around all night and wait for them to get tired and go home.

"You ready?" Weller reaches out and squeezes my shoulder.

An uneasy feeling settles in the pit of my stomach. I throw on a smile and look to the other players. "Absolutely. Let's go see what kind of shitstorm awaits."

Shitstorm seems to be the perfect description for the disaster awaiting us outside the arena. Security is lined up along some small metal partitions that, let's face it, won't hold back a five-year-old. Fans gather on either side, screaming out insults and throwing things on the ground. They push at the barriers and security guards, gaining more ground and closing off our passage. Local television crews stand on the outside of the crowd, no doubt waiting for a fight.

"Better get moving," Weller whispers in my ear before moving in front of me.

I can't agree more. Another minute spent out here with the hostile crowd is a minute too long. As if to prove my point, a fight breaks out to our right and the few security guards we had run off to intervene.

Being unguarded makes me feel so much better.

Taking small steps, I follow Weller down the walkway. Most of the insults hurled at us aren't the least bit creative. There are quite a few 'you sucks' and 'the Devils are losers.' Real brainiacs we've got in Phoenix.

I stop abruptly as hands from the crowd reach out in front of me to grab onto Weller. They latch onto his arm and jacket and pull him toward the crowd. My heart hammers in my chest. I reach out to grab him but am knocked backward. Pain shoots across my scalp as a hand grips my hair and pulls me from behind. I stumble backward and reach up, trying unsuccessfully to slap the hand away.

"Let go of me!" I try to spin around, but the grip in my hair is too strong.

"Stop struggling, bitch. You're only going to make this worse for yourself."

The hand in my hair tugs, forcing me to back up until my legs hit the barrier. Blood thumps in my ears, and a scream dies in my throat. A large hand circles the column of my neck and squeezes. I reach up, clawing at the hand, desperately needing it to loosen its grip. I can feel his fingers tightening, and it's getting harder to breathe. I gasp, struggling for air against the unyielding pressure.

My body feels sluggish, my hands meagerly clawing at his. I can't give up. I have to keep fighting. Stars creep in the corners of my vision, and I struggle against him.

Fingers scrape against my neck and the pressure disappears as strong hands grip my arms and pull me against a muscled chest. My eyes blink as Lincoln bands an arm around me, pushing me behind him. His other arm cocks back, and there's no hesitation as he punches someone, who I assume is my assailant.

The muscles in Lincoln's jaw tic, his lips draw in a tight line, nostrils flare, and eyes grow wild. I've never seen him so intense, even during a game. He looks capable of murder.

"Linc." My voice comes out hoarse as I clutch at his gray suit coat, trying to get his attention. As much as I want him to knock that fucker out, we're being filmed.

"Go to the bus," he grits out.

My feet are glued to the ground. I can't leave him there. Not surrounded by all these angry people. "Lincoln."

"Jazz. Go. Now."

Something in the tone of his voice has me bee-lining for the bus. Weller is sitting at the front and I throw myself down next to him. I glance out of the bus at Lincoln. He fists the front of an older, shorter man's shirt and has his face lowered to meet his height. I don't know what he's saying, but the asshole pales and tries to shrink back.

"Are you okay?" Weller looks me up and down, his eyes settling on my neck. His lip's busted and he has some light bruising around his jawline, but otherwise looks unharmed.

I reach up and feel my neck. It's sore and most likely going to bruise, but at least I'm not unconscious. "I think I'm alright."

"You scared the shit out of me." Weller hangs his head. "I'm sorry. I couldn't get to you. I saw that guy grab you and then he started choking you. Shit. Security guards were dealing with the fight. I couldn't—and then Lincoln showed up out of nowhere. I'm just glad you're okay."

I place my hand on Weller's back. "It's not your fault. I know you were being held."

"This was all my fucking fault."

I roll my eyes and give a halfhearted smile to make him feel better. "Weller. Mick. Stop. It's not your fault. It's the asshole you used to work for."

He takes a deep breath, blows it out slowly, and nods.

My eyes shoot up as Lincoln stomps on the bus. Even with all this craziness, I notice how great he looks in his custom-tailored gray suit with maroon tie. He holds my gaze, his face hardens, his fists clenching and unclenching. He radiates a palpable energy; his anger practically sizzles in the air. I open my mouth to ask him if he's alright, but he shakes his head and storms to the back of the bus.

I lay my head against the seat and close my eyes, trying to calm my nerves and my pounding heart.

We'll get back to the hotel where I can take a hot shower, call Gordie to assure him I'm alive, and crawl into bed. I'll feel better in the morning.

Everything will be better in the morning.

19

LINCOLN

BAM. Bam. Bam.

I can't tell if the noise is from the pounding on the door or my racing heart. I find myself outside Jazz's hotel room door, glad she's on a separate floor from the team, and overwhelmed with the need to make sure she's unharmed, as I pound on the hotel door with the same fist I used to pound that fucker's face. Logic tells me she's fine. I rode the bus with her back to the hotel for fuck's sake. But I have to see for myself. I have to run my hands over her to satiate the rage that burns underneath my skin.

I could have killed that man. I genuinely thought about killing him. It would have been easy. I had his pudgy face in my hands. I was close, so fucking close to losing it. I'd seen his hands close around the delicate column of Jazz's neck, her body going limp, and her eyes fluttering closed.

Then, I saw red.

No number of men, big or small, could have stopped me from charging off the bus and launching my fist at that asshole. It hadn't been enough. Even after feeling his nose crunch beneath my fist and seeing Jazz safely on the bus, my anger still simmered in my veins.

The door unlocks with an audible click, and the second it opens, I push Jazz into the room and slam it closed behind us.

I lean down, framing her face with my hands and stare, unblinking. Her eyes are glassy with unshed tears, and she bites her lower lip, but it still quivers slightly.

I smooth my hands down her neck, taking in the light bruises. Anger surges through me, but I hold it at bay. Leaning forward, I feather kisses along one side of her neck and then the other. Her body begins to tremble, and I raise up to meet her emerald gaze.

Her eyes darken, and she licks along the seam of her lips. Lust shoots through me, settling in my balls. The heat from her skin permeates my veins and chases away the remaining anger.

I feel an insatiable need to claim her, possess her, corrupt her in every way possible. I need to make sure she knows who she belongs to.

She. Is. Mine.

My mouth crashes down over hers. Teeth scrape together as we meet in cataclysmic fury. Our tongues twist and roll, stroking against one another. Our kiss is hot, wet, and hungry. Fueled by want and desperation. My mouth is ravenous in its exploration of hers. My body burning to the point of combustion, and burying my cock over and over in her tight little body is the only thing that will slake the flames.

She moans into my mouth, and her hips rock against my rigid cock. My balls ache with need, demanding release. Burying myself deep in her pussy is more essential than water.

Turning us around, I back her up to the door and press my body into hers. I tear myself away from her lips and trail wet kisses across her jaw.

"I'm going to fuck you against this door, Jazz," I whisper in her ear before flicking her earlobe with my tongue and sucking it into my mouth. "Anyone will be able to walk by and hear you screaming for me as you come on my cock."

She answers me with a whimper, her hands grabbing onto my tie, pulling me closer.

"I'm going to bury myself so deep in that tight pussy of yours, you'll still feel me tomorrow." I lick down the length of her neck and suck on the hollow above her collarbone. "You've got me so goddamn desperate. I'm gonna fuck you so fucking hard, kitten. I don't have any control tonight."

Jazz leans forward, resting her head on my shoulder. "I want it hard, Lincoln. Fast and hard."

I growl and tear off my jacket, throwing it on the floor behind me. "Naked. Now."

I watch Jazz scramble to remove her clothes as I reach in my back pocket and pull out my wallet. Maybe I'm cocky. Maybe I subconsciously planned this moment all along. All I know is, when this time came, I wanted to be ready. Condom out, my wallet joins my jacket on the floor. I kick off my shoes, unbutton my dress shirt, and have the rest of my clothes gone in record time.

Jazz's eyes are glued to my hands as they tear open the condom wrapper and roll the rubber down the length of my dick. She licks her lips, and my cock twitches.

I've dreamt about her taking me in her mouth, hips pumping my dick between her lips, making her swallow me down that pretty throat.

But not tonight.

I run my eyes up the length of Jazz's body, taking in her toned legs, the soft flare of her hips, her rounded full breasts, and her tight pink nipples.

She's fucking perfect.

I press against her once again, claiming her mouth and running a hand between us. She moans, as I run a finger into her bare slit and circle her clit. Her hips buck, and I plunge a finger into her, relishing how her walls tighten around me.

"You're so fucking wet, Jazz," I groan, fucking her with my finger. "You ready for my dick? I need to get inside you."

Jazz nods frantically, scraping her nails over my chest and down the muscles of my abdomen.

I pick her up, my hands grabbing on to her lush ass, and her legs wrap around my waist, tightening behind my back. Her hands clutch at my shoulders as I force her against the door and drive my cock inside her with one smooth thrust. She's so fucking tight I can feel the walls of her pussy quivering around me. She takes me perfectly.

It's so good.

Too good.

I have to slow down, or I won't last long. I'm already so close.

She pulls my mouth down to hers, using me to muffle the moans and whimpers she can't control, and I swallow them down.

I begin to move, tunneling in and out of her. Every time my hips draw back, her body clenches around me, trying to keep me in. She grabs at my shoulders, pulls at my hair, and runs her nails down my back. Her hot little cries have me fucking her harder. Faster.

"I knew your pussy would feel so fucking good. You're so hot, so tight. So wet. Fuck." I thought I knew how good this would feel. How good she would feel. But I didn't know. Not really. Now that I've been inside heaven, I'm sure I won't be able to get enough.

I angle my hips, pressing into her, and grinding my pelvis against her clit with every thrust. Her cries become sharper, louder, and I know she's close.

I fuck her harder, slamming my cock into her, claiming her. Taking what's mine.

"You like the way I give it to you? I want you to feel me, Jazz. Feel every fucking inch of me."

She peers at me through hooded lids, her chest heaving with every breath. "Yes, Lincoln, yes."

"That's right, kitten. You know exactly what you do to me, and I'm gonna be coming for more. This pussy is mine."

Her walls flutter around me, and I pull back from her, needing to see her come.

"That's it, kitten. I need you to come for me. Come on my cock."

That's all it takes to push her over the edge. She throws back her head, knocking it on the door, as she screams my name. Her pussy pulsates around me, gripping me like a vise. I can't take my eyes off her, even as my vision blurs. My cock jerks, my balls tighten, and my thrusts become erratic. I groan out her name as my hips buck and I empty into the condom.

She's torn me to pieces, and I can't find it in me to care. If I thought I was ruined before, I was wrong. Jazz just fucking destroyed me. After being inside her, I know I'll never be the same.

My hips still, and I lean my forehead against hers, our heavy breath the only thing between us. My heart beats frantically in my chest, and sweat lines my skin. I search her eyes, making sure there's no regret in their depths. Any doubt on her part will kill me.

Thank God, I see none.

I press my lips to hers in a soft kiss. "You okay, Jazz?"

"Wow. Just wow." Her words come out light and husky.

I nod before kissing her again, this time lingering, brushing my lips back and forth across hers.

"Can we do that again?" Jazz mumbles against my lips.

I laugh, trailing my lips along her jaw before releasing her and letting her slide down my body. "Give me ten minutes. I intend to do that at least twice more tonight."

"Two more times?" She looks at me, her eyes widening.

I cage her in against the door and trail kisses along each side of her neck. She runs her hands over the ridges of my abdomen and lets out a low moan.

"You're dating a professional athlete."

"We aren't dating." She smiles at me, and while she's serious, there's a playful air around her.

No, we aren't dating. At least not yet. I've got a little work to do to change her mind. Trade be damned. I'll take her ass with me if I need to. I can be convincing.

I give her a playful wink before I swat her ass and head to the bathroom to dispose of the condom. "I have stamina. Plus, just being around you gets me hard."

"Lucky me," she murmurs.

A smile stretches across my face. No, lucky me. I'll get to bury my dick in her all night long. Nothing else matters so long as I'm deep inside her pussy, right where I belong. Because whether or not she's ready to admit it, we belong together. She's mine and I'm hers.

Fuck, am I hers.

20

JAZLYN

Mmm. I moan, angling my hips, chasing the tantalizing pressure between my legs. I blink my eyes open. I must've fallen asleep after our second round of sex. If this is how Lincoln does wake up calls, I'll be falling asleep more often.

I stretch my back and rub my ass along his hardening length. His dick is amazing. The things he can do with it are out of this world. The guy attached to it isn't so bad either.

The more time I spend with Linc, the more I find that I like him. If circumstances were different, he'd be the kind of guy I'd like to date. Not that we aren't dating now. Actually, I'm not sure what the fuck we're doing.

I just know I'm not ready for it to end.

I turn around and peer into Lincoln's eyes. "Round three already?"

Reaching down, I wrap my hand around his shaft. His skin is silky smooth to the touch, and he looks huge underneath my narrow fingers. I begin to stroke his length in slow, methodical movements.

"I've been ready. I thought I'd let you sleep for a few. Seemed like you were a little worn out from our previous session." His mouth quirks into a smile.

I find myself smiling back. "I can't help it if your dick is magic."

He leans back and moans. "What you do to my dick is magic."

Well, if that's the case—

I lay my other hand on Lincoln's chest, pressing until he rolls on his back. I hover over him, laying a gentle kiss on his lips before kissing down his neck, pausing over his Adam's apple. "Then, you're going to love what I'm about to do."

His groan fills the room. "You're fucking incredible."

I continue my descent, roaming my hands across his chest and tracing my fingers in the ridges of his abs. His body is so yummy. It's like having my own personal playground. My tongue darts out, flicking one nipple and then the other before biting lightly. I lick down the length of his abdomen, drawing the skin under his belly button into my mouth and sucking. My fingers dance along his cock, exploring the veins of his shaft and the soft mushroomed head.

"Fuck," he hisses, as I dip down and replace my fingers with my mouth.

The sweet yet tart taste of his precum blooms on my tongue. I could lick him for days. I curl my fingers around the base of his shaft and guide him between my lips, my tongue smoothing around the swollen tip. I inch my mouth lower until my lips kiss my fist. I'm stretched wide from his bulk, and I love it.

I peer up at him, Linc is like a statue. His jaw clenched, eyes are closed, and hands are in fists at his sides. I relish in the power I have over him. Back and forth, up and down, I bob over him, sucking and licking as I move him in and out of my mouth. His hand tunnels in my hair, gripping the tresses and holding me steady.

"Oh, motherfucker. That mouth of yours is going to destroy me. And you love it. My little dirty girl likes having my big cock in her mouth. Can you take me deeper, kitten?"

I hum around his dick in response. I've never been a fan of blow jobs, but I love his dick in my mouth. Plus, I want to feel Lincoln bumping into the back of my throat. I flatten my tongue as he rolls his hips, pushing himself farther into my mouth.

"Goddamn." Lincoln groans. "I love seeing your pretty lips wrapped around my cock. I want to fuck that hot, wet mouth of yours."

Letting out a moan, I raise up on my knees and inch down until he reaches the entrance of my throat. I relax, breath through my nose, and reach around to give the cheeks of his ass an encouraging squeeze. He lets out an animalistic sound and begins to thrust his hips, pistoning in and out. Fucking my mouth like he can't get enough. My eyes water, and I grab onto his ass, wanting him to use me until he comes.

"I'm gonna—I'm gonna—" He growls.

My nails dig into his flesh. His words come out in snarls, and with one final thrust, his seed pours down my throat. My jaw's a little sore, but it doesn't put a damper on the satisfaction of knowing I cause him to come undone. He slips from my mouth, and I sit back on my heels.

"I think I forgot my name." Panted breaths accent each word. "Fuck, Jazz, I've never come that hard."

Lincoln pulls me down on top of his chest, and after a quick kiss on my forehead, he nuzzles his face into my hair.

"It was the least I could do." I press a gentle kiss to the hollow of his neck. "You've done so much for me."

"A few orgasms are the least I could do. I wish I could take you out on a real date. I would woo the fuck out of you."

"Woo me?" I wiggle my brows and give him a taunting smile.

He runs his hands up and down my back. "Oh, yes. I would

take you out and show you I can be as fun outside of bed as I am in."

"I have no doubt. But you know it has to be like this, right?" My body tenses waiting for his answer. He said he's fine with keeping us a secret, and I need to make sure. As much as I like spending time with him, it's not worth sacrificing my career. I won't do it. If it means making a clean break and walking away, I will.

"I told you, I'm good." He runs his hands over my shoulders, relaxing me.

I breathe out a sigh of relief. We can't go anywhere in public, but maybe we can have a date of sorts in private. "Linc?"

"Mm?"

"How would you feel about renting a suite or a cabin next weekend? We could stay together Saturday night and Sunday."

"Really?" His voice is laced with surprise.

I peer up at him and press a soft kiss to his lips. "Absolutely. If we can't go out on a date, we can stay in on a date. We can watch movies, play video games, I'll cook you dinner—"

He rolls us over, his hard body pushing me into the mattress. "We can fuck without worrying about someone hearing." He rolls his hips into mine. "I don't have to sneak out in the morning. Yep. I'm loving this idea. Don't worry about packing any clothes. You won't need 'em."

I open my mouth to respond, but his mouth slants over mine, his tongue sweeping in. Despite the multiple orgasms I've already had, lust has my body firing up. My nipples harden to points, and my lady bits dampen and clench with need.

"Now it's my turn to take care of you." He grinds his stiffening shaft against my clit.

I lean my head back and release a low moan. Lincoln had already taken care of me. Multiple times. He's a giver, and being with him makes the rest of the world fall away and my worries subside. He's quickly becoming my safe haven.

If I'm not careful, I may not be able to let him go.

21

JAZLYN

"Are you sure you're okay?" Gordon stops in the hall and looks at me expectantly, his eyes lit up with concern. The last time Gordon looked at me with those eyes had been after a particularly horrible parental lecture where my choice to hang up my skates in order to train future Olympians had been called into question.

I roll my eyes so hard I think there might be a good chance they'll fall out of my head. "Yes, Gordon, for the hundredth time, I'm fine."

"I know, I'm sorry." Gordon smooths his hand down the length of his narrow charcoal tie. "Thanks to that damn news video all I can see is that asshole with his hands around your neck. Is it sore?"

"Not really."

It is, but not like other parts of me. I suppress a shiver from running down my body. Lincoln didn't lie when he promised I'd feel him the next day. I didn't even know I had some of these muscles, but I feel a delicious twinge every time my thighs rub together.

"Come on." I push past Gordon and continue my trek to our offices. "We have work to…"

I stop abruptly right outside the entryway where my door has been left open. I never leave my door open. Gordon, who evidently isn't paying attention, runs into my back, propelling us into what used to be my well-ordered office.

"What the fuck?" Gordon's voice booms behind me.

What the fuck, indeed.

My office, which was pristine the last time I was there, now looks like a bomb exploded in the middle of it. Chairs knocked over, cushions slashed, legs broken. The crystal vase, a relic from my grandmother, is in pieces on top of a damp section of carpet. Trampled wildflower petals from the bouquet I'd put in the vase two days ago are scattered across the floor, along with a few pictures I had hanging on the wall.

The area behind my desk has seen better days. My computer has been jumped on by The Hulk, and it looks like someone shredded all the paperwork in my filing cabinet before pitching it in the air like confetti.

I spin around to face Gordon, my eyes wide, mouth opening and closing like a fish. I can't believe someone would wreck my office.

He grips my shoulders, holding my gaze. "I'm going to check and see if my office is trashed too. Don't move. I'll be right back."

Completely dumbfounded, I turn back, taking in the wreckage. There isn't a single thing left undisturbed. Even my computer keyboard has half the keys popped off. Who does that?

"Whoa." Adam edges into my office and stops beside me. "What the hell happened in here?"

I shake my head. "No idea. Gordie and I just got here and found it like this. I can't believe it." I narrow my eyes on him. "You don't know anything about this, do you?"

Adam throws his hands up in front of him. "Hey, hey! I know you and I haven't exactly seen eye to eye, but this—this is too far. I promise you, I had nothing to do with this."

"No?" I narrow my eyes. Adam likes to torment me, but it's always been verbally. Something like this is a whole other level of crazy.

Gordon darts in the room, injecting himself between Adam and me. "My office is clear. It's just you, Jazz. I don't get it. Any idea why someone would do this?"

My thoughts immediately go to the threats and my slashed tires. Lincoln is the only one who knows. It's too much of a coincidence for everything to be unrelated. I sigh wearily. Maybe it's time to come clean.

I hesitate, my gaze drifting to Adam and then Gordon. "Well, I didn't think it was a big deal at the time, but I've gotten a few threatening letters. And might have had my tires slashed."

Gordon's eyes flare. "What?"

"Are you serious?" Adam's words are clipped, and his mouth tips in a frown. "You should have said something. I'm calling security."

As Adam turns on his heel and makes a quick exit, Gordon takes a step toward me and leans down. "Why the fuck didn't you say anything?" His voice is low yet harsh in my ear. "This is ridiculous, you don't keep stuff like this from me. I can't look out for you if I'm in the dark."

I'm a grown-ass woman and don't need my big brother to take care of me. Last time I checked, I was doing just fine on my own. Except for this office disaster, of course. I open my mouth to tell him exactly what I think about him looking out for me when he cuts me off.

"I know you can look out for yourself and don't need your big brother around to keep you safe, but I can't let someone threaten you and do nothing. We have a full security team, and I'd feel better if you didn't go anywhere alone."

"Gordon." I cross my arms over my chest. "I'm not going to have someone following me around everywhere I go." The scowl on Gordon's face deepens, and I hold up my index finger to hush him. "How about we compromise? I won't leave the office or stay here alone, and we'll increase security at games."

"Already done." Adam breezes into the room. "Security has been told to double their personnel for all games, we're to have someone stationed in the executive suites at all times, and I have a team on their way. In the meantime, I suggest you let someone escort you to your vehicle and work from home today. Gordon and I will get everything cleaned up here."

Gordon and I stare at Adam in disbelief. Where the fuck did that come from? Did someone slip me a crazy pill? Never imagined I'd see the day when Adam would have my back. Gordon's wide eyes and slack jaw reveal a similar sentiment.

Gordon clears his throat and shakes himself, probably back to reality. "Thank you, Adam. He's right, Jazz, let us clean this up. You don't need to be walking around on broken glass, and your computer needs to be replaced."

"Fine, fine." I throw my hands up in the air. "I'll go home. Thank you, guys, for your help and concern. Adam, when I come back tomorrow, I expect you to be your usual asshole self. This nice guy routine is freaking me out."

Adam's lips twitch like he's fighting a smile. "Yes, well, if you weren't so damn incompetent, we wouldn't have to worry about this in the first place."

"Adam," Gordon rumbles.

Turning around with a light smile playing across my face, I pull out my phone. Better let Lincoln know what's going on before he finds out on his own and takes it upon himself to hunt me down.

Me: I'm ok, but someone trashed my office. Security's on their way to check it out.
The Missing Linc: Where are you? I'm coming up.
Me: Calm it down. You can't just come up here. We're a secret, remember?
The Missing Linc: I don't like this.

No surprise there. If his behavior yesterday after the choking incident is any indication, I'd guess he's fucking livid. I'm still not sure how I feel about that. Gordon has always looked out for me, but his behavior pales in comparison to Lincoln's downright possessiveness.

Through the years, I've always prided myself for *not* needing a man for any damn thing, including orgasms. Yet, knowing Lincoln has my back gives me a heightened sense of security I've not felt before. Plus, in bodyguard mode with all his intensity focused solely on me, he's sexy as fuck. I only hope I'm not left in the dust like I was six years ago.

"Alright, guys." I point to Gordon, then Adam. "Let me know if security finds anything."

Adam inclines his head in a tight nod.

Gordon sighs and pushes me towards the front reception area. "We'll let you know. Go home."

"Fine," I groan, drawing out the word like I used to when we were teenagers.

After blowing a kiss toward Gordon's bemused face, I turn and head to the lobby to wait for security. Yes, I do think about simply walking out to my car but don't want to give Gordon a heart attack. So, begrudgingly, I lean against the wall next to the reception desk and pull out my phone.

Me: Don't worry, caveman, I'm going home.

The Missing Linc: Good. Let me know when you get there. I'll be by after practice.
Me: Gordon will be home by then. How about you video chat with me when you get in your car? Besides, we have another away game coming up, and don't forget, you get me next weekend.
The Missing Linc: Two days...I want Friday too or I'm coming over.

Suppressing the world's largest smile, I hold my phone to my chest and look around, making sure I'm still alone. All clear. Thank God, the last thing I need is to get busted looking at my phone like a moon-eyed idiot.

Me: That's blackmail.
The Missing Linc: I'm not afraid to fight dirty for what I want. Friday?
Me: Ugh. Fine. It's a good thing I love your glorious cock. <Wink Face Emoji>

Dirty fighter, indeed. I can't help the smile tugging at my lips. That isn't the only thing he did dirty, and I'm ready for more.

22

The Missing Linc: Is it Friday yet?
Jaz-ersize: Not sure, let me double check my calendar.
Jaz-ersize: Nope.
The Missing Linc: Good thing I don't care.
Jaz-ersize: Are you always this horny?
Jaz-ersize: Wait...I think I know the answer.
The Missing Linc: For you...yes.
Jaz-ersize: I'm sure you say that to all the ladies.
The Missing Linc: What ladies? All I see is you.
Jaz-ersize: <eye roll emoji> How original, Dallas. After all the rumors and our near miss at the Olympics, my expectations were so much higher.
The Missing Linc: That's not what you said when I was balls deep in your pussy.
Jaz-ersize: OMG Lincoln!!!
The Missing Linc: I think it was something like I love your huge cock. <eggplant emoji><eggplant emoji>
The Missing Linc: I think you also mentioned something about being the best you've ever had.

Jaz-ersize: Your mother would be shocked if she saw your messages.

The Missing Linc: Haha. What are you doing?

Jaz-ersize: Looking over all the paperwork for the casino fundraiser Lucy sent.

Jaz-ersize: You?

The Missing Linc: Do you really want to know? <wink face emoji>

Jaz-ersize: I did. Now, not so much.

The Missing Linc: <downloading image>

Jaz-ersize: OMG. <shocked face emoji> <shocked face emoji> <shocked face emoji> You did not just send that.

The Missing Linc: Enjoy.

Jaz-ersize: I'm in a meeting!!

The Missing Linc: You mad you can't touch yourself? Oh! And tell Adam to suck my ballsack.

Jaz-ersize: You're not quite that impressive, Dallas. And absolutely not.

The Missing Linc: Such a little liar. And yes, do it and take a picture of his stupid face.

The Missing Linc: Video call me tonight. I want to see you finger that sexy pussy of yours.

Jaz-ersize: Maybe I will, maybe I won't, but I will not be telling Adam anything.

The Missing Linc: I'll stroke my cock for you, kitten. <cat face emoji>

Jaz-ersize: Strong maybe.

The Missing Linc: Here's a parting gift. See you tonight. <downloading image>

23

LINCOLN

Friday couldn't come fast enough. I have some rather wonderful and slightly romantic plans involving me and one particular skirt-wearing Devils owner. I wasn't kidding when I said I wanted to woo the fuck out of her. Instead of taking her out for a night on the town, we'll stay in. I'll cook her one hell of a dinner—recipe courtesy of my mom—followed by a chick flick, a massage, and a soak in the jacuzzi tub. If she finds me utterly irresistible and has to interrupt the planned activities to tear off my clothes and ravish me, I won't protest. Much. There's only one rule: no hanky-panky until after dinner.

Which is precisely why Jazz is pouting from the countertop watching me cook instead of laying across it while I feed her my cock.

"Who knew you could be such a prude?" Jazz muses, leaning back on the counter supporting herself with her open palms. Her shirt is tight across her breasts and the smug smile on her face hints it might be purposeful. "The way you jumped me after the away games on Monday and Wednesday made me think I'd be getting some good dick tonight. My mistake."

"Woman," I growl while stirring the bacon, mushroom cream

sauce for the pasta. "You'll get plenty of my dick tonight. I'm trying to make you dinner. You're going to need some energy for later. Can't have you throwing in the towel halfway through."

"Yeah, yeah. Does it help if I tell you it smells good?"

I point the wooden spoon at her. "No. Now I know you're just saying it to patronize me."

Jazz slides off the counter and saunters her way behind me. Her arms slip around my waist, and the weight of her head rests between my shoulder blades. "That's a big word for a hockey player."

I huff a laugh, turning around in the circle of her arms, and press a quick kiss to the tip of her nose. "Me play hockey. You beautiful. Me make dinner. You sit ass on chair."

Jazz's laugh goes straight to my balls. It would be so easy to peel off her jeans, bend her luscious ass over the counter, tug aside that thong I'm sure she's wearing, and fuck her until my legs gave out.

Dinner. I have to finish dinner.

I need to show her I'm more than a dick with legs. We've had four nights together, all of which involved me sneaking out early morning after an abundance of orgasms and not much time hanging out. The weekend retreat is about more than sex, and although admittedly, it's the best sex of my life, she needs to know there's more.

That I'm more than a good time.

More than just a deliverer of superior orgasms.

No woman has ever made me feel the things Jazz stirs deep within me. I'm not so certain any other woman would. She makes me feel accepted, completely comfortable in my own skin. I never feel like I have to adopt a different persona, act how people think a professional athlete should act. More than that, she makes me want a life where I have someone to come home to, to talk about our days and our problems. She makes me want a future with her because I've started to realize no one else will ever compare.

If she took her blinders off, she'd realize we could have a relationship, a future together. Hopefully not in Canada. Maybe in Chicago.

The place doesn't matter so long as she comes with me.

"Go sit down." I brush my lips against hers before turning her around and giving her ass a solid slap. "Dinner's almost ready."

Jazz peers at me over her shoulder with narrowed eyes. "And if I don't do as I'm told?"

A slow predatory smile spreads across my face. "Well then, kitten, I'd think that would make you a bad girl, and bad girls get spanked."

Her eyes sparkle as she moves around to the kitchen table. "We wouldn't want that."

"I know better, Jazz. Don't forget, I know exactly what makes you wet."

"So." Jazz keeps her eyes on me as I drain the pasta and start plating dinner. "Where did you learn to cook? It's not a talent most men have."

"My mom taught me." I spoon the sauce over the pasta, making sure everything is covered. I like my pasta like I like my women, saucy. "She always thought my brother and I should be able to take care of ourselves, so she showed us our way around the kitchen. Over the years, living on my own, I got a bit better."

"Have you made this before?"

I duck my head down, hiding the heat I feel on my cheeks. "No. I called my mom to get the recipe."

"What?" Her voice rises a few octaves. "You seriously called your mom? Did you tell her about me?"

"Of course not." Okay, so maybe I did, but I didn't give any specifics.

My mom's not entirely pleased she couldn't get all the juicy details about the only woman I've ever cooked for or mentioned to her. Knowing her, she's already shopping for what she'll wear to the wedding. I'm going to have to convince Jazz to actually date me first. And then to come with me after the trade.

She fiddles with the plate after I place it in front of her. "Is it hard being away from your family?"

"Yes and no. I go back when I can, but we talk every week. I'd like to be closer to them, but you go where your contract is."

Jazz nods. She knows how professional hockey works. "You must be close."

"Yeah, my dad left right after my brother was born, so it was Mom, Liam, and me. We were pretty tight. Liam was still in elementary school when I left after my senior year. He loves hockey, maybe more than me. He's good too. I imagine he'll get picked up after high school."

She takes a bite of the pasta and moans. "This is so good. Hats off to your mom."

"What about you?" I take a bite of my own, and damn, it is good. "What about your parents?"

She shovels another forkful in her mouth and then takes a sip of water. "You know my dad and how difficult he was?"

I bob my head and wave for her to continue.

"I told you we were never close. He preferred to spend all his free time with Gordy, shaping him into his image and all that. I was never good enough. Neither was my mom. He left her when we were little, and after that, he didn't have much time for Gordon and me with all the hockey and twenty-year-old bimbos."

"And your mom?"

"She had a hard time with the divorce. She kinda fell apart for a while, started drinking, popping pills. Then, she passed when I was training to go back to the Olympics the second time. Car accident. Gordon and I used to be close until he joined the NHL, but I'm hoping this ownership can bring us back together."

I reach over, covering her hand with my own. "I'm sure it will. And Jazz?"

Her gaze meets mine, and I can see the hurt and uncertainty within.

"You are enough."

"Thanks, Lincoln. You're not so bad yourself." Pink tinges her cheeks. Her gaze falls to her plate and then comes back to mine. "So, what happened to you six years ago? I thought everything was going great, but you disappeared when the Olympics ended."

I blow out a long breath. "Your dad kinda threatened my career. Told me he could get me kicked off the team and blackballed from the NHL. He promised me no team would touch me."

"Oh."

"Jazz."

"No. I get it, trust me. Hockey is important to you."

I want to bring up the inevitability of my trade from the Devils, but now doesn't seem like the time. Especially after I just insinuated hockey was more important than her.

Fuck.

We eat the rest of dinner in silence, sharing heated looks after 'accidentally' rubbing her with my leg several times. After the dishes are done and everything's put away, I challenge Jazz to one of my favorite PlayStation racing games. This weekend may have been Jazz's idea, but I've commandeered it to be my date to plan, and that meant checking into the suite early armed with groceries and video games. Not a lot of guys would bring video games on a weekend date with a lady, but Jazz is different. Growing up playing hockey, especially being good at it, means she has a competitive nature. I plan to use that to my advantage.

"What are we playing for?" Jazz rubs her hands together, bouncing back and forth on the balls of her feet.

"Let's see." I cross my arms over my chest and make a point to drag my gaze along the length of her body. "Clothes."

"Clothes?"

"Yep. Every race you lose, you also lose an article of clothing."

She points her finger at me. "You mean every race you lose. You're on, sucker. I hope you're prepared to have your ass handed to you."

Jazz grabs a controller and jumps on the couch. I turn everything on and sit down next to her. I fail to mention I'm pretty good at this specific racing game. If it wasn't my favorite before, it will be after she's shed all her clothes.

"Prepare to go down, Dallas." Jazz crosses her legs underneath her and leans toward the TV.

I smirk. "I'm always ready to go down, Benson."

She growls.

Actually *growls* at me.

I'm so distracted watching the intense look on her face as she stares at the starting countdown, I end up being the last one off the line. Well, shit. Jazz holds her advantage, hugging curves and staying on the track until she crosses the finish line and wins.

"I'll take your shirt, Linc," she says casually, holding out her hand.

Wow, she wins one game, and now thinks she's hot shit. I'm letting her off easy, but I'll have to up my game if I want to see some skin. Keeping eye contact with her as long as possible, I pull off my shirt and toss it directly into her smug face.

The shirt's only the first casualty. It isn't long before she has me down to my boxer briefs. Which wouldn't have been so bad, except she's still fully clothed.

"I don't know what you're doing, but you're cheating." I toss the controller on the table.

She huffs and puts a hand over her chest. "I would never

cheat. I'm just better than you."

I pluck the controller out of her fingers, and it joins mine. Grabbing her hands, I push her backward on the couch and pin her wrists over her head. My dick instantly hardens as I hover over her.

"Safe to say you won." I roll my hips forward, rubbing my cock over the seam of her jeans.

Jazz's head falls back on a moan. "Yeah, I kicked your ass."

"Position?"

"Huh?" Her gaze lands on me, and her brows knit together.

I rock my hips into her heat. One touch and I already need to get inside her.

"How do you want it, Jazz? Do you want me to fuck you like this? On your back with your legs on my shoulders. Or do you want on top? Do you want to ride me with that greedy pussy of yours?"

"Behind me," Jazz pants. "I want you behind me."

The rest of my blood leaves my body and goes straight to my cock. My balls are so tight I'm surprised they haven't exploded. I don't know what it is about Jazlyn that gets me so fucking hot so fast, but I've decided to stop questioning it. All I know is that I crave her, and right now, she's mine.

I lean back on my knees to give her space. "Get up and strip."

Without missing a beat, Jazz pushes up from the couch and holds my gaze. Her hands smooth down her stomach until she reaches the top of her jeans. Button open, she lowers the zipper and sways her hips as she pushes them down her thighs and off each leg. Her hands come back up and catch the hem of her shirt. It joins her pants on the floor, leaving her in a black lacy bra and matching thong.

My mouth goes dry like the Sahara. She is fucking gorgeous. I want to devour her. I want her to use me, to ride my face and dick until she can't take the orgasms. My fingers itch to plunge inside her, to bend her over and rub that sensitive area that makes her scream. Every. Damn. Time. My cock jumps, thumping to get free so it can sink into her wet fucking pussy.

"You better take off that bra and thong before I rip them off." I stand and shuck off my boxer briefs.

The bra falls to the floor, her little pink nipples drawn into points and begging for my mouth. They'll have to wait until later for attention. My dick has other plans.

"Lean over the end of the couch. Head down. Get that ass up and get ready for me."

Jazz whimpers, scrambling into position. Blood roars in my ears as she leans over the arm of the couch, giving me the perfect view of her heart shaped ass and her glistening pussy underneath. My hand slides along the length of her spine and pushes her head down toward the couch. With the tips of my fingers, I trail my hand back to her hips.

"Have you been waiting all night for this hard cock to fill you?"

"Yes," she answers on a moan.

I skirt my fingers to her stomach and down to her clit where I start to rub. "Your pussy is always so wet for me. Have you been wet all day thinking about me fucking you?"

A quiver runs through her body and she starts to rock her hips, chasing my fingers. I press my lower body tight against her, notching my cock against her entrance. I press in with my fingers, making tight circles around her clit. "I need an answer, Jazz. Has this greedy pussy been wet all day thinking about my cock? Thinking about me fucking you?"

Her hips push back into me. "Yes. Yes. Lincoln, I need—I need—"

"I know what you need, kitten." I thrust forward, pushing my cock into her tight channel. Her walls flutter around me, welcoming me home. "And I'm going to give it to you."

I draw back, pulling out almost to the tip before pushing back in again. My rhythm is slow as I start to pump in and out of her. She pushes back against me, silently asking for more, and I'm more than happy to oblige. Picking up my pace, I fuck her harder, the sound of my balls slapping off her thighs fills up the room.

Her moans and whimpers have lust pounding in my chest and thumping through my veins. I'm hot, so fucking hot for this woman. I reach up, wrap her hair in my fist and tug her head back. She lets out a loud groan and tightens around me.

She feels so good, too good, even better than before.

I know I won't last long.

"Shit, Jazz. Condom. We forgot a condom." No wonder everything feels better, tighter. I've never been bare with a woman before.

Jazz clenches around me. "Are you clean? I'm good, and I'm on the pill."

"I'm clean. I've never not worn a condom before. I'm sorry."

"Don't be sorry." Jazz pushes against me, grinding her ass into my lap. "Just fuck me. You feel so good like this."

My groan is ragged as I slam back into her, grazing her shoulder with my teeth. Knowing I can lose myself inside her, I don't hold back. My hips plunge forward, raw, deep, hard. I'm not just fucking. I'm claiming. The need to make her mine is overpowering.

"You like this, kitten? You like knowing my dick is bare inside you? You make me forget my own head. You and your tight little cunt. I want to come so deep inside you, this pussy will know exactly who owns it, who takes care of it, who gives it what it needs."

Her cries become louder, more erratic and her pussy clenches around my cock. She's close. I reach around to her front, pressing into her clit, rubbing it frantically. The buildup of my climax is so intense I can barely stand.

"Oh, God." She throws her head back and gasps. "Yes, Lincoln. Yes. Yes."

Her body trembles underneath me as her pussy clamps down on my cock, flexing around me, milking me. My climax pumps through me in waves as I piston in and out of her. I let loose a groan, loud enough to wake anyone in a neighboring room, and a stream of incoherent words, sinking into her as deep as I can get before spilling into her.

"Goddamn. Fuck." I lean forward, breathing heavy, resting my forehead in the middle of her back.

Jazz collapses on top of the arm of the couch, panting to catch her breath. We stay like this for several seconds. Minutes? Hell, at this point I have no idea.

She runs her hands along my arms. "What's next for our weekend fuckfest?"

I laugh, planting a kiss on each shoulder before wrapping my arms around her and holding her tight against me. "I figure once I can move my legs, I'll carry you to the bath and we can soak in some bubbles while I rub your back. Then, we can lay in bed and watch a movie with some popcorn and those Junior Mints you like."

"You gonna cuddle with me too?" she teases.

"Fuck yeah, I am."

Her soft groan has my dick hardening inside her. "You're something else, Linc. You're gonna make me an addict."

Well, that's the plan. Get her addicted to me because fuck, if I'm not already addicted to her.

Maybe then we can have that conversation about my trade, and she won't even have to think about ending what's between us. She'll see I can have both her and a good team.

One thing is certain.

The more time we spend together, the harder it'll be to let her go.

24

JAZLYN

WHAT IN THE ever-loving fuck is happening? Only me. There is no way something this unbelievably shitty would ever happen to anyone else. It's ridiculous. No. Correction. Ridiculous would've been them showing up right before the game. Or even just being late. What's happened instead is completely unacceptable.

It isn't just the coach. If it were, it wouldn't have been so bad. Adam coached before and could easily stand in. But no. All three of those fuckers—Weller, Adam, and Gordon—are stuck at an airport in Canada while we have a game starting in thirty minutes.

Or I guess, I have a game in thirty minutes because without a coach, we'll have to forfeit. I'll be damned if I'm handing over a game. Especially to Philadelphia. The cocky bastards already think they have this game in the bag, and I intend to give them a run for their money.

Even if that means I have to piss off all the chauvinistic hockey good old boys and pretend like I know how to coach a professional hockey team.

"I'm so sorry, Jazlyn. We were supposed to be back this

morning." Weller's voice pleads through the phone. "Who knew a fucking storm would shut down a whole airport?"

I couldn't have predicted the storm, but I fucking told him it was a terrible idea for the three of them to travel together. I don't care how good this player is. Even if he shits gold bricks in the middle of the hockey arena, it's not worth the three of them getting stuck somewhere.

I scoff. "Doesn't really matter now. We have a game and no coach. If we weren't the laughingstock of hockey, we will be now. I told you guys this was a bad idea."

"Does it help if I told you I think we found our new starting goalie?"

"No." I lean my head back and pinch the bridge of my nose. "It does not help."

Weller sighs. "Is now the time to ask for more coaching staff?"

"I think last week would've been better."

"Now that the coach has offered you his condolences, I'm going to need you to get that ass of yours in gear. We already sent you the starting line-up. Chris will be there to help, but God knows he hasn't been coaching long and you have far more ice experience than he does." Adam clears his throat.

"Was that actually a compliment?"

"Don't let it get to your head." Adam's tone is terse. "If we had adequate coaching staff, this wouldn't be an issue."

"Yeah, I get it. The coaching staff is too lean. I guess asking for your respect as your boss is too much."

"I'll tell you what. You manage to pull off a win tonight and there's a good chance you'll get my respect." Adam pauses, and I can hear all three of them murmuring to each other in the background. "Fine. I'm doing it. Also, we really appreciate you stepping up tonight. Not a lot of people would. They'd throw in the towel before the game even started."

A grin tugs at the corner of my lips. "Well, I'm not most people. You all get back safe. Tell Gordon and Weller they owe me big time."

"Good luck out there."

"Kick some ass, Jazz," Gordon calls out.

"You can do it." That was from Weller and yes, he does the Rob Schneider voice when he says it.

I hang up the phone with a shake of my head. It's certainly not ideal, but I feel a little better about the game. There's no reason the team can't win.

The second I step into the locker room, conversations die off and every pair of eyes turn in my direction. Some look hostile, but most eye me with open curiosity. Almost all of the players are already fully suited up and ready to play. I steal a glance toward Lincoln.

His gaze roams over my body, and the darkening of his eyes tells me exactly what he'd do to me if we were alone. He shakes his head as if clearing out the dirty images before crossing his arms over the front of his jersey and giving me an encouraging nod.

"Alright, Devils, we have a big change tonight." I clasp my hands in front of me and look around the room. "Coach Weller, Adam, and Gordon have all been stranded at an airport in Canada."

"What the fuck?"

"What about the game?"

"Are we forfeiting?"

The questions are coming in rapid fire without giving me a chance to answer, and they soon dissolve into voices blended together, as they all speak over each other.

"We are not forfeiting the game," I yell over them, and the room falls silent.

"But we have no coach. You said so yourself."

"We have Assistant Coach Miller." The guys start shifting around, looking at each other with wide eyes. If they're hesitant to have him coaching, they're gonna love this next part. "And you have me. Coach Weller has asked for me to step up and take his place out there on the bench."

"And what in the hell are you going to do?" Kevin stands up, gesturing toward me with his hand. "Hand out juice boxes and pat us on the head? This is bullshit. You can't coach us."

Fucking Kevin Craft. A perpetual thorn in my side. Not only does he have a shit attitude, but his playing has been garbage all season. "I'm not going to force anyone to play. If you want to go wait on the bus until we're done with the game, be my guest. I won't stop you. But for any of you who actually want to play some fucking hockey, I'll see you on the ice in ten. We've got a game to win."

With my head held high, I stride out of the locker room toward the ice. I'm confident everyone will be ready on the bench when it's game time, with the exception of Kevin. He could go pout on the bus for all I care.

Turns out, he did show up on the ice. As did every other player. And today, they're playing to win. In your face, Adam. We're halfway through the second period and already up by two goals. I'm so elated, I even let Kevin out of the box.

"Let's go, McIvers." I lean out of the players' box and shout. "Knock 'em into the boards."

"You don't have to be so loud." Lincoln straddles the wall, waiting to be switched out.

I chuckle quietly. "I'm in charge here, Dallas. I'll be as loud as I want."

"Noted." His eyes sparkle underneath his helmet.

"You gonna sit here and gab all day, or are you going to get out there and score a damn goal?" I nod to the ice. "Get your ass out there."

With a wink, Lincoln shoves himself out of the box and barrels down the ice to take control of the puck. Damn, that's sexy. That mountain of muscle, mine to command. I fight the urge to smile. Linc usually controls things in the bedroom, but I think it's time I take the reins.

Lincoln whizzes past me, Harris hot on his heels. The Bruiser Brothers are fighting their way off the boards when one of the Philly players flies by and hits one of them in the head with his hockey stick.

"Are you blind?" I yell at the refs after no penalty gets called. "High sticking, number sixty-three. My grandmother could have called that. Fuck."

The ref skates off with a shake of his head. The fucker. I'll high stick his ass if he doesn't pull his head out of it.

Harris and Linc pass the puck back and forth as they circle the net. The goalie rushes out to the front of it, defending his zone. Harris pulls his stick back to shoot, and the goalie dives to save. Only there's no puck. Lincoln skirts by the open side, and with a flick of his stick, the puck hits the back of the net and the buzzer goes off.

The roar of the stadium is deafening as Linc collides with Harris for a quick hug and points his stick over to me.

Calm down, big man, I saw the goal.

If he listens this well on the ice, we're both in for a treat later.

"Congratulations on your win, Jazz." Gordon relaxes against the headboard and holds the phone up to his face for our video call. "It was fucking awesome."

I lean against several pillows I have propped up around me and smile at Gordon. No matter how hard I try, I can't wipe the stupid smile off my face. We sent Philly straight down to Loser Town.

"I'm not gonna lie, I was a bit nervous. I wasn't sure if half the team was going to show up before the game."

"It is what we pay them for. I don't know if you know that."

I chuckle and run a hand through my hair, pushing it over my shoulders. "I may have told the team they could go back to the bus and wait for the game to finish if they didn't like the idea of me coaching."

"No, you didn't." Gordon's shoulders shake with laughter.

"I absolutely did. I had my mic drop moment and walked out not knowing if anyone would show up on the bench."

"Your rousing motivational talk must have done some good. The first line was on fire tonight." His eyes light up as he becomes more animated, waving his free hand around as he talks. "You must have said something Dallas liked, he was a force out there, and the other players followed suit. He's turning out to be a stellar team captain."

"I don't know about that. I don't remember saying anything particularly special."

It wasn't necessarily anything I said that had Lincoln playing his best. I'm thinking he liked me bossing him around. I also think he knew if we won, I'd be in a very good mood for him tonight. Not that I'm willing to divulge any of this information to Gordon.

He'd be traumatized, pissed, and traumatized some more.

"I was hoping to be back tonight, but the airport is such a mess right now. We can celebrate—" Gordon raises his eyebrows as he's interrupted by a few sharp raps on my hotel door. "Are you expecting someone?"

I sit up straighter and glance at the door. "Room service. I'm gonna grab a quick bite and then head to bed. I'm so tired."

That sure as shit isn't room service, and if Linc has anything to say about it, I'm not going to be going to sleep anytime soon. I stretch my free arm above me and fake a wide yawn.

"No worries, sis. Get some rest, I'll see you tomorrow."

My body hums as I say my goodbyes to Gordon and toss my phone on the nightstand. I stand, smoothing down my red blouse and black tight fitted skirt. I thought about changing when I got back to the room, but I know how much Lincoln likes these skirts. More specifically, snaking his wandering hands well past the hem or flipping them up to fuck me with them on.

I aim to please.

At least where Linc is concerned.

Not only is the man always there for me, he's sneaking around —which I know he hates—to be with me. He's truly a great guy, and I like him way more than I care to admit. I'm not sure I'm going to come out on the other side of this non-relationship unscathed, but I'm in too deep to stop now.

I pull open the door and peer up at Lincoln with a sly smile, batting my eyelashes a thousand miles a minute. "Hello, sir. Do you have some room service for me?"

He pushes through the doorway and slams the door shut behind him. "I believe I have something for you to eat. And I think I like hearing sir come out of that sexy mouth of yours."

"I hope you brought enough meat. I'm awfully hungry." I run a lazy finger up and down his biceps before I add with a smirk. "Sir."

"Trust me, kitten, it's a mouthful." He takes a step toward me, circles my waist with his hands, and pulls me to him. His cock hardens against me, and I want nothing more than to have him in my mouth right now. To feel his velvety soft flesh sliding past my lips and his salty taste on my tongue.

Running my hands over his hips, I push them under the waistband of his sweats. I groan, grabbing his plump ass before lowering myself to the ground and resting on my knees. I pull down his pants and boxer briefs, freeing his glorious cock. My mouth waters at the sight of his rigid, thick shaft.

"Let's test out that theory."

"Jazz." My name turns into a groan, as I flick out my tongue and lick along his length, teasing the head of his dick.

No, I don't have to, but I want nothing more than to be in charge of Lincoln's pleasure tonight. To know I'm the one bringing this larger-than-life man down to his knees. All while I'm on mine.

I take Lincoln in my mouth, moaning as the salty taste of his precum dances across my tongue. I slide down his shaft slowly, taking him to the back of my throat before pulling back and dragging my lips over the tip.

"You like the taste of my cum, don't you?" Lincoln gathers my hair at the top of my head and holds it in a ponytail with a tight fist. He jerks my head back, forcing me to meet his gaze. "Out in the world, you're prim and proper with your fucking skirts, but in here you're my little dirty girl, aren't you? You want my cock, kitten? Take it."

With a tight grip on the back of his thighs, I surge his hips forward, taking him deep in my throat. My tongue glides along the underside of his cock before I start to suck, bobbing my head up and down. I move slowly at first, licking and sucking, but then pick up the pace.

"I love your fucking mouth. Hot and wet, just like that little pussy." His words come out strained as both his hands weave through my hair.

I bring one hand up to grip the base of his shaft and pump as I work him with my mouth. I moan around his cock, sucking him hard.

"Fuck." Lincoln throws his head back, and his body tenses. "I'm so close. I'm going to come down that pretty throat of yours."

I hum around his cock, wanting nothing more than his warm seed running down the back of my throat. I increase my pace, pumping him into my mouth as I moan again, my throat vibrating around him. His grip tightens in my hair, almost to the point of pain, as his come spurts into my mouth and down my throat.

I pull back slightly, licking along his length until he shudders and releases his grip on my hair.

Lincoln stares down at me, and his lips twitch before they curl up in a smile. "Touch yourself. I want to see you play with your clit."

I lean back, and pull my skirt so it bunches around my waist, revealing the small red triangle of my thong. I tug it to the side and run two fingers between my slick folds before circling my clit in slow torturous movements.

"I love watching you fingering your own cunt." Lincoln licks his lips as he stares at my pussy. He reaches down, grabs his now erect cock, and pumps himself with his hand.

Throwing my head back with a moan, I increase the pressure on my clit, kneading it in tight circles. I lower my fingers, teasing my entrance before pushing them inside, fucking myself in measured strokes.

His eyes smolder with lust as he drops to his knees, reaches for my hand, and sucks my damp fingers into his mouth, licking my wetness from them. "I fucking love how you taste."

Without another word, he pushes me to my back and rips the thong from my body. Didn't need it anymore, it was about to incinerate anyway.

My pussy clenches, and I arch my back, as Lincoln plunges two fingers inside me. I'm already drenched, and I can feel another surge of moisture coating him while he moves inside me. I moan and whimper, writhing on the ground, as he finger-fucks me hard and fast. He surges forward, giving me no time to adjust before he fastens his lips to my clit and sucks it into his mouth.

I cry out and my hands dive into his hair, holding him against me. He has me close to the edge of orgasm, faster than anyone else before, and I can't get enough. My hips buck as his fingers tunnel in and out of me. His tongue flattens on my clit before he begins to stroke it with the same rhythm of his fingers. Hard and fast.

I close my eyes, and my body tightens. Shamelessly, I grind my pussy against his mouth. I'm grasping for control over myself, but I have none. My hips come off the floor, and my body jerks. A wave of pleasure crashes into me, vibrating through me. I can feel my walls clamping down on his fingers. My vision goes black, I can't see, I can't breathe, I can't...I can't...An orgasm rips through me, destroying me, drowning me in bliss. The waves of pleasure have my pussy convulsing until I'm nothing but a limp, boneless body.

Lincoln looks up from my core and rests his head on my thigh. "If I get this kinda welcome every time I win a game, you can bet I'm going to try a whole lot harder."

I'm sure there are a hundred witty things I could say right now, but I can't think of a single one. My brain is an oversexed ball of mush.

Not that I'm complaining.

I peer down at Lincoln, the haze of lust slowly lifting. He looks at me like I'm his world. And maybe in a different universe, a different life, I could be.

Unfortunately, in this reality, I'm his boss, and there's no way we can ever really be together. We can't hide in the shadows forever. Of course, it wouldn't be a problem if we didn't make the playoffs next year and Gordon and I lost the team. But I'm hoping that doesn't happen. I love Nashville and being a part of the Devils. And that may mean giving this up. Giving him up.

I went into this, eyes open, intending it to be a short affair.

Something to slake the lust that burned within me when he was near. To get him out of my mind so I could move on.

I didn't expect to feel this pull, this connection, this thing between us that just feels right. The more time I spend with him, the more hopeful I become. Hope for a future. Hope for different circumstances. Hope for the freedom to make my own choices. At the end of the day, I have none of those. Nothing to offer the one man who deserves everything. Nothing more than secrets and lies.

He deserves what I know he wants. A relationship and a future with someone he can bring out in public and introduce to his friends. Someone he can take on dates. Someone who can invite him over instead of just sneaking him into out-of-state hotel rooms.

I know—I fucking know—I'm going to have to give him up. I just don't know how to let him go.

25

LINCOLN

"You see that bunny over there?" Kevin is way too fucking loud. Even though he's sitting at the table behind mine, I'm sure most of the bar can hear him. "I had her bouncing on my dick two days ago. She's not much to look at, but she can suck the chrome off a bumper."

I take a deep breath and look to Tag, who rolls his eyes before giving an exasperated look. I thought team bonding over beer would be a good idea. I was so fucking wrong. The last thing I want to do is listen to piece-of-shit Kevin bragging about his sexual conquests.

Even with most of the team here at Whiskey and Rye, I'm somehow unlucky enough to be at the table right next to his. I'm thinking Ian and Owen had the right idea when they went over to the bar to get refills instead of waiting at the table for the waitress.

"If these bunnies have all touched *his* knob," Foster points his thumb over his shoulder in Kevin's direction, "then I don't want any part of them touching mine. You can't get rid of herpes."

"Amen, brother." I raise my beer and clink it against Foster's glass. "Antibiotics don't get rid of everything. And I wouldn't rule out leprosy either. There's a good chance your shit would just fall off."

"Can't have any of that. My trouser snake is in high demand and needs to be kept in tip top shape. You see—"

"I'm going to stop you right there, Foster. I don't need you to go into any more detail about your junk." I hold up a hand, interrupting him before I get a clear, mental image of his man region I won't be able to unsee.

Tag eyes me as he brings his beer to his lips and takes a healthy sip. "I notice you haven't spent time with any of the bunnies lately."

"Who are you, my fucking mom? Why are you keeping tabs on my dick?"

"No one's keeping tabs on your dick." Foster leans forward and drums his fingers along the edge of the table. "We've just noticed you've been a little different lately."

I look between Tag and Foster. "You too?"

Foster shrugs. "You've been disappearing after away games and no one sees you until the next morning. Your playing's been on point, but you're distant. Distracted."

So much for hoping no one noticed me sneaking off to sex up my walking distraction. You know the one. She comes up to my shoulders, wears sexy skirts, kissable lips, and has mesmerizing emerald eyes. No matter how many times I get her underneath me or on top of me, I can't get her out of my head.

She's it for me.

There's no one else that can even compare, and I don't want to try.

But I can't tell them shit. I can't tell anyone. I can't even take her out to dinner. I want to do all that and more, dammit, but I can't.

At least not until after I've been traded. I'm holding onto hope she'll come with me, although I've been struggling to find the right time to bring it up. Or maybe I'm afraid she won't even consider it.

"I've just got a lot on my plate right now." I lean back and fish my ringing phone from my pocket before quickly glancing at the screen. I use my thumb to swipe open the phone but instead of sending her to voicemail the damn photo album opens. Fuck. The picture I snapped one lazy morning of Jazz and I kissing in bed lights up the screen. Big ass fingers do not work well with a small screen.

Tag grabs the phone as I try to shove it back in my pocket. "What the fuck is this, Lincoln?" He holds it up, putting it on display for Foster. "Is this why you've been disappearing?"

"Jesus, put it down." I reach for the phone, but Tag holds it out of my reach. Maybe he won't recognize Jazz. "It's just some girl. No one important."

The lie feels dirty on my lips, and I tamp down the feeling of panic as Tag scrutinizes my screen.

"Some girl?" Tag drops the phone on the table, which thankfully lands face down, and glares at me. "Do you know who that is? Of course, you know. You have your tongue down her fucking throat."

I glance around the room with wide eyes. We've drawn some unwanted attention from the tables around us, and I want a hole to open up and take me out of my misery. It's bad enough these guys know, it would be a disaster if the team found out. "Keep your voices down."

Foster points to the phone, a knowing look crossing over his face. "Was she the reason for your walk of shame? I thought it was some random chick to help you get over your crush."

"What walk of shame?" Tag quirks his brows, his face marred with a frown, and his eyes look through me like I ran over his childhood dog.

"I caught this idiot," Foster hikes his thumb in my direction as

I sink down in my chair and run a hand down my face because I might just die of mortification, "coming home one morning wearing his clothes from the day before. Of all the women in Nashville, why that one?"

Tag leans toward me and whispers harshly, "Why wouldn't you tell us? And why the fuck would you risk your career for a piece of ass?"

My eyes narrow on Tag. This is exactly why I didn't tell either of these assholes. "Don't talk about her like that."

Foster sighs, rubbing his temples. "You have feelings for her. You have to end this before it gets out of control."

"Both of you need to settle it down. It's not out of control. I know what I'm doing."

Tag slides my phone across the table to me, pointing at the screen. "Care to explain what exactly it is that you're doing?"

I run my hands through my hair and bite back a groan. Where was that fucking hole when you need it? "Look guys, I wasn't exactly planning on—"

"Sexing up the boss?" Foster interrupts.

"On this turning into something more," I correct him. "But it has. I think she's it for me, I've never felt this way before. I couldn't tell you guys because she and I can't exactly happen right now."

Tag shakes his head before reaching up to push his hair out of his face. "I don't like this, Linc. Is she embarrassed to be seen with you? Is that what this is? Does she think you're not good enough?"

"Calm down, Mom, it's nothing like that. You hear it every day from morons like Kevin. Every decision she makes is still being questioned. What do you think would happen if people found out she was dating one of her players?"

Foster crosses his arms over his chest, some of the anger

leaving his face. "I get it, but I still don't like it, mate. It's not worth your career."

The last time I had a choice between her and my career, I chose the latter. I'm not sure if this time, I could pick one over the other if my hand was forced.

I need them both.

"No more secrets between us, but I need you to keep this one for me. No one can know."

Tag clamps his hand down on my shoulder and shakes his head. "I've got you, man. Just don't pull this shit again."

"What did we miss?" Owen sits down on the other side of the table, clunking several beer bottles between us on the table.

Ian grabs a seat next to him and hands me a fresh beer. "Why do you all look so tense?"

Foster grunts, and I hope he can keep his mouth shut. "Just talking about our next game. Linc here thinks we're going to lose."

"Dude."

"The fuck?"

I shoot Foster a grateful look before taking a quick sip of beer. "They're pretty good this year. I was just saying we have our work cut out for us."

Owen and Ian launch into a discussion, highlighting the New Orleans Fury's weaknesses and how we're going to dominate them on Tuesday. I nod and give my opinion when needed, but my brain is somewhere else. There's no way around it, I'm going to have to tell Jazz about Tag and Foster.

I'm not sure how she's going to take the news, but I don't have a good feeling. Secrecy has been her big thing from the beginning. I hope what her and I have is strong enough to move past this together.

I can't lose her now. Not ever.

26

JAZLYN

THE MISSING LINC: We need to talk.

I've been staring at those four words for the past thirty minutes, and they still slice right through me. Nothing fills you with fear, dread, and anxiety faster than those words. They should never be used together, definitely not in that exact order, and Lincoln should know this. But he's the one that needs to talk. Talk about what, I have no idea. Maybe it could be something simple like what he wants to do next weekend.

I scoff and toss my phone across my desk. The screen lights up, taunting me, telling me I've yet to reply. Of course, it's not something as simple as weekend plans. He would just tell me what he wants to do. We have to talk usually means 'I think we should break up' or 'my dick wandered into someone else's vagina'.

Maybe an ex-partner of his called him up and told him she had a disease that could easily be cured with a round of antibiotics. In this day and age, it could be entirely possible.

I never thought I'd find myself rooting for the clap.

I make a quick grab for my phone and stare down at the screen. What if he wants to break up with me? Can you even break up with someone when you aren't technically dating? It feels like we're dating. I guess we're kinda dating. Which means we can kinda break up.

Fuck me.

Me: Okay

It's not even close to the cleverest response I've ever made. I'm hoping it conveys what I don't feel inside—that I'm totally cool. Cool as a cucumber. Which yes, makes me sound like a total dweeb, but my brain power is focused elsewhere.

Me: Come up to the office when you can. I'll be here.

There.

Now, I'm calm. Cool. Collected. Waiting.

Very patiently waiting.

I better make sure Krista, my secretary, will send him back when he gets here. I wouldn't want to keep him waiting. Or worse, turn him away. I'd give the same consideration to any of my players.

My chair creaks as I push myself up from my desk and head to the front lobby. Krista is still fielding phone calls. It's been ringing nonstop since the game against Philly when I had to step in and become a temporary coach. I don't envy her or the job she has to do.

As soon as she hangs up the phone, I step up and catch her attention. "Good morning, Krista."

"Good morning, Miss Benson." Krista beams at me. Unlike most around this office, she's in full support of the female takeover of the hockey team. She also has a genuine smile that seems to be lacking around the corporate offices.

Ahem, Adam.

Except he's been in a good mood lately. Maybe he's finally accepted me into the organization. Either that, or him and Candance have had another late-night rendezvous. I will not be confirming with either of them.

"Lincoln Dallas is going to be coming up to see me for, um, a meeting. If you could just send him back to my office that would be great."

Her brows furrow together and her lips tilt in a frown. "He's already up here for a meeting."

"Wait—what?" I look around the empty lobby half expecting him to pop out from behind one of the chairs.

What could he be doing up here? There's no way I missed him on the walk to reception. How can you not see a six-foot-four wall of muscle?

"Yeah." Krista leans over the raised desk and lowers her voice. "Adam called an emergency meeting with him and Kevin."

A meeting with him *and* Kevin? That seems like an unlikely pairing for any kind of meeting. The two are polar opposites in every way. Lincoln is respectful, kind, sexy, a team player, and Kevin is, well, none of those things.

Although, I guess as team captain, it makes sense to have him present at any player meeting.

I edge closer to the desk and rest my elbows along the edge. "What do you think they're meeting about?"

"I don't know. Adam met with Lincoln first and then Kevin came up about fifteen minutes later." Krista looks around, no doubt making sure we're alone. "Kevin looked pissed. I mean, really pissed."

Maybe the wizard finally found Adam a brain, and he's putting Kevin on the probation he should've been on a month ago.

"Thanks for the heads up, Krista."

Krista gives me a tight nod. "If I find out anything else, I can let you know."

"Please do that." I push myself away from the desk. "And when Dallas comes out, can you make sure he sees me before he leaves?"

"Sure thing."

I head to my office, fully intending to wait for their meeting to be over, but as I pass Adam's office, the door swings open and Lincoln steps into my path.

His light blue eyes are hardened, and the muscle tics in his jaw. Tension rolls off his rigid body, and I have to stop myself from reaching out to comfort him. As I open my mouth to ask him what's going on, he shakes his head, turns and heads down the hallway, disappearing into my office.

I take a step forward to follow, but Kevin stops in front of me, halting me in my tracks. His hands are clenched into fists at his sides, and his eyes flash with anger as he glares at me.

"You better watch your back, you little bitch."

"What?" I take a step back. "This is completely—"

"You thought your tires and your office were bad, just fucking wait and see what's coming next. Someone has to teach you a lesson. You don't belong here." He bends at the waist, putting his face directly in mine, his vodka-tinged breath tickling my nose. "A cunt like you is good for two things, spreading your legs and opening your mouth. I'll put you in your place. Right on your fucking knees with my dick hitting you in the face."

"Kevin." Adam puffs himself up behind him, his voice deep and full of authority. "I thought we could do this nicely, but it seems you need to be escorted from the building. I suggest you get moving, I will blackball you from every team in the NHL. No one will touch you. Not even a team in the minors."

Kevin backs away from me but continues to stare at me for the next several seconds, his eyes full of malice. His jaw is clenched tight, and he takes a deep breath before shouldering past me and storming down the hall.

"Sorry about that. I'll fill you and Gordon in later," Adam murmurs, as he follows Kevin.

Holy shit.

Not only is Kevin being escorted from the building, which can't be good news for him, but he admitted to slashing my tires and trashing my office. I bet my left tit he was the one who left the notes too. Relief and fear battle inside my mind. Now I know who to look out for, but it sounded like he had something else planned. Kevin is a total wild card, and it's unnerving.

I take a deep breath of my own, closing my eyes and giving myself a moment before joining Lincoln in my office.

"What's going on?" I close the door behind me and sit in one of the two chairs in front of my desk.

Linc, who was pacing back and forth along the side of my desk, sits down next to me and runs his hand through his hair. "Adam just released Kevin from his contract."

"What?"

"He called me in to ask about his attitude and how I felt about his playtime, which for the record, all sucks. Then, he brought him in, sat him down, and released him."

"Wow." I push my hair out of my face and tuck it behind my ears. It would've been nice if Adam gave me a heads up before releasing a player. When he gets back, I'll have to explain the benefits of email and how I like being informed. "No wonder he went off on me in the hallway."

"What did he say?" Lincoln narrows his eyes on me and grips the sides of the chair.

"Well, he admitted to slashing my tires and trashing the office."

Lincoln shoots up, his face twisted in fury. I jump from my chair and barely beat him to the door. I back up against it, blocking him in, and put my hands on his chest to hold him at bay.

"He's already gone. Adam walked him out of the building. The last thing we want is to cause a scene." I trail my hands across the wide expanse of his chest, down his perfectly muscled arms, and link my fingers with his in an attempt to calm him down. "Come on, caveman. He's gone, we have nothing else to worry about."

I pull him back to the chairs and push him down, letting go of his hands and sitting on the edge of the desk across from him. It's a good thing I didn't mention everything else Kevin said. I wouldn't have been able to stop Lincoln from barreling through the door had I uttered another word.

That is, if he still cared. There was still the issue of *we have to talk*. Kevin and his bullshit shenanigans almost made me forget the bigger issue here.

Chewing on my bottom lip, I wring my hands in my lap and avoid Lincoln's gaze. "That is if there's still a 'we'?"

He slides his hands up my legs and grips my upper thighs in a comforting hold. His eyes search mine, his forehead creased with worry. "What do you mean?"

"Well." I swallow past the lump in my throat and throw it out there. "You said we needed to talk."

Before I can protest the inappropriateness of being so close in my office, Lincoln pulls me sideways onto his lap, wraps his arms around me, and rests his chin on my shoulder.

"Shit. I almost forgot. I hope you'll have me after I tell you this."

Oh, good Lord. His dick fell into an open vagina. I knew it.

I knew it was going to be bad.

"So yesterday, you know I went out with the team to get drinks."

Here it is. This is where he tells me about some young, hot bunny with a slutty name and big boobs that had an ailment only his dick could heal.

"I was with the guys when you called." He pulled me tighter against him. "I accidently opened up my photos, and Tag and

Foster saw your picture on my phone. They know we're together."

I breathe out a sigh of relief before irritation snakes up my spine. "You showed them your phone? What were you thinking? You told me no living, breathing person would ever lay eyes on those pictures."

His hand cups my cheek, and he brushes the pad of his thumb across my bottom lip before turning my head. His forehead rests against mine, and he presses a soft kiss to the tip of my nose. "I'm so sorry. I wasn't thinking. I explained everything to them, and they promised they won't say anything. I completely trust them."

"How can I trust them? I don't know them." The absolute last thing I need right now is for Linc and I to get outed to the media. Adam is just now at the point where he tolerates my presence. I might even go so far as to say he accepts me here at the organization. Everything seemed to change after the game against Philly. Even the media is nicer. They're not to the point where they're singing my praises every day, but they aren't verbally attacking me anymore.

All that would change if we were outed.

"They won't say a thing. I promise. These guys are like my brothers."

Brothers who could sell him out to the highest bidder on a whim. All it would take is a few phone calls to some tabloid journalists and our faces would be plastered all over the covers. I'll have to tread more carefully in the future.

"Alright." I nod. "There's nothing we can do about it now. Are you all coming to the casino fundraiser next weekend?"

"You'll be there, so I'll be there. Coach Weller made sure we knew our attendance was highly encouraged, so they'll be there."

"You do know we can't actually go together, right?" Even though, I'd love nothing more than to be on Linc's arm while he's sporting a tux.

Lincoln in a tux.

Instant lady boner.

He leans forward and murmurs against my neck, "I know the rules. We can't be together in public."

"Good." I close my eyes and enjoy the feel of his lips on my skin before I realize we're in my office, in the middle of the day, where anyone could barge in. "You better let me up before someone comes in here and finds me on your lap."

"As long as you promise you'll sit on my lap on Tuesday after the away game." He presses his lips to mine in a quick kiss. "I want your legs wrapped around my waist while my cock is buried inside your pussy."

"Deal."

27

LINCOLN

WE WON OUR GAME TONIGHT, which was great. I can't really complain. I mean, I shouldn't. But I'm down at the hotel bar celebrating with the team when all I really want is to be buried balls deep in Jazz's addictive pussy.

She's here too, making this even more tortuous. She's got on one of those tight little skirts I hate to love. This one's practically begging my hands to run up underneath, hike it to her hips, and finger-fuck her to oblivion. Especially since she's standing on the other side of the room, her back to me, and her hand resting on her hip. The pose isn't particularly sexy, but when she does it, her hip cocks to the side showcasing her incredible ass.

I crave the time we get to spend with each other during away games. It doesn't hurt that watching me play hockey gets her fifty shades of hot and bothered. After I attack the puck, she attacks me.

Over the past several weeks, we've developed a routine. If it's an early game, her and Gordon go to dinner while I hang out and eat with the guys. If the game is later in the day, I head straight to my room, change out of my game day suit, and wait for her text giving me the all clear. It's like the bat signal for sex, letting me know Gordon is safe and secure in his own room.

The brief overnight visits aren't nearly enough. Sneaking out with only a few hours of sleep gets real old after the first few times.

I need more.

"Linc? Did you hear me?" Tag waves his hand in front of my face, snagging my attention. I definitely missed something, or everything. "What were you looking—never mind. Maybe you can pay attention to us for a change."

"Sorry," I mutter, as I turn around in my chair to face the guys. "What are we talking about?"

"Ball maintenance." Foster answers immediately with a smirk spread across his face. "Do you trim, shave, wax or go all natural? Personally, I prefer a good shave. I'd love to be all smooth like a baby's bum, but I'm not letting anyone with hot wax near my knackers."

"Don't knock it till you try it. I've had many ladies compliment my silky balls. Or at least they would've, but their mouths were full." Ian laughs and gives his brother a fist bump.

I refuse his fist bump and instead shake my head. "Dude. Overshare."

"Actually, we were talking about the fundraiser this weekend, and these two fuckers," Tag points to Owen and then Ian, "somehow convinced a pair of models to go as their dates."

"Twins." Owen smiles.

I lean over the table, looking between them. "No fucking way."

"They're from Russia, only been here a few months. We met them at a photo shoot we were doing for some fancy ass magazine. I'm pretty sure they think we're actors."

These guys couldn't act their way out of a paper bag. They both had speaking roles on a commercial last year, and it was so terrible they ended up having a voice over. I can't wait to see how this unfolds. It's sure to be interesting.

"Are you bringing anyone?" Foster eyes me from across the table. He knows damn good and well I won't be bringing anyone to this shit.

"Nope. Figured I'd go by myself."

"No lady you want to bring? No one special?"

"Nope."

"Are you sure, mate?"

I narrow my eyes at him, not sure what he's trying to accomplish with his questions. "I. Am. Positive."

"Thought so." He leans back and takes a sip of his beer, eying me over the rim of his glass. "Tag and I decided to go with you, so you won't be too lonely."

"How generous of you."

I shift in my chair and scan the room so it's not so obvious I'm staring at any one particular person. At least, that's my plan until she turns around and her emerald eyes meet mine. Her lips quirk up in a smile, and she gives me a small wave. I still can't believe she's mine.

She can't help but capture my attention when we're in the same room.

Plus, I'm anxious. Anxious to put my arms around her. Anxious to feel her lips on mine. Anxious to find out how her fucking day was.

Jazz pushes through the crowd, and I lose sight of her for a second before she slips down an empty hallway and around a corner toward the bathrooms. I drain my beer, mumble something to the guys about having to piss, and push up from the table.

As I shift through the crowded bar, I clap a few guys on the shoulder and congratulate a few others on some good plays and make my way to the bathroom I don't really need to use.

In a matter of seconds, I'm standing in the empty hallway,

waiting outside the lady's room like some second-rate stalker.

Maybe I should turn around and head back to the table. The last thing I want is to expose our relationship to someone heading this way to take a leak. It's not like I won't see her later.

Fuck.

I'm a stalker.

Before I can turn around and make a hasty retreat, the lock clicks and the door to the bathroom opens. Jazz stands in the doorway, her widened eyes rake over me and then scan the vacant hallway. Vacant at the moment. I rush forward, push her back in the bathroom and lock the door behind us.

I run my hands up her arms and down her back, pulling her against me. Everything I've been thinking about doing since she walked into the damn bar. Leaning down, I rest my forehead on hers and press a long and hard but chaste kiss to her lips.

"Hi."

"Hi." She wraps her arms around my waist. "You know this is a bathroom. A girls' bathroom."

"I know. Humor me. How was your day?"

She huffs a small laugh and brushes her lips across mine. "It was good. Some hockey team I happen to own won their game tonight. I'm out celebrating with the team, but I'm getting ready to head to my room."

"Oh, got any plans?"

"I might be meeting my boyfriend. Are you interested in coming up after he leaves?"

I chuckle. "Cancel him. Unless you think he can give you multiple orgasms while you ride his face."

"Doubtful." She shrugs. "He thinks he's better than he is."

"Poor guy." I rub small circles into her lower back, and she moans, leaning into me.

"I've missed you."

"Me too, kitten. How's the room situation? Still going to be able to sneak me in tonight?"

Jazz nods and nuzzles her head underneath my chin, pressing herself against my chest. "I may have bribed the front desk to make sure Gordie and I are on opposite ends of the hallway. He's heading upstairs too, I'll text you when he's in his room."

"Sounds good. I'll see you soon." I pull her back and press a kiss to her lips. One that isn't chaste. One that makes her bend to my will and gives her a preview of what she'll get later. By the time I'm done, her legs are weak, and I'm sure her pussy is drenched. "You should head out first. I'll wait a minute."

"I need a sec. I don't know if I can walk straight after that kiss. Fuck."

After a hug that involved some ass groping and another quick kiss, Jazz heads out, leaving me alone in the lady's room. Which is a first for me. Worth it, even for five minutes of her time.

It makes me wonder if things would be easier for us if the media knew we were dating. I'm sure it would be a shock at first, but then the attention would die down, and we could go back to living our lives. Jazz is scared of the backlash and the judgement, and I'm not so sure it'll be so bad.

Once I think the coast is clear, I pull open the door and freeze, as I'm met with Gordon's hard stare, his big ass body blocking most of the hallway.

Well, shit.

I could say something. I should say something. Anything to defend the fact I'm walking out of a place clearly not meant for me. But I don't know if he saw Jazz leaving.

If he did, I'm fucked.

"Any particular reason you're in the women's restroom, Dallas?" Gordon tilts his head, pinning me with a hard stare.

In the dim light of the hallway, Gordon looks even more imposing. We're about the same height, but he's a much bigger son-of-a-bitch. Wider. More muscular. He was fucking intense on the ice, and he hasn't lost his edge. His fucking arms look like they could crush boulders. Or at the very least my skull.

I'm pretty tough and can hold my own in a fight, but I think he's a whole other level. He's like the boss you fight at the end of a video game. Though, my approximations may be guilt for railing his sister every chance I get.

"The men's room was occupied, and I liked the soap in here better. I have sensitive hands."

Oh, fuck me.

Gordon studies me for a moment, crossing his huge ass arms across his chest, and I'm a goner. But then he shakes his head and chuckles, and I can relax. If he was about to kick my ass, he wouldn't be laughing, right?

"Likes the soap." He shakes his head again. "Remind me to make sure the next hotel stocks your room with plenty of scented soap for your dainty hands. I wasn't aware you were so delicate."

"That's me. A delicate flower. As high maintenance as they come." I shuffle out of the bathroom, letting the door close behind me, and take off to the bar area, my shame following every step. "Catch you later. Enjoy your cheap men's room soap."

Great. That could have gone so much better, yet also so much worse. I'm sure now he's either questioning my sexuality or my sanity after professing my love for nice soap.

Although, it's a much better option than telling him I followed his sister in there for a rendezvous.

He would've been less questioning and more punching.

It's gonna be fun when he finds out I'm dating her. I wouldn't even say dating because we can't date, but when he finds out I'm *fucking* his sister.

Maybe he'll be happy we're happy.

Maybe if I'm lucky, he won't cave in my face with his gorilla fists. Maybe.

I'm so fucked.

28

The Missing Linc: I look stupid.
Jaz-ersize: That goes without saying.
The Missing Linc: <angry emoji> I'm not going to the casino night.
The Missing Linc: I'm going to stand out.
Jaz-ersize: I'm sure you look fine.
Jaz-ersize: And you already told me you'd go.
The Missing Linc: <frown face emoji> <frown face emoji>
The Missing Linc: <downloading image>
Jaz-ersize: I swear, Linc, this better not be another dick pic.
The Missing Linc: …
Jaz-ersize: Oh, look. It is a dick pic. At least this one's all dressed up in a tux.
The Missing Linc: Ha. Ha. I think you said, I can't get enough of your dick. I can't remember. I was pretty distracted while you were sucking me off.
Jaz-ersize: I think you misheard me, excellent example of why you shouldn't talk with your mouth full.
The Missing Linc: Liar again, Miss Benson. You keep doing that, and I'll have to wash your mouth out.

Jaz-ersize: I'm a little old for soap, don't you think?
The Missing Linc: I had a completely different white substance in mind. <tongue emoji> <eggplant emoji> <taco emoji> Maybe you prefer a spanking instead?
Jaz-ersize: I could get on board for that. But you are going.
The Missing Linc: I'm going to leave a permanent handprint on that ass of yours. And I'm not going.
Jaz-ersize: You're ridiculous. And you're going.
The Missing Linc: I look ridiculous. I'm not going.
Jaz-ersize: See you there <wink face emoji>

29

JAZLYN

I'M GOING to have to hand it to Lucy. She really did a great job. I had my doubts. I mean, I *really* had my doubts. When I first walked into the empty warehouse, I thought there was a good chance I was walking straight into a murder den where Lucy and I would either have to surgically remove a foot or cut someone open to get the key to our release.

Lucky for us, the warehouse was just an empty building and there were no little men on tricycles to taunt us.

And now it looks fantastic.

Elegant even.

Half of the space is filled with gaming tables, everything from roulette to blackjack, rivaling most Vegas casinos. The other half has a decent sized dancefloor with enough space left over for a small orchestra, silent auction, and plenty of room for mingling. Best part? Several small bars scattered throughout and waiters with trays of appetizers, whiskey smashes, and spicy vanilla lemonades all courtesy of the Sinful Gentleman.

But I can't seem to find one of those maroon-vested deliverers of happiness anywhere.

Which is a shame because rubbing elbows with all these rich

snobs is wearing on my patience. I dislike ass-kissers and tonight there seems to be a target directly on my right cheek.

This could be why my father drank so much.

If it was, I understand.

"I absolutely envy the courage you have, working around all this testosterone." One of the countless Stepford Wives in attendance leans over and lays a perfectly manicured hand on my arm. Her platinum hair, which is in waves down her back, brushes against me, and I fight the urge to bat it away. "It must be so hard not to be distracted all day. I wouldn't be able to get any work done."

The only work this cougar ever did was on her back to trap herself a rich husband. Her and at least half the women here.

Where the fuck is a waiter? I'm in great need of some alcohol to deal with all of them. Unlike my father, a drink or two would be enough for me. He would've consumed half the bar.

I smile at her, trying my best to make it look more genuine and less patronizing. "Don't worry, I have my own office I lock myself in when I find it impossible to control myself."

Her smile never falters, and I'm sure she's not used to the subtle art of sarcasm. "Maybe you wouldn't mind sneaking me in for a private tour. You know, just us girls."

I'd rather stab myself in the eyeball with one of those two-pronged meatball forks.

Seriously, where the fuck are all the waiters?

"We actually do have facility tours along with some player meet-and-greets, game tickets, and Devils swag available in the silent auction." I point to the other side of the bar, hoping she takes the bait and gives me a reprieve.

Her high-pitched squeal may have knocked out half my hearing. "That would be absolutely amazing. Are there any auction items for one-on-one time with any of the players?"

I'm sure she means a date but is too classy to say it out loud.

Wouldn't want her husband overhearing her. And now that she mentions it, I'm not sure what we ended up auctioning.

"Well, why don't I escort you over there, and we can find out together?"

"That would be great."

She whips around, giving me a faceful of her hair. I'm no hair stylist, but I think her ends are dry, and she uses too much hairspray. I won't even mention the extensions.

As I trail behind her, I sneak a peek around the room, looking for Lincoln.

I find him hanging out with a small group of players, the epitome of sex on a fuck-me-stick. My lady bits immediately go on high alert and let me know just how lonely they are right now despite spending the night with him a few days ago. That man wears a tux like nothing I've ever seen. It's not a traditional black, it's a steel gray I know will go perfect with his eyes, which are almost gray themselves.

The only thing that would make him more delectable would be him in nothing but a gray bowtie. His chiseled abs, his muscular chest, his arms that are better than any porn star I've ever seen. And that bowtie.

That fucking bowtie.

His eyes meet mine, and even from this distance, I can feel the heat of his gaze. I can practically feel his eyes moving over my body. I knew this low-cut backless dress would grab his attention.

The weight of his stare is oppressive as I move to the auction table, following this lady whose name I can't seem to remember.

Definitely not after I've pictured Lincoln in nothing but a bowtie and a smile.

"Oh my!" Her screech steals my attention. "I knew you'd have some individual time with the players on here. You were holding out on me."

The way she clutches that piece of paper to her chest tells me it's good, but I have no idea what it could be. I don't remember any individual player auctions.

That's weird.

"Do you mind if I take a look?" After she gives me an accusing stare, I add, "Don't worry, I'm not going to make any bids. I'm just curious. I didn't get to see everything."

She eyes me for a few more seconds before handing over the piece of paper.

As soon as my eyes scan the auction item, I have a true laugh out loud moment. Clever. This is very clever.

A handwritten note auctioning off a date with Tag Harris. His attributes are listed as:

- Devils' first line left winger
- Natural blonde
- ~~XXX-tremely Large~~ Massive dick (soda can...but like two...so, I hope you're thirsty...)
- You'll feel me for a week
- All around good guy

That's legitimately the description. All around good guy with a massive, soda-can-sized dick. His con is limited to him being a selfless lover who often tells inappropriate jokes. And there's a thumbs up next to the last point, drawn by what appears to be a kindergartener.

Perfection.

Is this a prank on Tag, or did he actually want to be auctioned off tonight?

It's pretty damn funny.

Either way, I'm putting in a bid for it.

Not because I want a date with Tag and his soda can sized monster dick. But because it's fucking hilarious. Maybe if I win, Tag and Lincoln can go on a bro date.

A glance at the auction clipboards tell me he is already the highest bidded item. All women. Most likely all married. Sorry. Correction. There's one guy. I don't know Roderick, but wish him the best of luck winning his item.

Come to think of it, this is a great idea. I'm going to have to discuss it with Lucy later. Our very own bachelor auction. You could win an entire date package. We could raise a lot of money if I can get the guys to agree.

With all the women surrounding the auction table, I slip away and head back to the bar area to either hunt down a waiter or wait in line. I'm still dying for that drink.

The further away I get, the more my shoulders relax, as does my face now that I don't have to wear a strained smile. My cheeks are going to kill me by the end of the night. After taking a deep breath, I remind myself this is for charity, we're helping kids, and we're going to make a big difference.

Before I can turn around to handcuff a damn waiter to my side, I feel the light press of fingertips to my upper back.

Dammit.

I plaster on my hostess with the mostest smile and turn around, ready to talk with the next housewife who, no doubt, wants to know what it's like to work with hockey players. The Stepford Wife wasn't my first and, I'm sure, won't be my last. I hate to squash their dreams, but most of the time hockey players are rude, crude, and they smell.

Especially after a game.

No exception.

One exception.

But he's taken. Maybe. No? Yes. He's definitely taken, and they better look elsewhere.

"I noticed your empty hands. Seemed like you were missing a drink."

Reed, the oldest Sinful Gentleman, gets a genuine smile,

mostly because he's providing me with alcohol. "My savior. Thank you very much."

He passes me a spicy lemonade, a slight blush dusting his cheeks. His traditional black tux looks good on him along with his slicked-back blonde hair and friendly smile.

"These things are always better with plenty of whiskey."

"I have no doubt." I chuckle. Plenty of whiskey sounds nice, but I think this one is good enough for me.

"So, what's a guy have to do around here to dance with the most gorgeous woman at the party?"

I laugh, a sweet high pitched fake laugh, and because I'm not sure how to respond, take a quick sip of my drink. A quick glance to the other side of the room tells me Lincoln is still in the same spot but now has a scowl etched on his face.

Calm down, caveman. I'm going to get rid of him.

"I don't know. You'll have to ask your brother. He's already stolen Lucy for two dances." I glance out to the dancefloor where Hudson is twirling Lucy. Her blonde hair and light pink dress swirl around her and then she laughs, putting her arms back around his neck and sways to the music.

Reed takes a sip of his own drink, one of his whiskey blends. If I'm not mistaken, it's the honey one. "I'm not sure she's what I had in mind. I was thinking about someone with darker hair. Maybe walking around in a sinful red dress. Have you seen anyone that fits that description?"

"Hmm." I tap my lips and look around the room. "I don't know if I see anyone fitting that exact description, but I'll keep my eye out."

"Come on, Jazz. Will you dance with me?"

I sneak another glance around. Lincoln's eyes are boring into my very soul, and I bring the lemonade to my lips for another drink.

It would be different if we could've attended together, danced together, even just talked without raising suspicions.

Although, it wouldn't look suspicious if I danced with multiple players. Reed too, for that matter. Then again, maybe not. I don't think Linc would be as receptive to him touching me as much as the others. He already looks like he wants to murder him.

"Sorry, Reed." I smile despite the ache in my chest. "I'm afraid I've got to mingle some more. Maybe try to drive up prices on the auction, and I promised Gordon I'd play a few games with him."

"What do you play?"

"Blackjack and poker. Although, I'm not sure if I should. I can get a little bit competitive."

"You?" His exaggerated gasp and comically wide eyes wound my ego. "I would've never guessed that two-time Olympic medalist Jazz Benson is at all competitive."

"There's a good chance I might have yelled at someone's grandmother last summer when I thought she destroyed my hot streak. In my defense, I was winning until she sat down."

Reed throws his head back and laughs, his hand brushing down the exposed skin at my back. "That's priceless. How about I come and find you in a bit? Maybe you'll have time for a dance later."

I nod because it's one dance. Lincoln will be fine.

What harm can come from one dance?

30

LINCOLN

"You'd think sleeping with the boss would give you special privileges." Tag pulls at his navy-blue bowtie with a frown. "I hate these fucking things."

"What did you want me to do? Ask her if we could show up in sweatpants?" I glance at him from the corner of my eye as I grab two glasses of whatever the fuck a whiskey smash is.

"Um, yes. Don't you know gray sweatpants are like women's kryptonite?"

I chuckle, handing him his glass before taking a quick sip of mine. I don't hate it.

Foster barrels between us, flips open his black coat, and smooths a hand down his matching black vest. It's a good thing he's not dramatic. "No, mate. These tuxes will lure them in every time. I've already been eye-fucked by at least eight ladies."

I hate to admit it, but Foster's right. Maybe not about the eye-fucking. I take a quick look around the warehouse and find several pairs of female eyes turned our way. Okay, it looks like he's right about the eye-fucking too.

At least I know how to pick my dates.

Even I'm man enough to admit we look good.

Although Tag, with his mane of shaggy blonde hair, is the closest thing to a girl I'll have all night. Jazz and Gordon are hosting the charity event, so she's been pretty busy. I've barely been able to catch a glimpse of her as she flits from person to person. There's also the minor detail about her not being able to be seen with me in public. Since this is very much a public event, Foster and Tag graciously agreed to go stag tonight to keep me company.

Best friends a guy could ask for.

Of course, they were afraid I'd end up in a corner, looking like a lost puppy and glaring at everyone that went near her.

They weren't totally wrong. All this sneaking around is starting to get to me. I just want to be a real couple and go out without worrying about getting seen or photographed. Or even do something simple, like taking her out on the dancefloor without people whispering behind our backs and getting the wrong idea.

Or the right idea.

But they don't need to know that.

I glance over at Jazz. Her tight, red, knee-length dress is pure torture for my dick. I want nothing more than to unwrap her like my own personal gift, throw her on my bed, and feel those sexy ass heels dig into my shoulders while I fuck her senseless. I turn to look away, to say something smartass to Foster, but freeze. My chest juts out, my spine stiffens, and my hand clenches hard around the glass in my hand. I'm surprised it doesn't shatter.

One of the brothers from the Sinful Gentlemen tosses back his head and laughs at something she says. His hand trails from the nape of her neck to her waist, the backless dress allowing his fingers to glide along her smooth skin.

Jazz told me about the brothers yesterday to warn me about their relentless flirting. She didn't want me getting upset if I overheard anything. So, of course, I looked their asses up.

I also want to let all these fuckers know she's taken, and they should think twice before laying their hands all over her. If he doesn't keep his hands to himself, the whiskey slinger might find himself with one missing. Let's watch him use a shaker after that.

"Drink this." Tag plucks the whiskey smash from my hand and replaces it with a lowball glass half-full of whiskey. "You look like your about to commit murder."

"I don't see what has your knickers in a twist—never mind, I see it." Foster claps me on the shoulder and turns me toward the casino area. "Let's go see if I can still count cards."

I drain my glass before handing it off to a passing bartender and grabbing another. "I'm pretty sure counting cards is illegal."

"Bollocks. When you're both British *and* charming, you can get away with most things."

"Sad to say, he's right about that." Tag grabs onto my arms and leads me to the nearest blackjack table. "I do have some good news, though. Not for either one of you assholes, but for me."

"I have to say, mate, I'm intrigued."

"Let's just say, you two may be my dates, but I'm almost guaranteed to go home with some lucky lady."

"What the fuck are you talking about?" Tag's been with us since we got here. He disappeared for about five minutes early on but claimed he was going to the bathroom.

Tag wipes some imaginary lint off the shoulder of his tux, his smile plastered across his face. "I might have taken the opportunity earlier to enter a date with yours truly into the silent auction. There's a fair number of cougars on the prowl tonight."

Foster claps him on the back as he laughs, and even I manage a chuckle. That's pretty good. I can just imagine some of these gold diggers fighting each other for a chance at an athlete. It could be a bloodbath. Maybe whiskey man will get stabbed in the face with a stiletto.

Stranger things have happened.

Blackjack isn't helping. Foster's incessant bantering isn't helping. The couple double shots of whiskey aren't helping either.

The burn radiating down my throat as I throw one more back does nothing to soothe the flames blazing within me, it only stokes them. Gives them the fuel to grow.

Fuck this fundraiser.

It's supposed to be fun. It's right there in the name.

This is not fun. This is fucking awful. A real cock up—thank you Foster for the phrase.

Fuck all those people out there dancing.

Fuck everyone for looking happy.

And fuck them for being with someone who doesn't have to shove them in the closet if someone walks by. Not an actual closet. A metaphorical closet.

That fucking guy is pulling Jazz out on the dancefloor. The whiskey dick who's going to lose his hand. Maybe both hands at this point. She's smiling at him. Like genuinely smiling, and I couldn't be more unhappy about it. I should be the one pulling her sexy ass around out on the dance floor. I should be the one making her smile.

But no.

No one can know we have a thing because the world is full of dicks.

He doesn't even look as good as I do. His tux is generic, like every other motherfucking black tux wearer here. Mine is a steel gray masterpiece. If you took one of those ancient Greek statues and dressed him in a metallic gray suit, he wouldn't look half as good as me.

"Dude." Tag grabs my shoulders and turns me around to face him and all the other losers at the roulette table. "You've got to calm the hell down. You're going to make a scene."

"How about another whiskey?" Foster waves his glass in my face as if that could even attempt to calm me down.

"No. The shit sucks."

It's really not that bad, but he doesn't need to know that. If one of the *gentlemen* wasn't out there manhandling Jazz on the dancefloor, I might be inclined to buy a bottle. But he is. So, I'm not.

"Fine," I mumble, handing my chips over to Foster. "I'll bet whatever you did."

"Yes, sir." The attendant smiles at me as Foster places my chips on the table. "That will be fifty on six and fifty on nine."

Tag throws back his head and laughs, one of those deep belly laughs, and his entire body shakes. Foster, of course, has a shit eating grin, and I swipe a hand down my face. I can't believe I'm friends with these assholes.

"What?" Foster bats his eyelashes in a false attempt to look innocent. "Those are my favorite numbers. Completely unrelated to whatever you're thinking."

I continue to stare at him. He remains unfazed.

"And it's just a coincidence that six and nine are both red, which is pretty close to the luscious pink—"

"Oh my God, we get it." Tag interrupts him with a raised hand. "We're at a black-tie event. You can't just go around talking about pussy."

"I was going to say a pink lily. The most delicate of flowers. Such a foul mouth. Don't you know we're at a black-tie event and there are women present."

I groan, running my hand through my hair. As distracting as Foster is, this conversation is not distracting me enough. I glance back over to the dance floor. The douche canoe has one hand clasping hers and the other perched very low on her waist. I don't know if you'd consider that a waltz or what, but I could do it better.

And I swear on my grandmother's grave, if he doesn't move his hand away from her ass, I'm going to lose it. I don't care if there's a crowd of people. I don't care most of the Devils are here.

I don't care.

I might care a little bit. But not enough to stop me.

I stomp across the warehouse and through the mess of people, ignoring the bullshit coming out of Tag and Foster's mouths and their outstretched hands as they try to grab me. I don't care about the housewives with too much makeup on trying to slip their numbers in my pocket. I don't care about the fan trying to talk to me about the game last week. I don't care about any of it. I don't stop until I reach Jazz in her black high heels and sexy-as-fuck backless red dress.

As soon as she sees me, her smile falters and her eyes widen in a silent plea I'm ignoring. She wants me to stop, I know she does, but I can't. I know what I'm doing is fucked up, but I can't do a thing to stop it. She's fucking gorgeous, and she's fucking mine. Regardless of what the whiskey man thinks.

"Mr. Dallas." Jazz's professional voice and the impersonal way she addresses me slashes me to pieces.

Whiskey man whistles, his hands still touching her. "Lincoln Dallas. Great season so far, man. You may be able to bring these boys to victory."

I force a smile. "Thank you. Do you mind if I cut in? There's something I wanted to run by the boss."

"By all means. I've got to check on the bars anyway." He turns to Jazz, raises her hand to his lips. I'm going to have a fucking stroke. "Thank you for the dance. I hope so see you soon."

Before Jazz can respond, I grab her hands and pull her away from him. Rude? Maybe. But, again, I don't care.

"Lincoln Alexander Dallas," Jazz hisses low in my ear,

wrapping an arm around my neck and gripping my outstretched hand with her free one. "What do you think you're doing?"

I stroke my thumb down her spine before splaying my hand possessively across her lower back and begin to dance. Because fuck you, whiskey man. I can waltz too.

"I'm dancing. What's it look like?" I murmur low in her ear.

"You know what I mean."

"You can dance with that asshole, then I think you can dance with me."

"Are you drunk?"

"Not at all. I had a few before I knew who *he* was. Now I'm boycotting the Gentleman."

"His name is Reed." Jazz peers up at me, her eyes turning into slits.

I pull her a little closer. "I don't care. You're mine, and I need you to know you're mine."

"This is not the time or the place to act like a Neanderthal."

I let out a long sigh and pull her a little bit closer, so her body skims mine. As I draw small circles on her back with my fingertips, I lower my mouth to her ear and mumble. "You're so fucking beautiful. Best looking thing here. I can't wait to put my babies in you."

Jazz pulls back, a frown marring her beautiful face. "I think we're getting ahead of ourselves here. I think we should save all this kind of talk for another time. Maybe when we're not surrounded by all these people."

"It drives me crazy we can't be together."

Jazz pulls me down and whispers in my ear, "Would it help if I told you I got us a hotel room for the night?"

"Did you?"

She nods, the small motion dissipating my anger. "I booked us a room at the Omni after you sent me the picture of you in this sexy ass tux. I can't wait to take it off you. Piece. By. Piece."

Take that, whiskey man. Thank God for camera phones.

"I think I want you to ride my dick tonight." I twirl her in a circle before pulling her back to me and whispering against her temple. "I want your tits in my face as you fuck me."

"That dirty mouth of yours."

"Don't pretend like you don't like it. Like it doesn't get that pussy all wet for me."

"Anyway," Jazz pulls back as the song comes to an end, "thank you for the dance. If you would be so kind as to send over a few of your teammates so we don't raise any eyebrows, it would be greatly appreciated."

"I can do that." The last thing I want to do is send men over to touch her in this sexy-as-fuck dress, but if it helps us blend in, then I'll do it.

"I'm leaving in thirty." She runs her fingertips along the length of mine before dropping my hand. "I'll see you in a bit."

I watch her walk off the dancefloor, paying particular attention to her swinging hips.

I'll be putting those hips to good use here soon.

I can't wait.

31

LINCOLN

She didn't leave in thirty.

It took her forty-two and a half minutes to leave the fundraiser. It was another seventeen minutes to get to the hotel, four and a half minutes to get to our room, and thirty seconds to unzip her from that dress and have her standing naked before me.

"Hold on." Jazz grabs my hands, pushes them away from my bowtie and unwinds it. "I thought I told you, I wanted to take this off you."

I grunt, palming her breast in both hands and pinching her hard nipples. My dick hardens and strains against the tuxedo pants. He wants out, and Jazz is taking her sweet ass time flicking open each button on my dress shirt.

"You're killing me, kitten," I groan, as she leans forward and flicks the tip of her tongue across my nipple.

One more button.

And another.

She slides the shirt off my shoulders at a torturous pace and tosses it on the hotel desk where it joins my jacket and her dress. "I don't care. I'm in charge tonight."

I didn't think my dick could get any harder, but I was wrong.

She's perfect for me in every fucking way. I want to be there for her, support her, satisfy her every need, and love her. Fuck. I love this woman. There's no denying it.

I was a goner the second she skated back into my life.

I couldn't help but have her. Touch her. Need her.

Maybe I don't need to be traded to be happy. I could make a home here. I could have a future in Nashville so long as Jazz is by my side and in my bed every night.

"You're thinking too hard." Jazz undoes the button on my pants, slides her hand inside, and strokes my erection.

"I'm trying to distract myself, so I don't come in my pants."

The need to be inside of her, to take her so thoroughly she'll feel me in her very soul, came over me.

I lean down and capture her mouth, tunneling my hands through her silky hair. She opens beneath me, and I sweep my tongue in her mouth, running it along hers, exploring her warmth. I grind against her hand as she moans and pumps my cock. Pulling away from her, I shuck off the rest of my clothing, climb across the bed, and sit with my back to the headboard.

She raises a brow, a smile spreading across her face. "Impatient?"

I don't know why she's still at the foot of the bed and not sitting on my dick, but she is. "Fuck yes. I'm always impatient to get inside your greedy little pussy. Come on, dirty girl, I'm ready for you to ride me until you come."

Torment must be Jazz's middle name. She gets on her hands and knees and crawls on the bed toward me, her breasts swaying with every subtle move, her gaze locked on mine. Inch by fucking inch, she gets closer.

The second she's within reach, I pull her on my lap. Her legs rest on either side of my hips, and her hands clutch at my shoulders.

"Too slow," I murmur, skimming my lips over hers in a light

caress as I reach a hand between us. With a groan, I plunge a finger inside her soaked pussy and fuck her with the same deliberate pace she used to unbutton my damn shirt.

Her eyes close and her head falls back as she bucks against my hand. Her soft moans have me increasing the pace, fucking her faster. I fasten my mouth around one of her pink nipples, circling the tightened bud before flicking it with my tongue and raking my teeth across the tip.

Jazz lifts up and pushes my hand out of the way as she grabs my cock and positions it at her entrance. "Fuck. Lincoln."

"That's it, kitten. Sink your cunt onto my cock. I've been thinking about you riding my dick all night. Own me. Use me. Fuck me."

A quiver runs through her body, and she moans my name, rocking her hips, taking me inside of her. I push forward, seating myself fully. Her walls grip me as she draws back and places a chaste kiss on my lips before thrusting forward and fucks me hard and fast, like she's as desperate for me as I am of her.

I plunge a hand into her hair, wrap it around my fist, tug her head back, and capture her mouth. Devouring her, spearing her with my tongue. Hard, deep, and commanding. She moans into my mouth, working her hips against me, riding my cock like a fucking champion.

I grab her ass, thrusting her against me harder. With a shift of my hips, I press into her and grind against her clit with every stroke.

Her cries become louder, and she flutters around me. She's right at the edge of orgasm, so I pull back from her mouth.

As I give her hair a yank, her eyelids flutter close. "Look at me, Jazz. I want your eyes on mine as you fall apart and take me with you. I want you to see me as I fill you with my cum."

Her pussy squeezes around me, gripping me like a fist and milking my cock. I groan her name as my balls tighten and my climax rips me apart. I jerk, releasing a few obscenities as I empty inside her, holding her gaze with mine.

"Fuck. Me." Jazz leans forward, breathing erratic, resting her forehead against mine.

I brush my lips across hers, my heart beating frantically in my chest. It could be because I just had mind blowing sex. Or it could be because of how much I love this woman, I'm balls deep in.

Her emerald eyes pin me in place, and I know there's not a thing we can't get through together. The media. Her position with the team. Her brother. We can face it all.

After a few minutes, we collapse onto the bed facing each other. Jazz lays alongside me, her head resting on my outstretched arm.

"You really went full on caveman tonight. You're lucky no one seemed to notice you stomping out onto the dance floor."

"I didn't mean to cause a scene." I run my fingertips up and down her back.

"Seemed like you did." She peers up at me. "Are you happy the way things are?"

"Of course, I am. Why would you think I'm not?"

"You made a comment about the future and—"

"It was nothing. Don't worry about it." I shouldn't have said anything about wanting to put my babies in her, but I was so pissed. And then having her in my arms, I got lost in the moment and lost my sense. "My prehistoric brain took over. I'm happy with us. With you."

It's not a complete lie. I am happy with her. Yes, I want more. I want exactly what I said with one addition, my ring on her finger. But if I said any of that shit now, I'd probably scare her off.

I know I should bring up the trade. To have a real talk about the possibility of a future. It's something we need to talk about.

But I can't bring myself to ruin this moment. Tomorrow. There's always tomorrow.

"Okay." She traces the ridges of my abs with her fingertips. "Did Tag enter himself in the auction, or did one of you do it as a joke?"

"I think he mentioned auctioning off a date." I curl my arm around her waist and pull her to me, closing the gap between us.

"So, you don't know what he said?"

"Should I?"

"It was pretty epic." She laughs. "The entry slip looked like a kindergartener wrote it, except for the part where he made a reference to his soda can-sized dick."

I kiss her forehead unable to help the chuckle that escapes my lips. Tag never said anything about mentioning his junk size. No wonder he was so sure he would be going home with someone.

"I did bid on it. Him."

My arms tighten around her, and I narrow my gaze. "You what?"

"Don't worry." She draws lazy circles on my chest. "I was going to try and win you a bro date but was quickly outbid by a very nice man named Roderick."

"Roderick?"

She nods. "I knew I didn't have a chance, so I padded his pocket to make sure he had that shit in the bag. Whatever he wants to do with Tag and his soda can dick is between the two of them."

My body shakes with laughter. I can only imagine the look on Tag's face as Roderick was announced as the winner. I'm sure he wasn't planning on the auction going that way. "Did he say anything when you guys danced?"

"Not really. We got to know each other a little bit and then he asked me what my intentions were with his best friend."

"He didn't."

"He did." She leans forward and feathers kisses along the length on my neck. "I told him it was none of his damn business, but I appreciated him being a good friend."

I don't know what I did to deserve her, but I will do it again every day for the rest of my life.

"Come on, let's get you cleaned up." I slap her ass and lurch forward to give her a loud, wet kiss on her forehead. "I've got a present for you in the shower."

"Is it your dick?"

"It might be."

She laughs, rolling over and pushing herself from the bed. "It's your dick."

"If you're a good girl, you can get my tongue too."

"That's a tough choice." Jazz taps her lips with the tip of her index finger. "I also like what happens when I'm a bad girl."

I chuckle, watching her exaggerated hip movement as she makes her way to the adjoining bathroom.

Tonight's perfect.

She's perfect.

There's nothing that can change that.

32

JAZLYN

"It seems your little dance moment last night wasn't your only interlude with the players."

Adam must have noticed Lincoln storming out on the dance floor. Before he dropped the bomb that he wanted to impregnate me. On the fucking dance floor. In front of literally everyone. We still haven't gotten to talk about that slip of his.

He wasn't exactly subtle when he stormed out there looking all pissed off and sexy as hell. He knocked through a few crowds of people and pushed past at least two dancing couples to get to me. He all but ripped me away from Reed to stake his claim on me.

I thought dancing with a few other players would lessen his display of possessiveness.

Fuck my life.

"What are you talking about, Adam? What other moment?" I stop rubbing my temples, it isn't doing shit for my headache anyway.

I blame Adam's presence.

I must be sensitive to assholes today.

I've also been feeling guilty since I snuck out of the hotel early this morning. It's getting harder and harder to leave him. I wish I didn't have this life. That I didn't have to sneak around.

And he wants to put his babies in me?

I don't even know how to respond. Part of me wants exactly what Lincoln offered, but the larger, more rational part knows how absolutely insane that is. For fuck's sake, we can't even go to a movie. I'm a fool if I think we can have an actual future together.

And what if he gets traded?

These guys have to move with such little notice, and I'm not sure our relationship would survive being in another state. With our schedules, we'd have no time to see each other until off-season.

"Please." Adam scoffs, stuffing one hand in his pocket while the other is perched behind his back. "Let's not pretend we're both idiots. You hid the whole thing very well until last night."

I sit up a little straighter, my heart pounds so hard it could be the drummer for Guns N' Roses. There's no way he actually knows anything. He just thinks he knows.

I can explain this.

"I can assure you there's nothing going on between me and... well, anyone. And I had several dance partners last night, so I'm not sure who you're talking about."

Adam takes a step past the threshold of my office, and I don't think I like that evil gleam in his eye or the way his mouth tilts up in a smirk that says he knows more than I think. But that's impossible.

Right?

"So, there's nothing going on between you and Lincoln Dallas?" There goes an eyebrow raise. "I saw you two dancing last night."

"I also danced with Foster and Harris." I'm thankful my voice even comes out because I am about to shit my pants.

"True. It would be a good cover up, though. So, there's nothing going on between you and Dallas?" He cocks his head to the side like he already knows my answer and is waiting for the next lie to roll off my tongue.

My palms are sweating, and I wipe the moisture on my skirt. Is it hot in here? It feels hot in here.

I swallow past the puck-sized lump in my throat. "Absolutely not. I don't really appreciate all this questioning, Adam. I don't think my personal life, or lack thereof, is any of your business."

"It is when it involves one of my players. I'm assuming you haven't seen the news. Gotten a newspaper? Browsed the internet?"

"No."

Dread settles in my stomach and ice snakes through my veins. I don't like where this line of questioning is going. Not one little bit.

Why is it so fucking hot?

"Didn't think so." Adam produces a newspaper from the hand that's been hidden behind his back and throws it down on my desk. "Seems some of your facts are incorrect."

I don't want to look down. I don't want to see what will surely be my demise, right there in black and white. No doubt an article full of speculation with a picture of Linc and I dancing last night. Granted, it's nothing concrete, but the speculation alone will be enough to put a dent in the reputation I've been able to build. I take a deep breath and slowly blow it out. I don't want to look. But I have to.

Pulling up my big girl panties, I glance down at the paper, and my mouth falls wide open.

Oh.

My.

God.

This is so much worse.

How did this happen? How would someone have gotten *this*?

I continue to stare at the paper, willing the picture to disappear. To be some cruel joke. I can't look at Adam. I can't acknowledge this. I have no defense.

Zero.

My breathing is erratic, and I swear my heart's about to beat out of my chest and flop across my desk like a fish. It's over. Everything is over. My reputation, my credibility, my relationship with Lincoln. All of which took months to build and seconds to destroy.

How the fuck did someone get this picture?

I can't stand to look at it anymore and turn the paper face down on my desk. Somehow someone took a picture of our first kiss on the airplane. A kiss that should've never happened, especially ten feet away from the rest of the team, but did. There's proof. Right here in the fucking Nashville Post. The angle is perfect too. We're pressed up against each other, his arms caging me in, and you know, with zero doubt, his tongue is in my mouth. You can see the damn thing.

I'm so fucked.

"Looks like the news was right about females in the NHL. You've turned this place into a circus, not to mention, your personal hunting ground. I'm so disappointed. And I know your dad would be too."

After banging my forehead against the desk a few times, I put my head in my hands, my heels digging into my eyes. I will not cry. I will not cry. Not in my office. Dammit, I'm going to have to start everything from scratch and I'll be under even more scrutiny than before. I've done nothing but prove women shouldn't be in power positions around athletes. I'm a disgrace. I've let down everyone.

I hope you're happy, vagina.

But it's not even her fault. Not entirely. My head and heart were in it just as much as she was.

Adam spins on his heel but turns back to look at me. "He used you, and you let him. I thought you had a better head on your shoulders than that."

I looked up and eyed him warily. Linc hadn't used me. Just last night he told me he wanted me to have his babies. I didn't want to ask, but I had to. "What do you mean?"

"I heard from a couple other GMs your boyfriend was looking for a trade." With a pitying glance and shake of his head, he leaves.

I choke down a sob and struggle to breathe with the weight settling on top of my chest. A trade is always possible—but Lincoln is looking at getting traded? I thought he was happy here. Maybe Adam is just trying to get under my skin. It doesn't matter anyway. I'm going to have to end things with Lincoln regardless of his trade status. I don't really have another choice. Not if I want to be seen as a professional ever again.

"I'd ask if this is true, but this is a picture no one can argue with."

Gordon.

Shit.

I was hoping to have a little more time to wallow in my mess before I had to start facing the music.

"What the fuck, Jazlyn? What were you thinking?"

I lower my hands, letting my fingers drag along my face. Gordon's gaze is laced with disappointment, his arms are crossed over his chest, and his mouth curved into a deep frown.

"I don't know. I wasn't thinking, I guess."

"I don't know which is worse." Gordon paces in front of my desk, running a hand through his hair, causing it to stand on end. "That you decided to date one of our players or that you hid it from me."

"I'm sorry."

"I don't care if you're sorry. They've labeled you the Puck Bunny Queen. You've compromised the entire organization. Do you have any idea how this makes us look?"

"Not great."

"Not great? It makes us look like amateur hour over here giving players secret blowjobs in the locker room and handing out special privileges to go along with them. How long?" He stops in front of me and pins me with a glare. "How long, Jazz?"

I shrink into my chair, hoping it'll make me disappear. No such luck. "About two months."

"Shit." He resumes his pacing, but this time smooths his tie over and over again. "Two months. Two fucking months. I can't believe you didn't tell me. You didn't trust me. I'm your fucking brother."

"I know. This is why I didn't tell you."

"Two fucking months you were seeing him behind my back. Doing—Oh, God." Gordon stops and runs both hands through his hair. "I'm going to kick his ass."

I don't have time to process what's happening because Gordon flies out of my office. I jump out of my seat, hot on his heels as I chase him down the hallway in mine. I'm struggling to keep up, this tight ass skirt not allowing my thighs to separate enough for an angry stride, nevermind a desperate chase.

"Gordon," I whisper yell, passing Krista and hightailing it out of the office suites. "You can't just go kick his ass."

"Watch me."

"This is as ridiculous as me chasing you in heels. Which, let me tell you, is pretty fucking ridiculous." Almost as ridiculous as the Lycra glue holding my knees together.

Gordon ignores me and launches down the stairwell. I'm trailing behind, trying not to fall on my face. Power walking down the carpeted hallway was a little easier than trying to navigate the stairs, and Gordon's gaining distance. Shit. Fuck. Shit fuck. The team is practicing on the ice. Surely Gordon wouldn't…

I better speed the hell up. I've never seen Gordon this mad. There's no telling what he'll do right about now. Predictable Gordon is flying off the handle.

"The team has practice. You can't just go out there on the ice."

Silence.

"Let's just sit down and talk about this like two rational adults."

The door in the hallway outside the arena is yanked open and then slams shut as Gordon leaves the stairwell. Holy shit balls. I kick off my heels, abandoning them in the stairwell, not giving two flying fucks about where they land. I've got to book it. I take the last several steps two at a time, and hike my skirt as high as I dare to get some kind of movement. The last thing we need is to make a scene out on the ice in front of the whole team.

But that's what he's going to do.

I finally make it in the hallway, but it's empty. I can feel sweat dripping down my back and my chest heaves as I struggle for air. I burst into the arena in time to see him stepping onto the ice.

He's so mad and all his stomping is making him slide. He catches himself the first time but falls down the second. If he wasn't about to out Lincoln and I in front of the entire team, I'd find this funny.

"You're going to break your other damn leg," I shout out after him.

"Lincoln Dallas!" Gordon shouts, springing to his feet, as if he's not yards from the team. "My fucking sister?"

Lincoln turns around. Hell, the whole team turns around. Everyone's taking their helmets off, looking at Gordon like he's lost his mind. Lincoln is frozen with his mouth hanging open.

"You don't have anything to say for yourself?"

"What are you talking about?"

"I'm talking about you fucking my sister for the past two months!"

The entire team is looking between the three of us and slowly shuffling away from Gordon, who's still half sliding, half stomping his way to Lincoln. I don't blame them for wanting to get as far away as possible from the dumpster fire about to go down.

I'm standing on the edge of the ice like a fucking statue as Lincoln glances over at me. His gaze whips back to Gordon and he throws his hands up defensively. "Look, it's not what you think."

"Not what I think? Not what I *think*?" The words hit an octave any soprano would be proud of between his efforts to stay on his feet, and it sounds like his brain is working at twice the speed of his mouth. "What I think is there's a picture of the two of you all over the internet with your tongue in her fucking mouth. I can see your fucking tastebuds, Dallas."

I could have gone without him divulging that information to the team. Of course, they all would've found out as soon as practice finished, and they pulled out their phones.

I can't believe this is happening.

I've got to do something.

After putting out a tentative step on the ice, I decide there's no way in hell I can go out there barefoot. I'd look as foolish as Gordon, and lord knows I already look foolish enough. I've never felt more helpless in my life. My knuckles turn white and my hands go numb as I grip the boards, my breaths coming faster. I can't seem to get enough air.

Could this be a panic attack?

What are the symptoms of a panic attack?

I need WebMD.

"Was this some fucking game to you?" Gordon shoves Lincoln, sending them both stumbling backward. "I noticed you have your captain's patch. Was this your attempt to fuck your way to the top?"

Lincoln tosses his stick and helmet to the side. "Of course not."

"But you sure got something out of it, didn't you?" Gordon cocks back his fist and punches Lincoln in the jaw.

My hands fly up to cover my mouth, and I can't help the gasp that escapes.

Lincoln puts his hands up again, dodging another punch as Gordon slips again. "Gordon, you've got the wrong—"

"Do you know what this has done to us? To her?" Gordon lunges forward, tackling Lincoln and bringing them both crashing down to the ice.

"Fuck. Gordon—"

"We're a fucking laughingstock again. All credibility we had is gone. For what?" Gordon lands another punch.

Lincoln grunts and attempts to push him off, but moving Gordon is like moving a mountain.

"A quick fuck?" Gordon connects with his side.

"It's not like that." Lincoln swings back, making contact with Gordon's chest.

"Maybe more money on your contract?" Gordon lands another punch, this time nailing him right in the face.

Lincoln falls back, and Gordon rolls off him, shaking out his fist.

And the team. The damn team that's still watching everything is being ushered back to the locker room by a very distraught Coach Weller and his assistant.

This right here is what I was afraid of. Why I wanted to hide everything. Why I didn't want anyone finding out.

Gordon pushes up from the ice, looks down at Linc, and

swivels his head to meet my gaze. "I thought you were smarter than this. The Jazlyn I thought I knew would never let some asshole use his dick to get ahead."

What if that's all this was? What if I was just a means to an end? He got his captain's letter, and I got the shaft. Literally and figuratively. Adam's remark echoes in my brain. He used me to get ahead with this team so he could secure a transfer to another. It makes perfect sense. I can't believe I didn't see it before.

Gordon spins around and continues his stomp-slide off the ice while Lincoln pushes up to his feet. When Gordon reaches the side of the ice, he pulls himself over the boards and escapes back into the hallway.

My hands are still numb, my chest still heaving, and my heart is racing faster than a horse at the Kentucky Derby.

I still need WebMD.

I was the idiot who opened her legs willingly. Very willingly. I practically served myself up as a ploy to advance his career, and now I'm a fucking joke on every TV screen across the US.

And Canada.

As Lincoln glides closer to me, I spin around and stomp my way to the hallway, back up the stairs, grabbing my heels on the way. I don't need to be fed any more of his lies.

Fuck this, and fuck him.

33

LINCOLN

Today is the worst day of my life. Correction: yesterday was the worst day of my life. The day when Gordon not only hurled his fists at my now bruised face, but swung accusations around I can't get out of my head. He thinks I was using Jazz to get ahead with the organization and the look of betrayal on her face right before she stormed out told me she did too.

Fuck.

This whole thing was a damn nightmare.

If only she'd stayed and given me five fucking minutes to explain, we may have been able to fix this mess. I'd tell her exactly how much she means to me, and I'd do everything in my power to help with the media situation.

But she didn't even give me a chance to speak. Didn't give me a chance to plead my case. Which is why I'm sitting alone in my apartment day drinking like some of the ladies I met at the fundraiser. While the drinking helps to dim the self-deprecating thoughts, it does nothing to subdue the ache in my chest. The ache, that started as a small throb the moment she turned her back on me to walk away, has done nothing but grow in intensity each passing moment she's not in my life.

All because of a single fucking picture.

I have no idea if our picture's still newsworthy. I haven't turned on the TV since I left the arena yesterday. Hell, I haven't even talked to anyone since yesterday when the team skulked off the ice. Unless, of course, you count the three times I listened to Jazz's voicemail when I tried to call and got no answer. Or the two times I called after that just to hear her tell me to have a nice day.

Newsflash—I'm not having a nice fucking day.

The thought of showing up on her doorstep to beg for some time came and went. If there was any press there, it'd make matters worse. There was also a good chance Gordon would answer the door. And he's a big son of a bitch. I have bruises and a busted lip to prove it.

So, I did the next best thing. I locked myself in my apartment and wracked my brain to come up with a plan. Something. Anything I could do to try to win her back. When nothing came, I started drinking. It's a little cocktail I made up consisting of one part glass, one part tequila.

My front door opens and closes with a slam, and I can't help but think karma is a bitch, and I must've wronged her in a past life. I had the door locked for a reason and regret giving Tag a key.

"Good Lord, it smells in here."

"Why don't you all just let yourselves in." I glance over in time to see the guys barreling toward me. Great. Company. Exactly what I don't want. Especially angry company. If the tight lips and fisted hands tell me anything, that's exactly what I have.

Perfect.

Tag stands in front of me, blocking my view of the blank TV screen. "I'm looking for a miserable bastard. Over six feet tall. Not as good looking as me. Have you seen him? Oh, there you are."

"Very funny."

"You know what's not funny?" Ian comes to stand beside Tag.

Owen joins his brother and narrows his eyes at me. "What's not funny is finding out that you're fucking our boss while our other boss is punching you in the face."

Foster throws himself on the couch beside me and turns my face toward him. "How is that pretty face, by the way? Not terrible. But it serves you right, you bloody wanker."

I drag my hands down my face, pick up my glass of tequila and drain it. I'm a little surprised neither Tag nor Foster told the brothers about Jazz after everything blew up. I figured their promise to keep quiet would have been negated after it all blew up. "I didn't tell you all because I fucking promised Jazz I wouldn't say anything. We didn't want it getting out in the fucking news."

A promise that was broken when a picture of our kiss on the plane hit the press. Fuck. I pushed her on the airplane. I knew damn well what the consequences were, and I did it anyway. Who fucking does that? Jesus.

Desperate, party of one.

I still have no idea who took the damn picture in the first place. My first guess was Kevin. Doing something super fucked up after getting let go from the team sounds like it's right up his alley. And I heard he'd been picked up by Florida. Probably thought he was untouchable.

"Well, you fucked that one up." Tag points a finger at me, as if I didn't know who he was talking about.

"Thanks. Super helpful."

"We could have found someone to wet your dick that would've been a whole lot less complicated." Ian picks up the tequila bottle and my empty glass, a scowl forming on his face when he gets nothing but a few lonely drops.

"Again, super helpful." I run a hand down my face before

grabbing the fresh bottle I'd stashed on the floor and my glass from his hands, then pour myself some more tequila and toss it back. The burn down my throat feels so fucking good. "It wasn't just sex so back the fuck off."

"Care to expand?" Ian narrows his eyes and reaches for the bottle, but I grip tight and extend my arm out of his range.

"Not really." If I don't give them any information, they'll only keep pestering me, and I'm not sure I can deal with that all day. I drop the bottle back to its place on the floor beside the couch and let out an exaggerated sigh. "But seeing as how you assholes won't leave me alone until I do, I don't see that I have a choice."

"That's correct. I'm glad you're catching on." Tag throws himself on the couch on the opposite side of Foster, blocking my access to the tequila. My only faithful friend at the moment.

"Fuck. I don't even know what it was. We had to keep everything secret, but it felt so real." I lower my voice to barely a whisper.

Tag pins me with a look, his eyes roaming over my bruised cheek and split lip. "I don't think you have any idea how much a stunt like this could cost the team. Did you think this whole thing would just be between you two? Did you not think there would be consequences? And I'm talking like big fucking consequences."

I fold myself over Tag, grabbing the bottle again, and fill my glass with another double shot, draining half of it. "What the fuck are you talking about? How does our relationship affect any one of you?"

"I'll take this one." Foster reaches for the TV remote. "Just let me turn on the telly."

Ian and Owen shift from their positions in front of me and sit down at the loveseat, unblocking the TV. Foster clicks to the sports channel and turns up the volume so I can hear the sportscaster loud and clear.

Turns out this is one of the few times I'm wrong. Not only

does this dickwad think *Miss Benson* is using the team as her personal hunting ground, but we are, once again, the butt of the joke. Two months of grueling hard work flushed down the toilet. No wonder these guys are pissed. I'm a little pissed at me too. I can go fuck myself.

"It seems some of our sponsors have lost the plot."

I stare at Foster, eyebrows drawn together, and head tilted to the side. I have no fucking idea what that means, but I don't think it sounds good.

"I don't know what the fuck that means, but some of the sponsors have pulled out." Tag snaps his fingers in front on my face, stealing my attention. "Do you have any clue what that means?"

I open my mouth to reply, but Tag cuts me off.

"It means a whole lot less money for the franchise. That affects all of us."

"Yeah, what he said." Foster takes advantage of my distraction and grabs my bottle of tequila, bringing it to his lips for a large sip followed by a wince.

Owen glances over to me as Foster turns the volume down. "No one is taking us seriously anymore. It doesn't matter what our record is or how many games we've won."

"They've all started predicting we're going to tank and come in dead last this season. No playoffs. No shot at the Stanley Cup. Worse than we did last year because you," Ian points a finger at me, and I feel the team's burden settle on my shoulders, "can't keep your dick in your pants. Don't tell me this isn't going to tank ticket sales."

Fuck me.

This is a bigger disaster than I thought, and I don't know how to fucking fix any of it. Not with Jazz. Not with the team. Not with the fucking sponsors. I've got nothing. Well, almost nothing.

I have my friend Codigo, providing me with my favorite kind of tequila.

"I didn't realize it was that fucking bad." I drain the rest of my glass, needing to feel the burn from the alcohol before I could continue. "What do you want me to say? I fucked up. I fucked everything up. I saw Jazz again right before they announced the change in ownership and—"

"What do you mean again?"

Shit. Of course, Tag would pick up on that. I'm such a fucking idiot. I completely forgot I hadn't told any of the guys about my history with Jazz. They're already pissed at me for all the trouble my secret relationship has caused the team, and rightfully so. No doubt this information will make them even more mad. My mom always says, out of the frying pan and into the fire. I don't think I ever fully appreciated that saying until now.

"Well." I hang my head and run my hands through my hair. "We knew each other before. You know, before she came here as an owner."

Five sets of eyes burn through me, waiting for me to continue before my impending crucifixion. The resounding silence is worse than the swearing I'd anticipated.

"I met her before the Olympics, a little over six years ago. We dated for a month or so before her dad caught us nearly going at it. Wouldn't have cared except he threatened my career. I know I fucked up. With her. With the team. With you guys. And now?" I huff out a humorless laugh. "Now, I've fucked it up beyond repair. She won't even answer my calls."

"No surprise there. You should see some of the shit in the tabloids. The sportscasters aren't being much better." Ian stretches out and thumps his big-ass shoes on my coffee table.

"It's really bad?" Who the fuck am I kidding? It's bad. Really fucking bad.

"It's bloody awful. I'd hate to be her right about now. They're

Forbidden Devil | 247

calling her everything from a puck bunny to a high-class prostitute."

"Shit." I snag the bottle from Foster and take several pulls before handing it back to him. My hands clench and unclench in my lap, and I fight to keep myself rooted to my spot on the couch. She doesn't want me chasing after her. She doesn't want me to save the day. She doesn't even want an explanation. Marching my inebriated and angry ass to the local news station to set some of these fuckers straight wouldn't earn me any brownie points.

It would feel good, though.

Especially if my fist just happens to connect with someone's face that called her any of those names.

No wonder she refuses to talk to me. I couldn't have fucked this up anymore if I tried. Not only has being with me tarnished her reputation. But thanks to Gordon's mouthy ass, she thinks I did it all for my own gain.

After stealing my tequila back from Foster, I take another shot, settle back against the couch, and pull out my phone. I'm sure she won't respond, but I need to reach out anyway. I can't leave things like this. Even drunk, I still feel the gaping hole in my chest. Before I can fire off a text, my phone vibrates in my hand.

Dan-Agent: Hey Lincoln, I've got some good news for you. Chicago offered you that contract we talked about. They're willing to overlook the media trouble. I'm emailing it over right now. They want it signed by end of day Friday and you on their ice in two weeks. Told them it wouldn't be in issue. Congratulations. I know you've worked hard for this. I'll call you tomorrow to discuss everything else going on. I think leaving is the best thing for you.

"You better not be textin'." Tag snatches the cell out of my hand and stares at it before shooting to his feet and throwing it on the couch where he was sitting. "What. The. Fuck. You want to talk your way out of this one, you selfish fuck? You wanna tell me some more bullshit about how you didn't know?"

"Now what?" Ian's eyes volley between Tag and me.

"This asshole has been trying to get traded. Got himself a nice little contract in Chicago."

"You cock up everything here and then you fucking leave? Is that how it is?" Foster shakes his head, his eyes filled with disappointment.

"Fuck this, and fuck you." Tag points at me, his finger inches from my face. "Leave us to clean up your mess. This was probably your plan all along. Get yourself some top shelf pussy to move your ass to the top. I hope you enjoy your new team, *Captain.*"

Before I can get a word in to explain myself, to let the guys know I'm not even sure if I want a trade, Tag stomps out of my apartment, taking everyone else with him.

Chicago had been everything.

My fucking dream come true, and I can't even enjoy it. But it's not my dream come true anymore. I had a new dream and lost her to a fucking picture. This is a backup I thought I wanted, but don't. A way to tuck my tail between my legs and run away. To leave this fucking dumpster fire in my rearview mirror and never look back. This contract offers me a way to get away from the heartache and the hurt because there's one thing that's certain, Jazz will never be mine.

Not ever again.

And now I don't even have my teammates. My friends. My brothers.

Fuck.

A fresh start may be my only option.

34

JAZLYN

APPARENTLY, I'm the Puck Bunny Queen. Too bad all I have to show for it is a pint of Ben and Jerry's Triple Caramel Chunk.

And a soggy pillowcase.

After the showdown between Lincoln and Gordon, I grabbed a few things from my office and drove home where I promptly dropped on my bed and cried my eyes out. Not literally of course, I don't think that's even possible.

But if it was, I'd have managed it days ago.

The days after were more of the same. I refused to talk to Gordon when he came home and ignored all the phone calls from Lincoln, Lucy, and Adam. I glance at my phone as it vibrates with what might be the hundredth text in the last hour. I suck in a breath and hold it. It could be another message from Lincoln. I want to hear from him again, to know he's okay. But it'll only make me feel worse.

I blow out my breath, this one is from Lucy, and I ignore it like I did the others.

I grab a tissue from the box by my bed, wipe under my eyes, and blow my nose before tossing the used Kleenex in the pile on my bed.

My phone vibrates again. Gordon. Ignore.

But I do open my phone. I can't help myself. I pull up the text messages from Linc. It's the tenth time I've looked at them, and it hurts every time. But I can't seem to stop myself.

The Missing Linc: I don't blame you for not answering, but you have to know...I didn't use you for anything. Gordon was way off base.

The Missing Linc: I was with you because I wanted to be. Nothing else. I wouldn't trade my time with you for anything. I wish I could talk to you, even for a few minutes. I think we can work this out. I want to be with you.

The Missing Linc: I'm sorry about the media and the sponsors. More than you know. I'm here for you, Jazz. I will always be here for you.

The Missing Linc: I don't know if you're seeing any of these, but I want to fix this. I need to fix this.

The Missing Linc: Jazz...I love you.

I stare at the last message like it's the first time I've seen it in days. I stare at it so long my vision starts to blur and tears threaten to spill over from the corners of my eyes. Not from sadness or a broken heart, it's eye strain from all the blue light coming off the phone.

At least that's what I keep telling myself.

Eye strain is a real bitch.

Thinking back, I really don't think Lincoln used me for brownie points. He worked hard on the ice and deserved all the good things that came his way. No one knew we were dating, and he asked me for no special favors. He was always about just the two of us.

Us.

I can't believe I let things with him progress to a level beyond casual friendship. I was lost in our own little world until it all came crashing down around us. The picture was only the catalyst. There was never a real future for us. Not with me being an owner and him one of my players. Of course, that's not an issue if the rumor about his trade was true. But he wouldn't keep something like that from me. If he did get traded to another team, it still wouldn't work out. Not with two very busy, very different schedules. We'd hardly get to see each other.

Not like it matters at this point.

If it came down to it, he'd likely choose hockey over me. He made that decision before. I'm sure now would be no different.

The media is tearing me apart. They're doing such a good job pointing out my inadequacies that several of our big sponsors have pulled out, killing a good hunk of our funding. I've lost my credibility. I've let down women everywhere. I'm the shining example of what not to do.

This, boys and girls, is what happens when you sleep with people you aren't supposed to.

"Jazz, we need to talk. I'm coming in." Gordon opens the door and leans against the door frame.

"I'm not sure I want to talk to you." I sweep the bunched Kleenexes off the bed and shove them in the nightstand drawer.

Gordon runs a hand down the length of his tie and sits on the edge of the bed. "I'd say I'm sorry, but I'm not. I may not have been entirely correct about his motives, but I don't regret what I did."

"You ran on the ice like a fucking crazy person and punched Lincoln in the face. Multiple times. In front of the entire team."

"I do regret doing it in front of everyone."

I lean back against the headboard and cross my arms over my chest. "What do you want, Gordie?"

Gordon scoots back to sit next to me and crosses his outstretched legs at the ankles. "I found out some news today."

"Oh?"

"I made a few calls to some of the tabloids, and they confirmed it was a former disgruntled player who leaked the picture."

That makes sense. I assumed Kevin was behind it because he's an asshole and warned me something else was coming.

"Guess he thought it was safe to get his payback. Jokes on him, though, no one will sign him knowing he's trouble."

"Apparently, he's already been picked up by Florida. The ink on the contract hadn't dried before he sold that picture." Gordon cracked a smile. "I wish them luck dealing with that piece of shit."

"Regardless, the whole thing was my fault anyway."

"It takes two to tango, and you were both aware there were risks. I wish you could have trusted me enough to let me into your life. At least I would have been prepared for all the fallout." Gordon lays a hand on my shoulder.

"Sorry. I'm not used to having someone I can talk to about this kind of stuff." On top of everything, now I feel like a shit sister.

"Don't get me wrong, I don't want any details." He chuckles. "But you can talk to me about the rest."

"If I decide to make another mess of my life, you'll be the first to know. What are we going to do about the sponsors?"

"Don't worry about them." Gordon waves me off. "I'm already working on getting them back. I, uh, I have one more piece of news, and I don't think you're going to like it."

I sit up straighter, my heart races, and my stomach plummets.

"What is it?"

He leans toward me, putting a hand on my shoulder. To his credit, he looks me straight in the eye. "Adam talked to the GM out of Chicago. Sounds like he's accepting the trade. If he does, Saturday's his last game."

35

LINCOLN

IT TURNS out drinking for several days leads to passing out face first on the couch before nine pm. Who knew? Other symptoms include a pounding headache, a slight urge to vomit, a mouth drier than the Sahara, and a pillow line down one half of my face. I saw that one when the urge to pee overrode my urge to stay on the couch.

So glad I have my shit together.

At least feeling like an overused asshole has made me stop thinking about Jazz. Nevermind. It just delayed things. I snatch my phone from the coffee table and scroll through my messages. Nothing from Jazz. No read notification. No three dots that tell me she's working out a reply. Nothing from the guys. Just the message from Dan that I've yet to respond to.

Congratulations. I know you worked hard for this.

As promised, the contract sits in my email, waiting for my signature. It's a four-year contract at seven and a half million a year. It's a little better than expected, and I'd be an idiot to pass up the opportunity. More money. Better team. A real shot at the cup. Close to home. But the more I stare at it, the more I'm not sure if I can bring myself to sign on the dotted line.

A knock on the door pulls my attention away from the blurring contractual terms, and I'm surprised to find Tag in the hallway.

"Grab your gear, asshole, we're going to the rink."

"Hello to you too." I hold open the door and usher him inside. "We don't have practice until later."

Tag pins me with a look. "I know when practice is. We're going early."

Looks like he's still angry with me. I grab my gear bag and follow him to his car. The ride to the arena is awkward and eerily quiet. Usually, I can't get Tag to shut up, but I refuse to be the first one to break the silence.

Once dressed and on the ice, Tag tosses the puck and takes off after it. Looks like we're playing a little one-on-one. In a few strides, I catch up to him, and he ditches the puck to ram me against the boards.

"What the fuck, dude?" I push him off me.

Tag drops his shoulders and pushes me back, pinning me between him and the wall. "What the fuck, indeed. Were the Devils just a steppin' stone for you to find a better team? Did you want to make sure you left with the team in the worst possible shape?"

I push him off me a second time and make a break for the puck. "Yes, I was looking for a trade, but I didn't plan anything else. Can you blame me? I want a shot at the cup."

"We all want the cup." Tag skates up beside me, muscles me out of the way, and slashes at the puck. "If you stuck around, we'd have a chance of bringin' her here. Maybe not this year, but we were startin' to look good."

"I grew up in Chicago. It's where my mom and brother live."

"What about your other brothers? Your team? Fuck us, right?" He takes control of the puck and sails it toward the goal where it clicks off a bar before landing in the net.

I round on the goal, snatch the puck out of the net and take off in the other direction. "It's not like that."

"Then, what's it like?"

"I can't stay here. Not after everything that's happened."

"You mean after you fucked our boss and hid it from us? What about the shit Gordon said? Was he right about all that too?"

I spin around, come to a stop in front of Tag and throw off my helmet and gloves. "Fuck you. You know me better than that."

"Do I?" He rips off his helmet and squares up to me. "The Lincoln I knew wouldn't just run off at the first bump in the road."

"It's a big-ass bump."

"It must be if you're willin' to abandon your brothers. The life you've built. The girl you love."

I take a deep breath and let it out slowly before bending down to grab my helmet and gloves. "She doesn't love me back."

"She tell you that?"

"She doesn't need to, her silence tells me all I need to know."

Tag pushes me, and my stick and gloves fly out of my hand. "Are you that fuckin' stupid? You really think she wants you to leave? She risked her whole fuckin' career to be with you. And you can't even stick around long enough to deal with the fallout. Did you ever consider that she may need some time considerin' her life is fallin' apart? Actually, you know what? You should leave. She deserves better than you."

My blood boils, as anger rolls through me, and I narrow my eyes. "You don't know what she wants."

"And evidently you don't either." He stands nose to nose with me, his shoulders thrown back and his lips flattened together. "If you're half the man I thought you were, you'd stay and fight.

Fight for your team. Fight for your girl. Fight for your future. You wouldn't run off like a pussy."

Tag snags his gloves and helmet and skates off the ice leaving me with a heavy heart and a view of his back.

I hate to admit it, but he's right.

The man I used to be wouldn't run away at the first sign of trouble. He also wouldn't be stupid enough to pass up a golden opportunity. Chicago is everything I thought I wanted. Jazz is everything I need. Tag could be right about her too. Maybe she really does love me.

Do I stay and lay my heart on the line in an attempt to work things out with Jazz knowing it could very well blow up in my face? Or do I salvage what's left of my heart and pursue a spot on my dream team?

Either way, if I chose wrong, I'd be making the biggest mistake of my life.

But I have to choose.

My dream trade…

Or…

My dream girl.

36

JAZLYN

I MADE the right choice not joining the team for their away game tonight. It's our first one since the split, and I'm not sure I could stomach seeing Lincoln on the ice knowing he wouldn't be showing up to my hotel room later. Or worse, he would show up and demand a conversation.

I'm strong. Independent. Don't need a man. Yet, I'm not sure I could turn him away if he showed up at my door.

He said he wants to fix this. Wants to make things right. But the damage to the organization, my reputation, and my career is irreparable. What was between us ran its course. There's nothing left to fix. Especially since he went behind my back and orchestrated a trade.

A man in love wouldn't do that.

He's going to Chicago. He made his choice, and it isn't me. I have no idea what he wants to fix, but it's hard to fix anything from a thousand miles away.

I'm doing the right thing.

Even if it destroys me.

"Thanks for the ice cream." Gordon digs his spoon into my chocolate chip cookie dough and pulls out a huge bite.

"I didn't get it for you." I point my spoon at him. "You crashed my pity party. I was all set to watch the game by myself tonight."

"Nonsense. I told you, if you stay behind, so do I." Gordon shovels another large spoonful into his mouth, and I have to hold the carton out of his reach to take a few bites of my own.

I wasn't prepared for Gordon to stay behind. If I knew, I'd have gotten him his own container of ice cream. I would have also reconsidered wearing the Dallas jersey that inconveniently arrived earlier this week. At the time I ordered it, I didn't think a several week delivery time was a big deal. I'm not going to admit wearing it most of the week, but it's starting to feel oily.

Gordon hasn't said a word.

On the TV, someone scores and people cheer. I honestly don't know if it's our fans or theirs. Every time I force myself to look away, my eyes wander back to Lincoln. To the number eight on his jersey, one identical to the one I'm wearing.

In a way, we're connected, but I couldn't feel further away.

"Are you going to the office tomorrow?" Gordon looks over at me.

I open my mouth to respond but quickly close it. I'm not sure how to answer. With the loss of sponsors and the hit to the franchise, I should have already been back. But it's a fight just to get out of bed in the morning, much less to fight through the throng of reporters. Much easier to stay home and wallow in self-pity.

Before I have a chance to say anything, my phone buzzes with a call from Lucy. After days of radio silence, I started returning some of her texts earlier today. If I'm honest, I could use a distraction from the game I'm not watching right now.

"I'll be right back," I murmur to Gordon before walking into the kitchen and answering the phone. "Hey, Lucy."

"Before I do any kind of reprimandin', are you doing okay?" I expected Lucy to be pissed, but her soft voice only sounds concerned.

I lean across the counter and rub a hand down my face. "Not really. But I made it out of my room. I'm sorry about all this mess. Is there anything I can do to help you?"

"Nah. I've got everythin' handled. This will run its course, just lay low for now." Lucy pauses. "A heads up would have been nice, though."

I sigh and rest my head in my hands. Add her to the list of people I've let down and hurt in my selfish pursuit. "I know."

"I knew there was somethin' there. I knew it from that first practice I watched with you." She pauses again. "Do you need to talk about it?"

Yes. No. I don't know. Maybe it will help. Isn't being able to talk about things a step in the grieving process? And Lucy sounds sympathetic.

I let out another sigh. "Lincoln and I met a few weeks before my first Olympics. The one in Sochi. We dated for a month." I shove away from the counter and pace the length of the kitchen while blinking back tears. "The connection was instant. We were drawn to each other on some other level. I've never felt that pull to another person before."

"What happened?"

"My dad walked in on us fooling around. He was drunk off his ass and chose that moment to be a fucking parent. Was pissed at me for losing focus on my career and threatened to basically force Lincoln out of the NHL if he looked at me again." I take a deep breath and switch the phone to my other ear. "I didn't know my dad threatened him, so I went back to Florida expecting to hear from him, and he never called. I spent years wondering what happened."

"Wow." Lucy puts extra emphasis behind the word, dragging

it out for several seconds. "And then you saw him when you came here."

"Yep. It all felt rather unfinished. But then, when I saw him again after my dad died, it was almost like we picked up where we left off. I knew it was stupid. I knew it wouldn't work. But I couldn't help myself."

"And now?"

"There is no now. Look at all this bullshit that's happening."

"What if there was no team? No hockey? If it was just you and Lincoln? Would you want to be with him then?"

"Of course," I answer quickly. "I love him."

My eyes widen, I snap my mouth shut and throw a hand over it for good measure. My heart thumps in my chest as I hold my phone in a death grip, waiting for a wave of denial that doesn't seem to be coming. I want to take it back. To shove it back into the dark recesses of my brain. But I can't bring myself to do it.

Shit.

I fucking love him.

Hell of a time to realize it too.

"Hello?" Lucy calls out into the phone. "Jazz? You there?"

"Sorry."

"Have you talked to him? Does he know how you feel?"

"What's the point, Lucy?" I raise my voice and a sob catches in my throat. I stop in front of the sink, letting a few tears drip down my chin and into the deep basin. "He initiated a fucking trade without telling me. Saturday is his last fucking game before he heads to Chicago."

"Jazz…" Lucy sounds worried.

I swipe at my cheeks, rubbing away the tears. "I have to go. I'll talk to you later."

Before she can respond, I hang up the phone and shove it in my back pocket. I wipe my face with both hands, run them into my hair, and fist the strands. What a mess I've made. I'm sure

Dad is rolling over in his grave. Not only did I commit the greatest mortal sin by touching one of his players, I let it interfere with my career.

A career that's now in the toilet.

Lucy said to lay low and let it blow over. There's no way the Puck Bunny Queen title will vanish. That shit will be etched on my head stone.

I may as well get t-shirts made.

Fuck.

"You know, I haven't seen his new contract, so there's a chance it doesn't exist yet."

I jump at the sound of Gordon's voice and spin around, placing a hand over my racing heart. "You scared the shit out of me. I thought you were watching the game."

"I was, but then I heard you yelling." His lip twitches, and he crosses his arms over his chest. I open my mouth to speak, to tell him I wasn't yelling, but he holds his hand up, halting me. "Look, I know what it's like to find that connection with someone. To love them with your entire being and then walk away with nothing but pain and regret. Life moves on, but the regret...it stays with you."

"Gordon. I had no idea. Who—"

He shakes his head. "It doesn't matter. It was a long time ago, and it's too late to fix it. But you still have a chance to make things right."

"What about the team? The sponsors? The media?"

"Lucy has it handled. Let her do her job."

I swipe at a few more fallen tears and lean against the sink. Is it really that simple? Except I don't know if I can look the other way while the sponsors pull out and we lose all our funding.

I can't be the reason the Devils fail.

The reason we lose the team.

Yeah, I love Lincoln, but it doesn't mean everything else

ceases to exist. All of our other problems can't be swept under the rug.

Love makes everything more difficult.

Complicated.

Gordon walks over and rests his hip against the counter next to me. "And while you're at it, you might want to wash that jersey you've been wearing for the past couple days. It's starting to stink."

37

LINCOLN

THE GAME TONIGHT fills my gut with dread. I can't help but wonder if I made the right choice. For me. For my future. I thought I'd feel better after I made my decision, but the weight of it is heavier than before.

As I walk out of the coach's office, I'm met with the intense gaze of the entire team. Things have been tense with some of the guys since Gordon beat my ass in front of them. Most of the second string have been uncharacteristically quiet. I can only guess they think I used my dick to get the captain's patch and edged out some of the other guys in the process.

"Nothing like playing Boston." Tag breaks the uncomfortable silence and claps me on the shoulder. Hard. "Hope we don't get our asses handed to us like last time."

I grunt in response, sitting down to lace up my skates.

Foster flings himself down next to me and taps me with his stick. "Don't worry, mate. You made the right decision."

Ian sits down on my other side, puts his arm around my shoulders, and tugs me to him. "As much as I loved helping you make this decision, next time you make me talk about my feelings like a teenage girl, I'll get Gordon to kick your ass again."

"I thought you liked braiding Tag's hair." I remove his arm from my shoulders and give him a shove.

"No." Owen comes up behind Tag and punches his arm. "Tag likes it when we braid his hair."

"Fuck off. It feels good. It soothes me." Tag runs a hand through his hair for emphasis before sliding on his helmet.

I shake my head and laugh. I'm glad I made up with the guys after Tag knocked some sense into me at our one-on-one practice time. Not all teammates become family, but these guys have.

Even Foster.

My only regret is Jazz and how I handled things with her.

I never mentioned the trade, even though I had countless opportunities. I didn't talk to her about what I wanted. About the future I wanted with her.

Except for my slip where I might have mentioned putting my babies in her.

She still hasn't talked to me or responded to my text messages, and I can't say I blame her one bit. I should have been honest and laid it all out in the open.

I'm still not sure how I'm going to fix things. Maybe showing up on her doorstep, Stanley Cup in hand, will make her reconsider being with me. Or maybe convincing our sponsors to come back, doing promos for free if that's what it takes. Whatever I have to do to make things right.

Whatever I do, staying in Nashville—tying myself to the Devils for the long haul—is step one.

The music in the arena kicks into high gear. The X Ambassadors' *Jungle* usually kicks me into high gear as I skate out on the ice, but today it's been replaced with Motley Crue's *Kickstart My Heart*. I don't remember them playing any eighties music at any of the other games. I'd be more curious about the change except the guys are grabbing their sticks and heading out on the ice.

Even Foster and Ian have left me on the bench.

Time to focus. Man up. Take charge.

I've got a game to win.

I push my helmet on, force myself from the bench, and grab my stick before heading out to the ice. The music fades into the background and is soon replaced by cheering fans. They're going nuts, and the game hasn't even started.

Did I miss something? Where are the announcers?

My brows draw together, and I look around. Half the team is on the bench, looking as confused as I feel, and the other half have stopped on the ice, staring at the Blazers.

Tag catches my gaze and shrugs.

The cheering on the other side of the arena gets louder. The Boston players part and Jazlyn skates between them and heads for center ice. She's in leggings and a Devils' jersey.

If I didn't have this strap under my chin, it would be hanging on the ice. My pulse races and my stomach drops to my balls as she lifts the microphone I didn't realize she had.

"I'm Jazlyn Benson, co-owner of the Devils, and I'd like to welcome you all to the game tonight." Her voice wavers, and I fight the urge to skate over there and wrap her in a giant bear hug. "You may have seen me in the news recently. I've been accused of having an affair with one of my players."

She glances over at me, and I hang my head. I'm not sure why she's coming out on the ice to deny the allegations. As if I need her to skate over my heart after she's ripped it from my chest.

"This is usually the time for excuses and denials, but I'm not going to do that. I'm done lying to all of you and myself. If you can't tell from my jersey, the rumors are true."

I glance over at Tag, gripping my hockey stick so hard I'm afraid it may snap. "Did she admit it? Am I having a stroke?"

Tag chuckles and punches my arm. "Stop being a dumbass."

I turn back as Jazz turns her back to me. My stick falls and clatters on the ice. I rip off my helmet, which Tag grabs before it joins my stick.

Fuck. Me.

She's wearing my jersey. My number. My name.

Mine.

Possessiveness floods my body and awakens that primal part of me that wants everyone to know she's mine. Mine and mine alone.

And she's confirming this fact.

I'm going to mark every piece of clothing she has with my name or number.

Jazz completes her circle, facing me, and raises the mic again. "Lincoln Dallas and I had a relationship. A relationship I wanted to hide away from the world because I was afraid of what everyone would think. Afraid I would lose all credibility and respect, and I thought I had to choose between him and my career. It took me a little bit to realize I don't have to choose. I don't have to live up to anyone's expectations."

Her eyes meet mine and all I can do is stare. I've never loved her more. She's beautiful. Brave. My girl's a fighter.

My girl.

"I love you, Lincoln. I love you more than I've ever loved anyone. You're a part of me I never knew was missing until you came into my life. I thought I had to hide you away, that you were off limits, but that was a bad call. You're everything to me. I lost you once, and I'll do whatever it takes to get you back into my life and keep you there." She takes a deep breath and addresses the crowd. "I've stepped down from my position as owner. Effective tomorrow, Gordon Benson is the sole owner of the Nashville Devils."

I straighten as a wave of shock runs through me. She gave up her career. Her position as owner. The one thing she fought so hard to protect. The only good thing her father ever did for her, and she's just walking away.

For me.

I've never loved her more. I've never felt so unworthy. I've never given fewer fucks whether or not I deserved what was being offered.

Because I want her and she wants me, and that's all that matters.

I need her. In my arms. And I really don't care if we're surrounded by the team. If we're on the fucking news. If her brother sees. Because it doesn't fucking matter.

The gloves come off next which Foster takes from me. Don't know when he skated over and don't give a fuck.

I get to her in three long strides, framing her face with my hands, brushing my thumbs over her cheeks. She looks up at me, eyes brimming with tears.

"Are you sure? Giving up the team? Everything you've worked so hard for?"

"I'm sure. I want you, Linc. Forever. You're my future. I—"

My mouth crashes down on hers. The crowd is cheering, egging me on, as I grip her high ponytail and tug, tilting her lips to mine and curl an arm around her waist, tugging her to me. Her curves press against me, her breasts against my chest. The mic echoes as it drops on the ice, and Jazz clutches the front of my jersey. Our tongues duel for control, and my fingers skim along the curve of her ass.

Remembering that we have an audience, and I have a game to play, I pull back and rest my forehead against hers.

"I love you, Jazlyn."

"I love you."

The music kicks on and the players start moving to the bench. I'm not ready to let her go. But at least this time, I know it's only temporary.

"We're going to Whiskey and Rye after the game. Can you meet me there?"

She nods, giving me a quick kiss before sliding back. "Go win your hockey game, caveman. I'll see you tonight."

Jazz turns, giving me another look at my name across her back, and skates off the ice. I return to the guys and grab my gear with the biggest shit-eating grin across my face.

"Let's win a hockey game."

38

JAZLYN

"THAT WAS the ballsiest thing I've ever seen." Lucy clinks her soda to mine before taking a drink.

Gordon mumbles under his breath as he sits down on the bar stool next to mine, crossing his arms over his chest.

"What's that?" I take a sip of my soda. "I couldn't quite hear you. It sounded something like you're the best sister ever and I love you so much."

He mumbles again as Lucy laughs from my other side. I can make out the words *idiot* and *kick his ass* before he takes a long, steady pull from his beer and peers around the almost empty bar. The three of us snuck out of the game a little early. With Lincoln on fire tonight, our win against Boston was secured well before we left.

I can take a pretty good guess whose ass he wants to kick. Namely, the reason he's stuck running the team alone. I'd like to say I regret giving up the one thing I fought so hard to keep, but I don't. I no longer have to constantly defend who I am or the choices I make. I don't have to wake up every morning preparing for a battle I'll never win. I can just be me. No sneaking around.

No worrying about being caught. No fretting over a future I can't have. Now I can enjoy hockey again.

Gordon clears his throat. "I respect your decision, and I want you to be happy. But I don't like running the team without you. I liked working together."

"Aw, Gordon."

"That's all you're getting out of me." Gordon stands up, smoothing his tie, and heads to greet the arriving players.

"Your brother's a charmer tonight." Lucy nudges me with a chuckle. "I was tryin' to get a rise out of him the whole time you were gone from the booth, and he wouldn't say two words to me. I think he was worried you'd get turned down."

I scan the group for Lincoln and come up empty, then turn to Lucy. "I mean, the thought did cross my mind."

"Not mine. I saw it all over his face that first practice."

"I seem to remember you calling me out."

"Doesn't sound like me at all." Her eyes flick to the door. "Speak of the devil. He just walked in."

I swivel on my stool in time to see him muscle his way through the door. Before he can make it two feet in the bar, Gordon pulls him to the side. I have a split second of panic before I realize Lincoln can handle himself.

Lucy leans toward me. "I think your brother is threatening your boyfriend."

"Looks about right." I nod. "The last time they saw each other, Gordon was a bit feisty."

"You mean he punched him several times in the face?"

"Exactly."

I breathe a sigh of relief as Gordon extends his hand and takes Lincoln's to shake. I'm glad no more punches had to be thrown. Gordon shoulders his way through the crowd to meet Weller, and Lincoln turns, meets my gaze, and stalks to me.

"Oh, Lord." Lucy fans herself. "It's getting hot in here."

"Uh huh."

Lincoln stops inches from me, leans down, and cages me in with his arms. His gaze never wavers from mine. "Hey, Lucy."

"Hey, yourself." Lucy trails off, as she's interrupted by the phone ringing in her purse. The theme song from *Halloween*. Interesting. "Oh, look, saved by the phone. I've got to get this. I'll be out front if you need me. Not that you will."

Lincoln is still hovering over me, staring down at me intently, his eyes a soft blue. Only a small space separates his lips from mine, and I'm suddenly a desperate bitch that needs it gone. The need to touch him is overwhelming, and I lean forward to run my hands over his chest and up his shoulders.

"What did Gordon have to say?"

Lincoln snorts, the corner of his lips twitching. "He said he wasn't sorry for punching me the first time and that he'll do it again if I do anything to hurt you." He pauses, reaching up to cup my face with his hands. "I can't believe you really gave up the team."

"I did." I smile at him, looping my arms around his neck. "You're more important to me than some hockey team."

"Even if we get the Stanley Cup?"

"We?" My eyes widen as I search his face for answers that aren't there. "But your trade…"

He shakes his head, running his hands up my back. He tugs on the end of my hair before undoing my ponytail and winding his hands in my hair. "I turned it down."

"But why?"

"You're more important to me than my quest for the cup."

I don't know how I got so lucky, and I'm not stupid enough to ask. Even though I have a home here in Tennessee, I would've happily moved to Chicago with Lincoln. But I'm glad I don't have to. I'm not sure what the next chapter holds for me, but I always envisioned it in Nashville.

"I love you, Jazlyn."

"I love you."

His fist tightens in my hair, pulling my head back. He leans down and skims his mouth over my bottom lip. A second time. And then a third.

My body is on fire, consumed by love and powered with my need for this man. With his hand in my hair, I'm at his mercy. Unable to deepen the kiss I so desperately crave.

"Lincoln," I moan, clutching at his shirt, trying to pull him closer.

With a groan, his lips crash to mine, his tongue sweeping into my mouth, stroking against mine.

I pull back, panting against his lips. "We need to stop before I climb you like a fucking tree."

"I'm not opposed to that." He sucks my bottom lip into his mouth, and I think my vagina just imploded.

In a matter of seconds, we're surrounded by Lincoln's friends as they shove their way around us.

"Get a room."

"Are you two thinking about shagging right here?"

"Look, Tag, she has prettier hair than yours."

"Not possible." Tag shakes his head and looks over at us.

I bury my face in Lincoln's rumbling chest, muffling my laughter and hiding my heated face.

"Fuck off. Can't you see we're having a moment?" Lincoln trails his hands up and down my back.

"We can have our moment later. How do you feel about spending the night and having an awkward breakfast with Gordon?"

A smile stretches across his face, but Foster answers before he does. "I'm jealous. I want an awkward breakfast with Gordon. We all get pretty hungry in the morning."

"I love waffles." Ian throws his arm around Foster and winks.

Their presence might ensure no blood is shed at the breakfast table. However, Lincoln's growled response makes me think he'd like it to be the three of us. However uncomfortable it may be.

"Sorry. Sorry," Lucy calls out, as she pushes through the team.

Lucy's phone call must've been a bad one. Her eyes are glassy like she's trying not to cry, she's chewing on her bottom lip, which I've never seen her do, and she's fidgety. "What's going on?"

"I...uh, I've got to run." She looks down at the ground, her grip tightening on her purse. "I've got to go back home for a family emergency. I'll be gone for a few days."

"What's going on?" I reach out and lay a hand on Lucy's shoulder. She's always so well composed, so it must be something big to have her out of sorts.

"It's my sister. She's havin' a huge crisis and doesn't adult very well."

"Is there anything I can do to help?"

"I'm not sure what she needs yet. I'll give you a call when I get there. I've got to talk to Gordon." Lucy smiles weakly before she spins around and disappears into the crowd.

Lincoln wraps his arms around me and rests his chin on the top of my head. "I hope everything's okay."

"Me too."

Foster sits down and signals the bartender. "Is she single?"

"How does she feel about soda cans?" Tag pushes himself between Foster and me.

With these guys, things are sure to never be boring.

Ignoring Tag and Foster arguing about which one of them Lucy would find most irresistible, I pull Lincoln down for a lingering kiss.

This right here is all I need.

Everything else can be figured out.

39

The Missing Linc: You. Me. Tonight. Date night.
Jaz-ersize: Ok. Casual or fancy?
The Missing Linc: Hmmmm casual. And be prepared.
Jaz-ersize: For?
The Missing Linc: Lots of public indecency. I make no promises to keep my hands to myself.
The Missing Linc: We may get arrested.
Jaz-ersize: Is this all part of the wooing process?
The Missing Linc: Fuck yeah, it is.
Jaz-ersize: I'm not sure it's entirely necessary since I'm already yours, but I'll play along.
The Missing Linc: Can you repeat that?
Jaz-ersize: I'll play along.
The Missing Linc: <Laughing Face Emoji> The other part.
Jaz-ersize: I'm not sure it's necessary.
The Missing Linc: <Angry Face Emoji> <Angry Face Emoji> You know damn well what I want.
Jaz-ersize: You mean the part where I said I'm already yours?
The Missing Linc: Yes. Now say it again.
Jaz-ersize: I'm already yours.

The Missing Linc: One more time.
Jaz-ersize: I. Am. Yours. Is your inner caveman happy?
The Missing Linc: Not yet. I have to go beat my chest around other males to intimidate them.
Jaz-ersize: Watch Gordon. He might punch you again.
The Missing Linc: Fuck no. Your brother scares me. I'd like to say he punches like a girl, but I know for a fact it's not true. His fists hurt my face. I'll intimidate Tag. He's an easy target.
Jaz-ersize: That's not fair. You're bigger than him, and he has long hair. He's more sensitive.
The Missing Linc: I don't play fair. <Downloading Image>
Jaz-ersize: This better not be what I think it is!!!!!
The Missing Linc: <Shrugging Emoji>
Jaz-ersize: OMG those flowers are so beautiful. This is way better than an unsolicited dick pic. Thank you so much. <Heart Eyes Emoji>
The Missing Linc: My dick is offended. And you're welcome. Consider the wooing officially started.
Jaz-ersize: Hahaha I'll see you tonight. I can't wait.
The Missing Linc: <Face Throwing Kiss Emoji> I love you.
Jaz-ersize: I love you.
The Missing Linc: PS-Don't wear any panties tonight. I want easy access to your pussy.
The Missing Linc: <Downloading Video>
Jaz-ersize: Lincoln!!!

EPILOGUE
TAG

"Oh God, get a room."

Lincoln looks up from humping Jazz to peer at me over the couch. "This is my room. This is my apartment. In fact, I've been meaning to ask you for the extra key so I can give it to Jazz."

I flop myself down in the oversized armchair, pull my lips in a pout, and give Linc my best puppy dog face. "That wounds me. You know you gave me that key because I'm your first. Jazz wouldn't appreciate it like I do."

Jazz pushes Linc off her and sits up, tugging her dress down. I may have gotten a flash of upper thigh, but I'll never tell. Doesn't matter if she's hotter than the hinges on the gates of Hell. He'd kick my ass. For some unimaginable reason, Jazz is stuck on that asshat. Clearly, I'm the better choice between the two of us. She's a hell of a lot more mouthy than I like, but Linc doesn't care.

He's entirely pussy-whipped and loves it. I think he cut off his own balls to put in her purse. I could have sworn I saw him rubbing her feet yesterday. Who does that? Willingly?

But if it wasn't for her, he'd have taken the trade and I'd have lost my best friend.

That would've made for a very unhappy Tag.

Which would make everyone else unhappy because, let's face it, I'm a fucking ray of beautiful sunshine. Without me, they'd just be playing hockey and hanging out at home.

Not going out.

Not meeting ladies.

Boring.

I don't get the whole girlfriend, *I'm in love so now I have a vagina* thing. That shit is not for me. Being tied down to one woman. Only having sex with *one* woman.

No, thank you.

Bunnies and random one-nighters are good enough for me.

"I gave you that key to use for emergencies." Linc puts his hand up to his forehead and looks around the room like he's a fucking Boy Scout. "Where's the fire? Who's dead?"

"The emergency is go fuck yourself." I pause, taking in Jazz's dress and Linc's button down shirt. "Why are you two dressed all fancy? I thought we were going to Whiskey and Rye for a bite to eat and a drink."

Jazz moves to stand up, and I get an up-close view of Linc's boner as he tucks it in his pants. Jesus. I get enough of that monster in the locker room. I should feel bad I interrupted his quickie, but I don't.

"We are." Jazz smoothes the wrinkles from her little black dress with both hands. "Lucy's sister just moved up from Georgia. We're trying to give her the impression we're civilized before she meets the rest of the team."

A smirk stretches across my face.

Fresh meat.

"Lucy has a sister? Is she single?"

Jazz rolls her eyes and walks over to get her purse. "I don't know. I think so. I think she just went through a break-up." She lifts her purse and points it at me from across the room. "Do not get any ideas, Tag."

Too late.

She's just my type. Emotionally unavailable and ripe for a rebound. If I had one of those handlebar mustaches, I'd be twirling it menacingly.

The last time my dick was offered a good time was the night of the auction, though it wasn't at all what I'd hoped. I don't know how the fuck it happened, but some dude named Roderick won. As tempting as it was, I did not take him up on his offer to give me *the best night of my life* while he took the liberty of groping my ass.

I glanced down at my worn jeans and T-shirt. If I'm going fishing, I'll need something a little nicer.

"I'm going to go change."

"Tag," Linc groans, pushing himself up from the couch. "You are not going to hit on Lucy's recently single sister. And you look fine. If you change now, we're going to be late."

"I'll be right back." After giving them both a princess a wave followed by duel middle finger salutes, I make my way to the door, ready to put together the perfect attire to package the *package*.

The last thing I hear before I shut it is his exasperated swearing and Jazz's loud sigh. Doesn't matter. I may be going to the bar with them. But I won't be leaving that way.

Hello, Lucy's sister.

Thank you for reading FORBIDDEN DEVIL—I hope you enjoyed Lincoln and Jazz's journey as much as I enjoyed writing it! Do you want more Nashville Devils Hockey? Tag and Elle will be up next in UNTAMED DEVIL!

Want to stay in the know about all my upcoming releases? Just sign up for my newsletter HERE.

As an Indie Author, I would love your help spreading the word about FORBIDDEN DEVIL. If you enjoyed the story please consider leaving a review on Amazon, Goodreads, or even referring to a friend. Even a sentence or two makes a huge difference.

Thank you for taking this journey with me.

Melissa

UNTAMED DEVIL - PREVIEW

From CHAPTER ONE

Tag

What I need right now is a distraction from my distraction.

Linc and Jazz are great company, but I expected there to be more people here. A few guys from the team, maybe a couple people from the Devils' front office. The whole purpose of this little gathering at Whiskey and Rye, was to welcome Lucy's sister to the city, and they haven't even bothered to show up. Instead, I'm impatiently playing third wheel to Linc and Jazz's happily ever after.

My leg bounces under the table and I check my phone for what seems like the hundredth time. I double check to make sure the volume is turned on and then check again. I had several missed calls from my sister because my dumb ass had forgotten to turn it off vibrate after practice. I tried calling her back—multiple times—and sent her *several* text messages. Crickets. If it were anyone else, I'd say 'fuck it' and move on with my life.

But Finley? There's no telling what kind of trouble she's in, and Finley is always in trouble.

"What's up with you?" Linc nudges my foot with his before throwing an arm around Jazz. "You're not your usual annoying self."

I lean back and glance over at him, giving him the best smile I can muster before deflecting. "So, where's Lucy and this sister of hers? I need a bourbon. Stat."

"How the hell should I know? They're not even ten minutes late. If you want a drink, order a fucking drink. Maybe it'll calm your ass down." Linc relaxes in his chair and presses a kiss into Jazz's hair, but not before throwing me a look that says we'll be talking later.

I make a show of rolling my eyes, and that's when I see the blonde beauty at the bar.

Hello, distraction from my distraction.

Watching Linc dry hump Jazz all night isn't going to stop me from thinking about my fucked up family.

Now, this girl...

She could be a night of no strings sex to occupy my time. Forgetting about my problems is easier when I'm face first in a nice set of tits. Make me focus on something else for a while. Or in this case, two something elses.

The honeyed hair falling in waves down her back would be perfect for wrapping around my fist as I lose myself in her luscious body. She's perched on one of those rounded bar stools, forcing her to slide back just enough for me to see an ass rounded to perfection in a pair of form fitting dark blue jeans.

Curvy girls are my weakness, and she has 'em in all the right places.

I strain my neck to get a better look and hold back the groan building in my throat. I really want to bite down on that ass, but I don't think it's appropriate in the middle of the bar.

At least not until we've been properly introduced.

Consider me properly distracted.

"See you losers later. I've got someone to meet." I push away from the table, the chair scraping against the wooden floor, and make my way toward the girl who's going to wake up in my bed tomorrow morning. Hair tousled, cheeks flushed, and thoroughly fucked.

She's hunched over the bar, her eyes never leaving the bartender as he pours three shots of Jäger right in front of her and two empty seats. The first she tosses back immediately, exposing the length of her delicate throat, and giving me a new appreciation for the curve of a woman's neck. Her whole body shivers, before she slams the bar-top with her free hand, and sets the empty shot glass upside down. She looks at the next one for a moment, laughs to herself, and then downs it as easily as the first.

The last one. She stares at it like I'm staring at her, like she's in desperate need of regret, and I'm only happy to oblige us both.

With my tongue. My hands. My cock.

All of the above.

"Rough day?" I slide onto the barstool next to her, with as much finesse as I have on the ice, and when she turns to look at me with an arched brow, I extend my hand. "Tag."

Her eyebrows shoot up and she squints, her bright blue eyes narrowing on my face, before reaching out to poke my shoulder. "You're it."

"Ha. Ha. Very original. Haven't heard that one before." I roll my eyes, pushing the tauntings of several prepubescent boys from Oliver Lewis Elementary out of my head. Suggesting a game of tag during recess had been a favorite pastime of theirs growing up and it got real old, real fast. "Maybe I can hear you say it later. Much later. And louder. Who might you be?"

She sucks in her lips and blushes a magnificent shade of pink. For a second, I don't think she's going to respond. Then, she flips her hair over her shoulder and gives me an appraising look. "Elle."

I know the second her small hand slides into mine, and her ruby lips tip in a smile, that she'll be leaving Whiskey and Rye and going straight to my bed. And the couch. The kitchen counters. The shower. All of the above. Not necessarily in that order, but definitely all by morning, because that's when this relationship expires.

I'm not above using the bathroom stall of the bar, either. I'm sure it's clean...enough.

"So, is it a rough day or do you always pour yourself three shots of Jäger?" I smirk at her, gesturing to the shot glasses with an index finger.

Her bright blue eyes meet mine, her lashes flutter, and the air sizzles around me. She's only said three words to me and I'm already on the edge of my seat waiting for more.

"You have no idea." She throws back the last shot, her eyes never leaving mine. You can take me out of the country, but as soon as her smooth southern accent hits my ears, it brings me right back to the Bluegrass state. Rolling hills, sunny days, and home. "But I'm sure you don't really want me to carry on all about my day."

I don't.

"I do."

"Well, I moved out of my ex-boyfriend's house this morning. We'd been together two years when I found out he'd been cheatin' on me with Brittney, Summer, and Caraway." She pauses, her nose scrunching up. "What kind of name is Caraway? That's not even one of the good spices. More of a seed, really."

What the fuck is a caraway? I didn't even know it was a word let alone a spice. All I know is, it's not a *Spice Girl*. "Not even in the top ten spices, I agree."

"Anyway." She waves her hand around erratically, and I'm in

range to inadvertently take a hit to the throat. Me, hunched over, grabbing my neck and struggling to breathe isn't a sexy look, so I back up a few inches. "I threw some stuff, broke a few things, and after being called a few disparagin' names, I high tailed it the hell out of there. I'd like to say I feel bad for going full crazy. But I don't."

"Bless your little broken heart."

I heard something about spices, and she broke some stuff. The take home is, her asshole ex cheated on her, and now she's on the rebound. She might be a little bit crazy, but who isn't?

Maybe it's because my family is a *little* fucked up, but I like crazy.

I like rebounds even more, they never want more than a friendly fuck, and I'm the master of casual. In. Out. Repeat a few dozen more times. No one catches any feelings, and I keep my status as a perpetual bachelor.

ALSO BY MELISSA IVERS

Devils Hockey
FORBIDDEN DEVIL (Lincoln and Jazz)
RECKLESS DEVIL (Tag and Elle)
BROODY DEVIL (Rhett and Lucy)

Love in Aspen
MISTLETOE AND MISCHIEF (Nash and Jules)

ACKNOWLEDGMENTS

Just as it takes a team to play hockey, it takes a team to write a hockey novel and I am so grateful to have great people willing to be with me from start to finish. I've pulled people to just sit with me and talk things out, read through something I'm not sure of, critique me when I think something's garbage, and help make it better.

So, all you bitches that helped me, I want to say thank you, from the bottom of my heart. You know who you are, but in case you need me to say it, because you're a drama lama. A huge thank you to Beth, Krista, Mary, Siby, Victoria (My Catique Kitties), my girls over at the Hockey Round Table (Aurora, Danica, Kat, Kathy, Kelly, and Isabella), the Lady D's Danielle, Marissa and Rachel, and my family for putting up with all my deadlines and hours I dedicate to writing.

A HUGE thank you to all the reviewers and bloggers for reading the story and helping me spread the word about my story.

And I especially want to thank you! Thank you for reading. Thank you for making it to the end. And hopefully thank you for loving it.

Melissa

ABOUT THE AUTHOR

Lover of all things romance and hockey, she also loves to bake extra delicious treats. Melissa Ivers loves to write steamy stories with all those hot, alpha men and women who can bring them to their knees literally and figuratively. Melissa lives in Kentucky with her eye-rolling teenage son and two of the laziest dogs known to man. She has numerous fictional boyfriends, but—shhhh—they don't know about each other.

When she isn't writing or working, you'll find her under a blanket on the couch reading a book off Kindle. She also likes baking yummy treats for family and friends, binge watching shows off Netflix, such as the *Office* and *Vampire Diaries* and being an all-around joy.

To keep current with what Melissa is doing stalk her on social media or check out her websites.

Facebook

Instagram

Website

Click to join my Newsletter and my Facebook reader group Melissa's Sweet and Sassy Readers. I'd love to see you there.

Printed in Great Britain
by Amazon